D0006997

THE SHIP OF STOLEN WORDS

AMULET BOOKS • NEW YORK

Winner of the Nebula Award
Fran Wilde

THE SHIP OF STOLEN WORDS

Cataloging-in-Publication Data has been applied for and may be obtained from the Library of Congress.

ISBN 978-1-4197-4950-6

Text © 2021 Fran Wilde
Illustrations © 2021 Shan Jiang
Book design by Marcie Lawrence

Printed and bound in U.S.A.
10 9 8 7 6 5 4 3 2 1

Amulet Books are available at special discounts when purchased in quantity for premiums and promotions as well as fundraising or educational use. Special editions can also be created to specification. For details, contact specialsales@ abramsbooks.com or the address below.

Amulet Books® is a registered trademark of Harry N. Abrams, Inc.

ABRAMS The Art of Books
195 Broadway, New York, NY 10007
abramsbooks.com

To everyone who wishes
for adventure

Chapter One

Sam

On the last morning of fifth grade, Sam Culver lost his favorite word. Right after that, he lost two more words.

Sam didn't notice at first. But then his sometimes-best friend, Mason McGargee, and his teacher, Ms. Malloy, noticed. And after that, *everyone* noticed. Which was embarrassing.

"Sam! Easy on the screen door!" His stepmother, Anita, had called as he ran from the house. Too late—the door hit the frame with a WHAM right between *screen* and *door*.

"Sorry!" he shouted over his shoulder, hoping that would smooth his exit. He heard Anita say something about Mason, but he was already late. He'd see Mason in a minute anyway, because they walked the three blocks to school together.

But today, she wasn't waiting for him.

Just in case Mason was running late, Sam strolled slowly toward Ursula K. Le Guin Elementary alone. He took his time stepping over cracks and dodging the ants making lean trails across the already-hot pavement. Mason and her mom had missed their families' latest Saturday movie night and the first meeting of the Mount Cloud summer baseball league, which they'd been waiting for all year. He had a lot to tell her.

As Sam walked, he whistled. He wasn't very good at whistling, and the notes sounded flat. He tried to remember the bad guys' theme in the monster movie that he, his sister, Bella, and their parents had just watched. But he couldn't quite get it right. Mason would have known which notes he was getting wrong, because she never forgot things like that. But she hadn't caught up to Sam on the way to school yet, so he couldn't ask her.

Sam was also thinking about baseball—how could he not? The first practice of the summer was that afternoon. At the end of last season, he'd played second base instead of his usual right field position, and he and his dad had been working on his throws ever since. The Mount Cloud coaches, Mr. Lockheart and Mason's dad, Dr. McGargee, had hinted Sam might move to the infield for good.

Sam was so busy thinking about baseball and movies that he almost tripped over a miniature white pig rooting around the base of Mrs. Lockheart's Little Free Library, two doors up from his house.

The pig's snout was deep in the last of the tulips, upending the flowers and pushing dirt onto the sidewalk. *Boy, Mrs. Lockheart hated when her flowers got messed up*, Sam thought. Then he realized there was a bigger problem.

The pig's leash—a long, leather strap that matched the saddle it was wearing—had gotten tangled around Sam's ankles. He'd blundered right into it when he was looking at the wrecked tulips and wondering who was going to get in trouble and have to apologize to Mrs. Lockheart.

Mrs. Lockheart hated apologies. Sam knew this for a fact, having messed up her tulips before.

The surprise pig was very odd, and its leash and saddle even more so. But what most immediately concerned Sam was the small, silver-haired old woman poking a willow stick at his face while trying to untangle the pig's leash with her other hand.

Her skin—both on her hand, which was way too close, and her face—was wrinkled like a dried apple. When she shook the stick, the end almost scraped Sam's nose. And then she started scolding him.

"Watch where you're going, young man!" the old woman bellowed; her voice was much bigger than should be possible for someone so small. Even Bella—who was five and taller than this woman—couldn't get so loud. The old woman waved the switch at Sam again. "Kids should be more careful, especially—"

"Sorry!" Sam said for at least the second time that morning.

He tried to back up and pull his foot free from the leash. The pig made a watery snuffling sound and gazed at Sam doubtfully, sideways, with one black-ink eye.

Sam couldn't free his foot fast enough. He ended up splat on the sidewalk, next to the tulips, where he couldn't avoid the old woman's stick. She tapped him on the cheek with it, which itched. "Hey!"

Something shimmered near Sam's cheek, like a spiderweb or a long piece of ribbon—the kind Bella sometimes tied to Sam's backpack. He pushed it and the stick away. Sam waved at his hair too, for good measure. Leaves and spiderwebs sometimes fell from the big oak onto the sidewalk near the Little Free Library.

For a moment, Sam felt the same way he did when he'd just pulled a tooth out—where that one raw spot was just *lacking*, before it became a point of pride to stick his tongue through. And then the feeling went away, and he grabbed for the ribbon. Mrs. Lockheart didn't tolerate littering any more than people messing with her tulips, and if she caught Sam on the way to school doing both, he was going to have a lot of explaining to do.

But the ribbon—or whatever it was—sparkled just out of reach. Then the white pig snorfled it up gleefully. Most of it disappeared before Sam could grab it. "Hey!"

"You shouldn't be so careless!" the old woman scolded him. She glowered and yanked at the leash. The pig snuffled, and Sam finally freed his foot. He was going to be so late for school.

"I really apologize for running into you! I have to go," Sam shouted over his shoulder as he sped off, a little embarrassed that he'd managed to get so tangled up with the pair of them. The strange woman waved at him with her stick. And Sam got the missing-tooth feeling again, but then it went away.

A pig! With a saddle—in Mount Cloud! Sam almost stopped and turned around again to make sure they were real. But that would make him even more late. And who would believe that he was late because of a wandering grandmother and her miniature pet pig? No one. Especially not Ms. Malloy, his fifth-grade teacher, who lived right next door to the Lockhearts and likely had never seen an old woman walking a tiny pig on a leash. Sam knew he hadn't.

But then he did look back. And when he didn't see the old woman or the pig—or anything other than the Little Free Library and a few uprooted tulips—he wondered if maybe he had imagined it all.

He quickened his pace and made it to the school's front steps just as the bell rang. He'd climbed two of the five big stone stairs that led up to the blue doors of Ursula K. Le Guin Elementary before Mason caught up with him.

"What is that you're whistling?" Mason asked. She wore her hair in curly pigtails and had one of last year's Mount Cloud baseball jackets wrapped around her waist so that it cinched her yellow sundress in a blue hug.

Sam hadn't realized he was still whistling the song.

"There you are! I can't remember the tune right—it's from *Ghostbusters IV*, which you'd know if you'd been able to come watch the movie last weekend," Sam teased. He and Mason had been teasing each other a lot lately. Sometimes not so nicely.

"This one?" Mason repeated the tune and did it perfectly. She was so good at remembering. And at whistling.

Sam felt his face go red. He didn't really know why, but Mason barely having to try to remember made him want to turn invisible. She was better at everything than he was, really, except reading and baseball. And maybe fixing stuff, when Sam had Anita's help. He spoke without thinking. "It's hard to tell. You whistle kind of like a goldfish." He puffed his cheeks and pressed his lips into a fish face.

Mason's smile fell.

One thing Sam liked about Mason was that he rarely had to worry about hurting her feelings. She was tough and always said she could give as good as she got. But today felt different.

"It's not like you can whistle well either, Sam. You should practice more instead of teasing people." Mason was blinking hard, and her face was scrunched. "Can we not fight today?"

Sam winced. Mason knew he was touchy about having to do extra work to get stuff right, like with math this year, but she still teased him about practicing. It wasn't fair. Even though he did wish he could unsay the bit about the goldfish.

He tried to smooth things over. "Sure. And I'll definitely practice. As long as it's practicing baseball!" He opened Ms. Malloy's classroom door. It was the first room down from the principal's office, just after the main entrance. A wave of air-conditioned coolness washed out, smelling a little like very cold tin cans. "Instead of spending all summer doing math problems, like a nerd!"

Mason elbowed him. "It's called Math Olympics, and I like it." Now she grinned.

Sam smiled too. He started to describe what had happened on his walk. "You'll never believe . . ."

But with a few words, his mostly best friend made him forget all about pigs and grandmas. "Don't worry, you're getting a lot better at math too," she said with a wink.

Mason wasn't letting up! Even if she'd dropped the joking tone and was trying to sound nice. Sam focused on his shoes, betting he was turning bright red and that everyone in class could probably see it. Math *had* been hard this year, and Mason knew it.

His parents had even talked with Ms. Malloy about extra summer work, but he'd managed to pull his grade up before the end of May. Unlike Mason, who ate math for breakfast, Sam wished he could disappear every time the subject came up. Why didn't she get that?

Mason took her seat and Sam slid into his desk right in front of hers. His embarrassment simmered, then quieted. Why had they been fighting? He couldn't remember how it started. Now he felt a little sad. Mason would have loved hearing about the pig.

She'd have said the old woman was a witch or a fairy, probably.

Sam almost turned and tried again, but Mason was already talking to her neighbor, Gina. And Gina thought Sam was weird. So he decided to leave it alone for once. His dad said that it was good to leave well enough alone sometimes.

Maybe when it's summer, I'll tell her about the pig, Sam thought as he stared at his desk. *Meantime, only a few more hours of school to get through and I'll be free.* He knew he'd earned it: the bell was going to sound like a winner's gong.

That final bell took a long time to chime.

School ground from math (games, thankfully) to history (a movie, with everyone dozing off, including Ms. Malloy) to English. The playground outside Ms. Malloy's classroom window shimmered with waves of heat. Sam couldn't take his eyes off it.

That shimmer meant freedom. Schools in Mount Cloud's district weren't built for this much summer. The air conditioner—an old window unit with colored strips of paper in the vents that let the students know it was still working—coughed and sputtered. It couldn't keep up with the heat.

Sam could almost taste the lemonade Anita would set on the porch after the last day of school. She'd done that every year since he was six. He could feel the sweaty surface of a baseball—Mount Cloud Community League (MCCL) Sharpied in fading black ink near the red stitching—as he caught it and tagged a runner out. Summer was less than an hour away.

On the playground, a tongue-red kickball someone had left out after recess seemed to deflate a little and stick to the pavement. As he stared, the curl of a pig's white tail appeared behind the ball.

He blinked to clear his eyes. Then he heard a snort.

The pig, not the ball.

When Sam looked again, after giving his head a good shake, the pig was gone.

"Sam! Pay attention!" Ms. Malloy waved a fan-folded worksheet in his direction. The less-warm air cooled the sweat on his cheek. "We have forty-five more minutes of your time, my friend. We're going to make it count. Let's take a look at your summer book projects."

"Yes, Ms. Malloy," he said, while his sixteen classmates, including Mason, snickered. Sam momentarily considered tacking a half-hearted apology onto the end of his sentence, then looked up at his teacher with wide eyes.

Sorry was the kind of word that had always rolled off Sam's tongue like a bright coin and made everyone relax. Before he said it, he'd think of something sad, like chocolate melting uneaten or Bodie Jacobs, the youngest player ever for the Mount Cloud farm team (who might get to play for the Mets someday), striking out with all the bases loaded. That was Sam's secret formula for getting out of trouble. It wasn't just the word that mattered. It was the delivery: Say *sorry* and look really sad or serious. Adults ate that stuff up.

But it was the last day of school, and when he said certain words around Ms. Malloy, he had to mean them. She was strict. Sam learned that from the first three-paragraph essay he wrote for her: wasted or excess words got him extra work, like looking up things in her huge classroom dictionary. But Ms. Malloy said Sam was a great storyteller, so she'd wanted him to fix it.

No, she'd said she *expected* Sam to fix it. So he had.

When anyone did what Ms. Malloy expected, she never said thank you. She just nodded like they'd finally lived up to her standards and moved on. That made her a little scary, for a teacher, but also as a neighbor.

Ms. Malloy, when she left Ursula K. Le Guin Elementary, would walk the five blocks to her house, which was catty-corner to Sam's, and sit on the porch fanning herself all summer, except when she disappeared inside.

She wastes summer, Sam had told Bella once. She didn't come to baseball games or go to cookouts; she didn't go to the neighborhood parties either, his parents said. She sometimes chatted with people on her porch, but that was it.

Sam couldn't imagine anything worse, and neither he nor Bella could figure out what Ms. Malloy did at her house for three whole months. They'd spent some time the previous summer imagining that Ms. Malloy's house had hidden tunnels and secret portals to the other side of the world. Like in the stories that Sam's sister loved.

But Ms. Malloy didn't seem like the kind of adult who would have secret tunnels. She was the kind of adult who could sit on her porch all summer long without the perfect bun on top of her head getting the least bit out of place.

In the classroom, the heat-damp curls of Sam's own too-long hair already stuck to his neck.

"Sam!"

He stopped staring at the small holes in the ceiling tiles and smiled at Ms. Malloy.

She shook her head, then returned to discussing their summer book projects. "You'll be partnering with someone in your neighbor-hood to take care of the nearest Little Free Library and make sure it's stocked with books for the community. Ones you've read. I want you to write recommendations too. And if there isn't a Little Free Library near your home, I can help you find a way to build one."

Sam grinned. This would be easy. Ms. Malloy's neighbor, Mr. Lockheart, had built his block's Little Free Library—with Sam's help—and it was always well stocked. The recommendations? Those depended on who Sam was teamed with. He liked sharing sports and comic books. He hoped he got someone who liked a lot of different things.

"Sam, your partner is Mason."

His smile faded. This wouldn't be so easy after all. While Mason liked science fiction and graphic novels, she also liked to read math and science books. Maybe, Sam decided, we can add in some of Bella's favorite recommendations too, and it would work out.

The whole summer might still have gone great if Mason hadn't decided right then to whisper something about Sam and math to Gina Dulaney that sounded like more teasing.

And if Sam hadn't decided to fire back.

"I hope you won't have to spend the whole summer with your grandmother again, Mason," Sam whispered, trying to get her to be quiet. At least about him. "I don't want to have to do the whole project myself."

Mason's face folded shut like a book. She looked hard at her desk.

And *WHAM*, Ms. Malloy's hand came down loud on *Sam's* desk. "Apologize, Sam. Immediately."

His stomach cinched up. He'd gone too far, probably. Somehow. He had no idea how. But it was definitely too far.

As the window-unit air conditioner hummed loudly, stirring the chalk dust and sweaty-feet air of the classroom around without actually cooling anything off, someone pig-snorted near the window, and Mason glared at Sam.

He thought of Bodie Jacobs striking out with three people on base. Then he reached for his trusty word.

"_____ . . ."

Sam gaped, tasting the empty space where the word should have been. He couldn't for all the summer baseball games in the neighborhood make the sounds that formed his magic get-out-of-trouble word.

He'd used it just that morning, for bumping into the old woman with the pig!

But now? The word was gone.

So was the other word he could think of that meant the same thing.

Sam's mouth hung open and he stared at Mason, and she glared back. He tried to say the word again. "S____" is all that came out. Nothing more.

The word wasn't just stuck, it was gone, and the place where it had been was a hole no sound could escape from.

What was happening? He opened and closed his mouth experimentally. "I can't," he said.

Talking was fine. His voice wasn't gone. He didn't have laryngitis.

It was just that one word. He tried again, opening his mouth wider. "I'm _____." Nothing.

"Stop fooling around, Sam. This is serious." Ms. Malloy's tone had a brittle edge to it.

Just then the bell rang, and everyone lurched toward summer.

Everyone including Mason, who whispered, "My gran passed away, you fish-face jerk," as she gathered her bag and swept out of fifth grade in a storm of dark curls and worn-out sneakers.

Everyone except Sam, held in his seat by Ms. Malloy's restraining hand. His stomach churned. Was that what Anita had been trying to tell him that morning?

Probably that's why Mason hadn't been able to come watch movies last weekend. Sam blinked hard and stared at his desk. He wished he hadn't said anything.

Out of the corner of his eye, Sam saw the white pig and the old woman—her willow stick held straight up in the air—and beside her a boy, silver hair sticking up every which way and wearing a long green shirt under a short vest and canvas pants. They strode past the kickball field, across the playground, and then toward the baseball diamond.

When Sam listened really hard over the air conditioner, he heard one of them whistling the tune he'd been trying to figure out that morning.

The classroom's air-conditioning unit ticked slower and slower until it stalled. Down the hall, Sam could hear his friends opening and closing their lockers and running, shouting toward the big doors at the front of Ursula K. Le Guin Elementary and freedom.

He looked up at Ms. Malloy, and she looked down at him.

"You can't apologize? Why not?"

"I don't know," Sam said. Tears made his eyes prickle, which was frustrating. He shook his head hard. He *didn't* cry, not over something as dumb as this. "It's just gone."

Ms. Malloy got down to eye level with Sam. He knew that when a teacher did that, something was really wrong.

"Listen, Sam. This isn't a game. You must apologize to Mason. I can't let you end the year like this."

"What do you mean?" Panic rose. Getting stuck in fifth grade was just a story that sixth graders told at lunch to scare fifth graders. Even Mason had never teased Sam about *that*. "I did all the work. I passed math."

"You did. And you did it well too, once you applied yourself. You're bright, Sam, when you do the work. But this? This is unacceptable behavior. I don't want to spend my summer in this hot building any more than you do, so write Mason an apology note if you can't say it, and we'll be done."

One of Ms. Malloy's grammar posters (It's = it + is) wilted, a corner peeling away from the wall. She smoothed it back, her charm bracelet jangling against her jacket sleeve. Sam was wearing a T-shirt and shorts and he was hot. He couldn't imagine how sweaty the adults were. *Yuck.*

Ms. Malloy turned back to her desk, opened a drawer with a loud squeak in the quiet room, and then handed Sam a piece of lined paper and a pencil.

He started to write. *Dear Mason, I'm very very* ____

And that was as far as he got. Sam stared at Ms. Malloy. "I can't find the word."

Frowning, she pulled her enormous dictionary from the shelf and put it on Sam's desk with a *thunk*. She walked back to her desk and sat down. "I'll wait."

This dictionary was legendary at the elementary school. The words were so small that it came with its own magnifying lens, and Ms. Malloy had to supervise students when using it, so they didn't break the lens or try to fry bugs with it.

Now, though, Sam didn't even know where to begin. He was getting a little scared.

He'd forgotten things before. His mind had gone blank at the blackboard when he was trying to calculate a word problem. That had been awful. But he'd never lost an entire word and all its synonyms.

He kicked the desk leg, nervous energy finding its way to his feet.

"I'm not kidding, Ms. Malloy. Even the word you said just now: a_____? That's gone too."

Sam knew what she meant when she'd said the word, but he couldn't say it, and it was starting to be hard to even think it.

Gone. Lost.

He felt as bad as the day he'd frozen over the math problem, the chalk getting damp in his hand as the substitute math teacher prodded him with, "Come ON, Sam, this isn't hard." His classmates had whispered—not quietly, either—and Mason had shushed them.

Mason had been really nice to him later, also. But he'd been so embarrassed that she'd had to keep people from teasing him, and he'd snapped at her. Called her a name, in front of people.

Ever since, they'd been not-as-good friends. And today might have wrecked them entirely. She'd been nice, even though she was sad. He could see that now. Which made him feel even worse.

If he could make it up to Mason, he would. Once he got out of school. *But*, Sam wondered, *if I can't say the word, or write it, how can I possibly fix things?*

Ms. Malloy studied her watch. Ten minutes past summer.

"I want to get out of fifth grade, Ms. Malloy," Sam finally said. "But the words you want? I mean it. They're really gone. I think they were stolen."

Ms. Malloy frowned. Her forehead wrinkled and she pressed her fingers to the spot beneath her glasses where they rested on her nose. "I'm going to call your parents."

Sam swallowed hard. No one wanted to hear a teacher say that.

"Come on, Sam, all you have to do is apologize."

He tried a new tactic. "I regre—" he began. That word would probably work as well as other words he suddenly couldn't say. But that missing-tooth feeling happened again, and the word unspooled even as Sam said it. As if it had been pulled from his mouth, a shimmering ribbon flickered near the air conditioner, then flew out the window.

Sam shut his mouth angrily and stared out the window, blinking hard, trying to figure out what was happening. Then, that willow stick waved below the sill.

Just beyond it, past the school's playground, the neighborhood league was starting to set up on the now-impossible-to-reach baseball field. Coach Lockheart put a canvas bag of aluminum bats by home plate. He kicked at the dusty diamond. Dirt and lime puffed up, then settled in the heat.

And closer to the building, that same wild-haired boy skittered away from the window, holding the stick and trailing a sparkling ribbon. Sam thought the boy shouted, "I did it, Nan!"

But when Sam blinked and rubbed his eyes, the boy was gone.

Sam looked at his teacher. "Honestly, Ms. Malloy. This morning, there was a pig by Mrs. Lockheart's yard and an old woman with a stick, and I think I saw them just now—"

Ms. Malloy blinked. "A pig? What does that have to do with your apology?" Then she sighed heavily. Finally, she waved him out of his chair. "Let's go, Sam."

With loud footsteps, accompanied by the click-pop of her cane, Ms. Malloy headed down the hall to the principal, with Sam in tow. He'd been right: she didn't believe him.

Right before Sam and Ms. Malloy reached the doors that led outside, they turned into Principal Vane's glass-walled office. He was packing up his bag when Sam and Ms. Malloy entered.

Sam glanced behind him, through the glass doors, out to the playground one more time. There, the old woman and the young boy were crossing the field with the snow-white pig.

"Wait, there they are! Ms. Malloy!" Sam pointed, but by the time Ms. Malloy and Dr. Vane stopped talking and came to look, the old woman had waved her willow switch and they'd disappeared.

"What is it, Sam?" Ms. Malloy asked, concerned.

"Nothing. I thought I saw–" Sam couldn't understand it. Maybe there was something really wrong with him after all. *Maybe I'm getting sick?* he worried. *On the first day of summer, oh no!*

"Mr. Culver?" Dr. Vane said. "I hear you won't apologize. And *who* is where, exactly?"

Dr. Vane was new, and his white hair was cut close to his head, which was almost square. He was even stricter than Ms. Malloy.

"No one's there," Sam said. "And I think I might be sick. I mean, I feel okay, but something's ... not right?" Maybe he should have spoken up about the pig, but he didn't think Principal Vane would believe him either.

Ms. Malloy interceded. "Sam is an excellent teller of stories, Dr. Vane, but this *is* unusual, even for him."

"Can I go home if I'm sick?" Sam couldn't help trying it. Dr. Vane could have let him off with a warning.

Ms. Malloy looked worried. "Maybe it's best."

Sam heaved a sigh of relief. Summer was only moments away.

But Principal Vane frowned. "Ms. Malloy can walk you home, Sam. I'll call your parents to let them know. And you'll all come back here on Monday to meet with me again unless you either apologize or bring a doctor's note."

What?

"Dr. Vane's decided you'll need to come to school until you can apologize, Sam. We both will." Ms. Malloy sounded a bit mournful.

"I'll explain it to your parents. The school is serious about mean-spirited behavior. You could spend all next week here, Sam, or as little as one minute, right now."

Sam tried once more, but the word _____ just wouldn't come.

Ms. Malloy sighed, then handed Sam his backpack.

"I'm sorry that's your decision, Sam. See you Monday." Principal Vane frowned at him, and then at Ms. Malloy, and shut his door.

Ms. Malloy made him wait by the doors of Ursula K. Le Guin Elementary while she locked up her room. Then Sam and his teacher began the long walk back to Mount Cloud village. Together.

It was the worst day, kind of ever.

As they walked home, Sam kept an eye out for anything weird.

If he could show Ms. Malloy that strange things were afoot—for instance, a word-stealing white pig—maybe she'd let him off the hook.

But they crossed the big street leading away from the modern brick-and-stone elementary school and turned into their neighborhood—streets lined with Victorian cottages, brightly painted, two green parks with benches and bird feeders and a community garden, all so much older than the school and the bright city that Sam's dad took the train to every day—without seeing anything strange.

"Sam, I know the past few years have brought a lot of change for you, but you've been doing fine. Now you're fighting with your best friend, you're distracted, you're snooping around your neighbor's hedges—is everything okay?"

The thing about living down the street from your teacher, Sam thought, *is they know too much about your life.*

He stopped searching the hedges for the old woman, the boy, and the pig. It was important to look adults in the eye when he wanted them to believe him. "Everything's fine, Ms. Malloy."

Sam's teacher was tall and what his dad called bird-boned. Her wrists were knobby, and her fingers too, and all her clothes hung straight down like curtains. Her charm bracelet was big and jingly, and her cane was as black and shiny as her hair.

Sam liked her cane—Ms. Malloy had stuck glow-in-the-dark stars on it when they studied the solar system. She was pretty old, Sam thought. More than thirty, maybe even close to forty, like Sam's dad and Anita were, but nowhere near as old as Principal Vane.

She might not have much to say when students did okay, but when Ms. Malloy was really pleased with their work, she'd smile, and her eyes would sparkle. She'd say, "Brilliant."

But she wasn't smiling now.

"If you want to talk," she said.

"Honest." Sam tried to fill in the silence. "Everything's fine!"
Except for a couple of lost words.

Not lost. They'd been stolen. He was sure of it now. How could Sam explain that this wasn't his fault? He wished he could prove the theft without Ms. Malloy thinking he had made it up.

Her cane and heels click-clack-clicked on the sidewalk, and the summer breeze blew the tree leaves into a long shushing sound. They turned onto Calloway Drive—their street.

The first house on the corner, the Lockhearts', was the biggest and oldest Victorian in all of Mount Cloud village. The glass windows—Anita, an architect, called them "mullioned"—and gingerbread porch of the house appeared in all the community posters.

Last summer, Coach Lockheart built the street's Little Free Library to resemble his house, painting it the same four purple shades—light to dark—with cream gingerbread trim. He'd let Sam and Anita help.

The box was a lot bigger than most Little Free Libraries because of all the additions. It sat outside Mrs. Lockheart's low green hedge, which was bordered on both sides with tulips.

Ms. Malloy had tulips too, but no hedge. Just a big oak tree. Her flowers had gotten crushed in the same incident as Mrs. Lockheart's, but she hadn't minded as much. Just tossed the ball back.

Sam wondered if Ms. Malloy was going to walk him past her house and all the way to his. This was another problem with living down the street from your teacher.

"I'm okay, Ms. Malloy," he said in his most serious voice.

"Okay, Sam. I won't press. But I'd like to get this figured out," Ms. Malloy said. "Sixth grade is a big responsibility. You set the example for the rest of the school. You can't be so cavalier about your friends' feelings."

"I know Ms. Malloy—" Sam began. But right then, on the other side of the Lockhearts' hedge, he saw a pig's tail and then a snout sticking through the branches. "*There* you are."

"*Who?*" Ms. Malloy looked around, but Sam was already scrambling under the hedge, trying to grab the pig. His backpack jammed in the bushes and he got stuck and scraped. Meantime, the pig leapt away, snorting, just out of reach. "*Sam!*"

He wriggled his backpack free and crawled from the other side of the hedge, determined to show Ms. Malloy that there really had been a pig. Sam was sweating, and the dirt clung to his knees and arms. When he stood up and chased the pig, the old woman emerged from the bushes and started chasing Sam too. She raised her arm, trying to swat him with the willow stick again.

The pig, with a tendril of ribbon dangling from its jaw, ran straight for the Little Free Library. Its Victorian gingerbread-trimmed door hung open. When the pig got there, it and the old woman took an enormous leap, shrunk rapidly, and then disappeared inside the library. The door slammed shut.

Sam stumbled, stunned. *What had happened?* But he couldn't let them get away.

"Oh no you don't." Sam grabbed the frame of the miniature house, knocking pieces of trim loose. He opened the door and stretched his hand into the Little Free Library.

When something caught Sam's fingers and pulled, he tried to yank his hand free.

Sam pulled, and the something yanked back, until his arm was good and stuck in the Little Free Library. His backpack dropped to the ground as he grunted and struggled. The grip on his fingers grew painful as the library rocked on its purple-and-white-striped post.

"Sam?" Ms. Malloy's voice came through muffled from beyond the Little Free Library. "What are you *doing*?"

At that moment, whatever had his hand released it, and Sam tumbled backward to the ground.

He looked up to see his teacher, frowning.

"Nothing! I thought I saw a—" Her eyes narrowed. She hadn't seen the pig. Maybe Sam *was* seeing things. "A wasp! I wanted to get it out before any little kids got stung!"

Ms. Malloy continued to look dubious. "You should be more careful."

"I will be," Sam assured her.

But even as he said the words, Sam glimpsed two dark eyes and a puff of silver hair peering over the pile of free books inside the library. The boy—though the creature looked like a bug deep in the shadows—wasn't wearing a green shirt after all. That was his skin. He was green, with silver hair, like the old woman. And he had dark, beady eyes like a bug.

Except he was too big for a bug. And his hands were as strong as Sam's. And he was glaring at Sam.

Sam glared back. He lunged at the face behind the books.

"Sam!" Ms. Malloy squinted at the library, fumbling for her glasses. Then she grabbed Sam's shirttail and pulled. A twisting, yanking, tumble later, the Little Free Library's door swung, dangling, on one hinge.

Below the door, five figures sprawled among the remainder of Mrs. Lockheart's tulips. Five. Not two.

Ms. Malloy. Sam. A small, fuzzy, green boy with silver hair. A very small silver-haired old woman who raised a long switch into the air threateningly. And a tiny white pig with a pink snout and a brown leash. The edge of a sparkling ribbon inscribed with gleaming letters dangled from the pig's mouth.

"Got you!" Sam yelled. "Ms. Malloy, can you see? This is what stole—"

Ms. Malloy stared, her mouth hanging open.

The pig grunted and struggled. Sam's fingers tightened around the pig's leash. With his free hand, he reached for the ribbon.

"Give that back!" The old woman shouted, then blushed nearly invisible when Ms. Malloy turned toward her, shocked.

Sam hadn't expected his teacher to see the creatures. To his surprise, Ms. Malloy's eyes widened. Sam didn't expect her to react the way she did, either.

On a normal day, an adult like Ms. Malloy ought to have said, "What IS this?" or maybe, "Who is *that*?"

But instead, his teacher shrieked "YOU!" at the top of her lungs and lunged for the tiny old lady. "GIVE IT BACK!"

Now it was Sam's turn to be shocked.

Ms. Malloy's voice suddenly sounded so young and out-raged. In fact, she sounded a lot like Sam.

The old woman, in reply, struggled to take the leash from Sam's grip. She stuck out her tongue at Ms. Malloy. "I can't, and I won't."

The pig rooted around in Ms. Malloy's school bag until she smacked it away with a loud, "THIEF!"

And then the younger creature, whom they had all forgotten in the chaos, bit Sam's hand.

"Ow!" Sam let go of the leash fast.

Then he and his fifth-grade teacher sat on the sidewalk in shock as the green boy, the tiny old woman, and the white pig disap-peared into the Little Free Library.

"Well, I never thought I'd see that wretched thing again," Ms. Malloy grumbled.

Sam shook his stinging hand and stared at his teacher.

"What did they take from you?" Ms. Malloy asked, her voice shaking.

For the third time that day, Sam was left speechless.

Chapter Two

Tolver

Tolver had never been made to vanish before—that sort of magic didn't work at home.

He'd never been allowed on the other side, where the humans still lived, either.

But apparently when Nan did magic on that side of the worlds, it *itched*.

Tolver never thought his first adventure to the other side would itch. Or require so much disappearing.

The itch from disappearing wasn't *nearly* as bad as falling. Which was what he was doing now, while *also* itching.

The silver-haired boy spun and tumbled through the air, his arms and legs windmilling until he landed with an *oof* on the wet, and thankfully soft, ground of a marshbog island so small it didn't have a name. He'd dropped into the mud beside a thatched cottage suitably small for the tiny island. One where he'd lived with his grandmother since he was a baby.

In the distance, a bell rang on Schoolhouse Island. Closer by, Nana's laundry flapped noisily on the line strung from her cottage roof to a post by the shore. The air smelled of salt and mud.

Home.

Like nothing had changed. Especially the mud.

But Tolver had changed. He knew that much.

Tolver scratched his chin triumphantly. His first time on the other side might have ended with him falling into a puddle, sure, but it was filled with victory. He'd followed in Nana's footsteps and stolen his first spoken word. "Come here, Starflake!"

The white pookah grumbled at him but spat out the silver ribbon so that it landed in Tolver's muddy lap. *Regret* glittered silver across the length of it. They'd taken three words from that terrible boy, and this one was his.

Tolver forgot about the itching. He'd done it all by himself! Well, almost.

"Maybe tomorrow we can go back," Tolver mused aloud. Going back meant getting more words, which would help with every difficulty he and his Nana had.

"Tolver, you did very well! But if we have enough, we don't *need* to keep going back." Nana's patient voice came from the sky above. "We only gather spoken words when we need them."

"But what if we do need them? And when can I get my own switch? And . . ." Tolver bit his lip as he watched his grandmother drift gracefully to the ground. They could get printed words fairly easily. But Nan used those only for spells; they disappeared so fast. Spoken words lasted much longer, especially if they'd been really poorly used by their owners. Nan had taught Tolver everything he needed to know about that before they'd gone to the other side, but she hadn't yet taught him how to work the spells necessary to get there and back.

Now his grandmother held the white pookah's leash in one hand, and her basket rested in the crook of her elbow. She was much better at moving through the portal and hadn't fallen like Tolver. "I'm proud of you."

Tolver forgot about the itching and the mud altogether. He smiled at his grandmother. "Thank you." He'd been practicing so hard, ever since he finished school. Studying maps of Mount Cloud, learning how to hold onto a pookah while it jumped. Which he could do now, most of the time.

The other twelve-year-old boglins had each joined their family's lines of work. Now he'd done the same. His chest puffed out a little, fraying his torn shirt more.

"I'll get you the mending kit," Nana tutted at him. But she seemed as pleased as he felt. "I told you if you practiced enough with Starflake, you'd make a good word-boglin. And now you have."

Real spoken words—the overused ones, at least—could be converted into hot air, and that helped power ships and machines. And that meant it could be traded for something big, like Nana's island. *And then maybe a fine ship*, Tolver thought.

"And if I get good enough, maybe I can be a *full-time* word-boglin! No more delivering the mail! No more chores!" Tolver crowed. "Now that I can help you, we'll buy your island, and someday—"

His grandmother chuckled, as if she could read his mind. "Don't get too ahead of yourself. We'll deliver mail, as we always have, so long as there are islands to deliver to. And we'll do what word-gathering needs to be done, us and the pookah, both. But only what needs done, and no more than that."

But that's part of the problem, Tolver thought. *We never have more than just enough of anything.* "Delivering mail gets us eggs and fish, plus a magic word now and then, on a grimy piece of paper. That's not going to help save the island, or–" Tolver stopped again. He'd nearly said, "Get me on an adventure."

"Tolver. You know I want the island to be yours one day. I hope we can make that happen. But slow is how we do it. Remember your studies."

It was unlikely Tolver would forget his classes on School-house island: Trading and Economics. Ethics. How to behave when you visited the big city, Felicity. Boglin history. Nana, who was the eldest goblin in the marshlands, taught that one herself. He hadn't wanted to go to a city for further study like she had, though. He'd been eager to start work with her, ever since he realized that boglins could buy things like islands and ships. "What I learned was that we'd need to shift from slow and steady to faster progress if we want to keep the island, Nan," he grumbled.

Other islands were already becoming extensions of the city–with factories and warehouses rising from the mud. Only those boglins who'd bought their land back from the city had managed to stay independent: Schoolhouse, Roe Island, and Wanderer's Reach.

If I manage it, Tolver thought, *Nana won't have to worry so much. And I won't have to feel guilty when I go on my own adventures one day.*

Nana shook her head, "We'll get there." Starflake, the white pookah, grunted agreement.

No matter how tradition-bound she was, Tolver loved his Nana, and the pookahs too. If they would just take him seriously. "Once we can stop giving our earnings every half year to the city and stop worrying that they're just going to move a factory here, *then* we'll be able to go slow, I promise. I mean, look at the prospectors—they're full time. And the city can't tell them what to do—"

He regretted saying that much when her smile faded.

"The prospectors! I don't want to hear another word about those miscreants. Reckless, obsessed with expensive, dangerous machines..." Nana tried to keep her voice light, but she was nearly bubbling with rage. "No more about them, Tolver. They take too much of everything because they've gotten so big. And because they've gotten so big, they have to take more. I refuse to deal with them."

Tolver bowed his head. "I know, Nana." She was talking about his parents. She'd had to worry a lot about him, in addition to the pookah and the island's rent, once his parents had disappeared on a lost prospector ship.

As an apology, Tolver removed Starflake's leash and saddle, then brushed the sweat from her back while the white pookah snuffled and grunted loudly. From behind Nana's cottage, a black pookah and several small baby pookahs emerged from a fenced paddock and mud bath.

The family of pookahs—which looked a lot like pigs—nuzzled each other while Tolver tried to clean himself up at the pump. He brushed off his clothes after the pookahs trundled back to the mud. Some boglins liked mud a lot more than others. Pookahs, it turned out, liked it most of all.

Then he handed his first word over to his grandmother. She took two more ribbons out of her basket. They said *Sorry* and *Apologize.* "Maybe this will be enough," he said hopefully as she poked through her basket, making sure nothing had been left behind.

"Maybe," she murmured hopefully, not looking at him. "If they haven't raised the price again. But even then, eventually we will have enough."

Tolver sighed, some of his exultation draining. Learning word-gathering was slow going. Tolver had been clumsy at first and hadn't realized how hard it was to find mis-used words, even with a pookah's help. Which was why Nana wasn't teaching him magic yet.

And though they both daydreamed about buying the island, musing about it over supper and out in the mail boat, the longer they took getting enough to trade, the more the cottage seemed to cost.

He tried one more time. "We only need to be a little more efficient, to have a plan when we go foraging, to use some of the new machines," Tolver said. He'd heard rumors, the last time they were in Felicity, about something better than pookahs and switches and magic words.

Nana clucked at him, then patted his cheek. "You're a good boy, looking out for me. But word-gathering isn't something that is done well if it's done fast. And well is the way we do things."

"I know, I know. It's *always* the way we do things. Switches and pookahs and portal-words." Tolver tried to smile, but his heart sank. *It* was *too slow*. His gran wasn't getting any younger.

The prospectors used ships and machines to help them get everything done faster. They had, he'd heard, big metal word hogs. Ones that could sniff out the best word wasters on the other side twice as well as regular pookahs.

Everyone knew pookahs were slow. Even the pookahs knew it.

But, like everything else, the prospectors liked to keep their technology to themselves and charge others for using it. Those word hogs, Tolver guessed, probably cost more than an island.

Meantime, with only a switch, two pookahs, and a few magic words, Nana had kept everything around the tiny cottage going. She'd fenced the mud bath all on her own, before Tolver had come to live with her, when the pookahs decided they liked it. She'd even built her own hot air converter after studying with the inventor on Brightside island down-marsh.

Tolver had heard that the prospectors had better converters. Ones that could turn any word to hot air, even if it wasn't really mis-used. But whatever the prospectors used would upset Nana.

At least boglin pookahs were good at sniffing out mis-used words. Starflake had traced the boy who'd been wasting those words so easily. He'd been wasting them for a long time. The scent of it was all over the neighborhood, even on the Little Free Library. Even Tolver could smell it a little.

Once they'd found the boy, Nana had set up a careful trap. Tolver had watched every step. But the setting of the trap, and the gathering of each word, did take a lot of time.

He wished they could be faster, that's all.

"Do you want to do the honors, Tolver?" Nana stood by the converter, holding one of the ribbons out to him. His word.

Tolver jumped at the chance. The family's converter was a bit wobbly, and it leaked. But Tolver had always loved converting the words Nana brought home, and now he'd get to do his own first word.

He carefully put the ribbon into the brass cup on the top of the converter and closed the lid. Nana began to turn the crank on the side, and Tolver waited for the canvas bag on the other side to

fill with hot air, like it always did when Nana came back from one of
her adventures.

Instead, the bag stayed flat and the converter made a click-
ing noise.

Nana flipped the lid open and examined the ribbon.
"Hmmmm."

Then she opened the side of the box, carefully. "HMMMM,"
she said again. This time sounding gruffer, the way she'd changed her
voice to scare the boy.

"That's not good. A cracked gear." She lifted the ribbon from
the cup. "We'll have to take the words to the Depository and get
them weighed there."

Tolver groaned. That would be at least another day, if not
more. The Depository was in Felicity. And the Depository charged a
fee for weighing and storage. Which would make buying the island
even more of a distant dream.

"There, there." Nana patted his hand.

She'd always done that to make him feel better, and usually
the touch of her fingers on his skin did calm him. But today, Tolver
pulled his hand away. "It's not fair."

"We'll ask Julius if he can help fix the converter. Don't worry.

Meantime, it's just a little longer wait." Julius was the inventor on Brightside, and Nana's friend. Nana smiled at Tolver, and then put a hand to her forehead. "Oh! I made a tea cake before we left! You must be starving."

Tolver sighed as the old woman carried her basket into the cottage. He was hungry, but that wasn't the problem. He tried to do what Nan told him. She was the wisest person he knew. But she had lots of rules about what was good and what was bad. Slow and steady? That was good. Getting ahead of yourself? Bad. The marshbogs and the pookahs and the way things had always been done? Good. The prospectors who sometimes came through the marshlands on their enormous ships? They were bad.

Nana emerged from the cottage with three plates. She put the largest plate on the stoop. Gilfillan and Starflake snorted happily and trundled over. Pookahs loved cake.

Tolver took a bite and felt his mood ease. "I wish we could have gathered more words. Maybe even taken a few from that woman with the sparkly cane—"

"Leave *her* out of this," Nana said quietly. She put her cake down. Her creased face seemed to close in on itself just a little.

That was strange. "Do you know her?" The woman *had* seemed to know Nana.

"Not in the least!" Nana gave her cake to Starflake. She wasn't smiling any longer. "She reminded me of someone I met long ago. A mistake I made once. Plus, she got in our way!"

Even stranger. Nana rarely got upset. And she never made mistakes.

Strangest of all, Tolver had enough schooling and training from Nana to know that word-gatherers weren't supposed to do things that might get them recognized by humans.

Word-boglins were supposed to clean up the over-used words on the other side and get home fast; a service done for humanity—making sure that most of the words in circulation continued to mean something—and a help to goblin-kind as well. Poorly used words over there turned to many useful purposes over here. Everyone won. That was the way boglins always did things. Goblins who lived in the city, rather than the marshbogs? They did things differently.

Nana was definitely upset. And Tolver was fascinated. He scratched a still-itchy spot on his arm and watched his grandmother closely as she turned back to the small, bright cottage kitchen. "More tea? I'll put the kettle on again."

When the blue teakettle whistled on the stove, Nana finally stopped banging pots around. From inside, sipping a sweet grass tea, she said, "You are a good boy, Tolver, and you did well. We'll be fine. Please don't ask about that woman again, all right? We'll do our best to avoid her." She still looked upset.

Tolver nodded. He wouldn't ask, but he would wonder.

Nana pointed at the carved safe box above the stove. "We'll keep your word here until we can go to the Depository or fix the converter." She piled her own ribbons inside, and Tolver put his in too.

Nana waved her switch over the box while reading a word she'd taken from a nearby basket: "protect." That locked them up and out of harm's way. She crumpled the now-blank paper and threw it in the hearth.

Nana knew so much useful magic. How to open up portals. How to organize the pookahs. How to use words to do things.

All Tolver was really good at so far was steering the mail boat and falling. "Soon, we'll have enough."

His Nan nodded. "These words could make years of hot air. Starflake wouldn't lead us astray. Finding good sources is getting harder now and more expensive. Those terrible prospectors are racing to grab them all first. We're lucky we have such lovely pookahs. We won't waste a syllable on a broken converter."

Nana went to rest while Tolver began his chores and had a think.

Years of hot air—with a few more words like those, even with the broken converter, they should be able to buy Nana's island. *And then, perhaps,* Tolver thought, *a ship.* Or some machines. If they got enough, Tolver wouldn't have to stay a mere word forager and mailboat driver for the rest of his days.

Tolver looked out across the small marshbog island, over the water turning deep blue in the evening light, and to the bright lights of the high-and-low city in the distance.

Half of the city rested on the largest island in the marshlands, and half floated far above. The lower half was factories and practical things. The upper half of Felicity was filled with adventure. Giant ships moved around its edges, and trains zoomed between the buildings, and the Depository itself glowed from within.

The city glittered in the evening light, and Tolver's dark eyes glittered too.

~~⊃

As night fell in the marshbogs, Tolver fed the pookahs and began to load the mail boat. Three lumpy sacks jangled with boxed trinkets, many bound up in ribbons and colorful seals. Every one of the packages had an address carefully lettered on it, in strange scripts: Schoolhouse Island, Roe Island, Wanderer's Reach Island, Brightside Island. Four stops tonight.

That would take until nearly dawn.

It was safer to deliver mail at night, even if he was tired from his first word-gathering trip. Sometimes, prospectors liked to raid mail boats and take what they pleased.

Tolver knew the mail route kept them in tea and fish, and every so often, a magic word or two—the printed kind. And the pookah in cakes. Not a terrible job to have. But it wasn't the same as word-gathering.

Tolver put the last of the sacks in the boat. For a moment, he felt very sad. "Nana, you and my parents delivered mail all over the marshlands. Now all we've got is a few islands."

Nana thought before answering. In the distance, a ship detached from the floating city and began to sail closer. Were those prospectors? Coming for the mail? Tolver shivered. The old boat bobbed in the shallow water.

"Our family's always been good at getting messages anywhere they need to go, Tolver," Nana said, carrying the broken converter to the boat. "We're good at staying out of sight, crossing borders, that sort of thing. We did it in the human world quite a bit, even helped set up the first mailboxes and post services. It doesn't matter how much or how little mail there is. Only that it gets where it's going."

Another ship had detached from the upper city, following behind the first. While Tolver was curious about the prospectors in broad daylight, he didn't feel as interested in coming across them at night. He didn't want the boat to be attacked or Nana to be hurt. "We can go later. It's just the mail."

Nana frowned. "These are not just the mail. They're our duty. They're our neighbors' hearts. We must be careful with them."

Tolver scowled at a letter that had slipped from a sack. "Some are pretty flat for hearts." But he finished settling the bags and packages in the boat. Then he held the craft steady as Nana climbed in and took the starboard oar. He wrapped his hands around the port oar—smooth from years of use. The boat had a hot-air motor that could help speed things up, but they didn't want to use any fuel if they could help it. It was too valuable. And noisy. It would draw attention.

Water lapped the boat's sides as they rowed, a soft, slick sound, interrupted by the occasional *thunk* of a larger wave. In the dark, Tolver and Nana headed toward distant lights that could have been even more distant stars. That was how delivering the mail often went. Sometimes, as they rowed in the quiet, she told him stories of the worlds before or of his parents.

This night, though, Nana was tense. One of the prospector ships had turned. It cast a shadow their way as it left the city and began circling the marshbogs. She eyed it as she thought aloud. "It's been a long time since we've seen Julius on our rounds—I hope we can find him on Brightside tonight."

Tolver remembered the inventor being kind to him when he was young, while Julius and Nana worked on projects together. The boglin was a bit of an island oddity, having gone to a university in a distant goblin city. He liked to make gadgets. Most boglins on the marsh preferred to fish or farm. And to lift the occasional word.

Not Julius. He'd made Tolver a tiny ship once that floated all on its own. Tolver had taken it apart to see how it worked and hadn't been able to put it back together. Tolver sighed, thinking about it.

"Tell me how we quit delivering mail on the other side again?" Tolver asked to distract himself. He loved this story.

Nana chuckled, her voice calming. "My grandfather told me that we didn't quit. We used to work side by side with humans, delivering notes, finding secret places to put messages. We were very good at it. The shape-shifters—the pookahs—were especially good at getting secrets where they needed to go. When humans started building houses all across the countryside, they set up mailboxes with our help. Then they didn't need secret places. And they began wanting to deliver their own mail. And then—*boom*, said they didn't need us anymore. Retired, thanks for your service, that kind of thing."

"Did we steal words then too?" Tolver had never asked this before.

"Never!" Nana said. "Mostly!" She waved her arms widely, making the boat wobble. "We got a bad reputation from one or two missing secrets. A code book or two. That was when their world started to get noisy with fighting, and goblins began talking about leaving. And then all of a sudden, humans didn't want our help, so we did leave. They changed all their stories about the mail so that we vanished. We were too small, too strange. They didn't trust us anymore. Even though we didn't take things. Not much." She looked out toward the next island. "Only when it was necessary."

Tolver rowed and rowed, thinking about what was necessary and what wasn't. Good boglins, he knew from school, were careful with magic and words. They tried not to interfere too much in the lives of humans. "So when we left, we took all the magic with us, right?" That would be fair.

"Oh, no," Nana chuckled. "Humans don't realize it, but they still have a lot of magic. Their words are very powerful. When we left, they forgot a bit, that's all. They were so busy fighting. So sometimes, we magic good places for them to hide notes. You saw the tree next to the portal this morning?"

Tolver rowed and thought back to their passage through the portal. The box filled with books—which Nana said they couldn't steal from, because the books were in a mailbox, and they didn't steal from the mail (much)—and beside it, a large oak tree. "Was there a cemented-up spot in it?"

Nana nodded. "A long time ago, children used to leave messages in that knot. That's what makes a good portal—spaces where people leave things for one another. There's a particular energy." She quieted as they approached the first island, Schoolhouse.

She and Tolver handed over packages by the water's edge. The islanders there and on Roe gave Nana more packages, plus a few words torn from books or a basket of eggs or fish in payment.

Then their oars splashed the water again. The stars spun in the sky, and as they paddled, the water began to glow each time the oars struck the water. They rowed between rivers of stars, stopping again at Wanderer's Reach to drop off more packages at sleep-quieted cottages.

"Almost done," Nana said. Tolver's hands hurt and his eyes were heavy. Though he was used to this route, he'd been awake for so long. The sun was nearly up. The final island was Brightside. The inventor's island. Even from a distance, he could see lights in the factory and hear the clanging of machinery being built. Rumor had spread that the prospectors were keeping factories like the one on Brightside very busy. As if the city's factories had spread.

By the time the mail boat ground against the shoal, two young boglins waited with lanterns in the predawn light. They grabbed the bow and helped haul the small boat up on shore. "How many letters? Any for me?" The smaller boglin child's high-pitched question echoed through the dawn. Five more goblins emerged from the factory buildings, and another from a well-lit house. The only cottage on the island that remained dark was up a steep hill. The inventor's cottage.

A puppy barked from inside one of the buildings. The boglins stood on shore, waiting. They were all silver haired like Tolver and Nana. But some had goat horns, and some, small wings. Two of the factory workers had skin that looked purple in the lamplight and sparkled with phosphorescence. *Kobolds*, Tolver thought, *always liked to dress up.*

He began handing out carefully wrapped packages and hand-lettered envelopes. Some had flowers and sketches of strange machines hand-drawn on the envelopes, signifying payments: a new saddle for wild pookahs; a kind of calculator that ran on curses.

A young kobold, who was missing two teeth, took a package from Tolver's bag. "My name! Mine!" She tore it open right there in front of him. "Look!" Inside the package was a locket. "My gran sent me this from all the way across the marshbog." Tolver helped her put the locket on. As he slipped the clasp closed, he heard a soft, sad sound. The little boglin's mother held a letter tight and clutched a hand over her mouth. "What's wrong, Mum?"

"Such good news." The woman turned away. "Your brother's all right."

Nana bent close to the woman for a moment, talking quietly. When the woman straightened and walked down the path between cottages, Tolver noticed that Nana's face was gray and resolved.

"What happened?"

"The prospectors took her son out of school in the city. Convinced him to work on one of the rigs. He finally earned enough fuel to be allowed to write a letter."

Tolver stared, trying to make the words make sense. "They stole him? Like pirates do?"

Nana shook her head. "Not pirates. Not really stealing. What's that old word. Conscription. The boy had some debts, and they said he needed to work them off. Kind of like what sailors did during human wars." She sighed and folded the mail bag. "I've told you, those prospectors have too much machinery. Airships, fast ones, require more and more goblins to help keep them going. That poor boy."

Maybe, Tolver worried, *prospectors' efficiency is hard won, and not as easy to mimic as I'd thought.*

As they neared the bottom of the second bag, Nana prepared to go find the inventor. She set the converter in a basket on her back.

"I'll stay with the boat," Tolver offered. He hadn't seen any more ships leave the city, but it was good to be safe. Especially given what he'd just heard.

"I'll leave you my lantern," Nana said. So she was worried as well. She read a word to it that Tolver couldn't hear. "If you need me, wave it in the air and I'll come."

He wished she'd have given him a spell to use, but he took the lantern anyway.

The little boat rocked in the shallows while she waded ashore toward the darkened cottage on the island's leeward side.

When her footsteps faded, the marsh frogs and crickets picked up their evening concert: deep croaks and high chirrups. Then the music ceased.

Tolver thought he heard splashing in the shallows. A low chuckle.

Prospectors? He lifted Nana's lantern.

"Don't come farther. I've got words to spare." He didn't, but he'd heard Nana say as much when the prospectors had come too close before.

A reply came back. "You wouldn't waste words. You're a boglin."

Whoever it was, they were close. And they knew who he was.

"What do you want?" he called. "Show yourselves."

Two goblins stepped into the light. They wore boat clothes and canvas pants, and their feet were bare. One had a long, silver braid. The other was as broad as a cottage door and as expressionless. "Tolver Boglin—we've brought you a gift from Julius, the inventor."

Tolver narrowed his eyes. He liked presents. All boglins did. But this one felt wrong. "What's the catch?"

"No catch. Though if you're interested in something more, let us know. Julius is making lots of things these days—most very inexpensive."

Tolver shook his head. "My nan's up looking for Julius now. Maybe he'll tell her this himself."

The city goblin with the braid said, "Aye, if he's there. He's got responsibilities. Perhaps you don't need a gift. Perhaps you need a job? Wish to have adventures?"

"Not interested in a job." Tolver leaned back as casually as he could. "Won't leave my nan."

The first goblin sniffed, offended, but the second chuckled and held out a small, round object. The metal-and-glass surface glittered. "No job. No strings. Just a gift, then."

"What does it do?" Tolver asked. He tried to keep his hands behind him, but he wanted to reach out. The "gift" looked like a compass, but without any directions. It glowed faintly green in the marsh light. Or perhaps that was magic.

Tolver put out a finger to touch the compass. Just to see.

The goblin with the silver braid pulled her hand back so the compass was just out of Tolver's reach.

She smiled. "This? It helps you find the best words all on your own. You can use it to open a portal. Julius's own spell."

So I won't need to know how to do magic? Tolver's fingers twitched, but he crossed his arms. This had to be a trap. "We don't need that. We have pookahs. And my nan does portals the old-fashioned way."

"This is better. Faster. Just give it a try." The goblin extended the compass on a flat palm.

Since Julius had made the compass, Tolver was definitely curious. His fingers curled round the cool metal. "No strings?" The other two nodded.

He wanted to believe them. And that wanting was enough, at least right then, to make what the two goblins said feel like the truth.

At the sound of his nana's shoes on the reeds near the water's edge, Tolver slipped the gadget into his pocket. The two goblins faded into the darkness. By the time Nana appeared beside the boat, Tolver could hear the faint thrumming of an airship passing overhead. Prospectors indeed.

"Julius wasn't home," Nana said, sounding disappointed. "We'll have to fix the converter ourselves. Or buy help in the city."

Tolver frowned. That would take even longer. But Nana sounded so dejected and tired, he didn't say anything about the compass. *Perhaps*, he thought to himself, *I can trade their gift for a new converter gear. Or for a whole converter.*

Quietly, Tolver rowed Nana back home, put the boat away, fed the pookahs, and climbed, exhausted, up into his soft bed in the cottage loft. Before his head hit the pillow, he was nearly asleep. In the room below, Nana was already snoring softly.

Well into the next day, Tolver dreamed of the prospectors and their shiny new tools. He dreamed himself onboard one of their ships that stopped off at different cities to trade goods. That's how the prospectors knew so much more than regular marsh boglins.

In Tolver's dreams, they offered him his own ship, and he accepted.

Near the middle of the day, Tolver woke with a start, the feel of the wind still in his hair, his heart pounding.

Nana would be so upset if he left like that. That could never happen. He would have to get rid of the gift somehow.

He tried to get settled again, but the noise of the air baffles on the dream prospector ship still thrummed in his ears. Nana snored softly in the room below the loft.

Perhaps instead of getting rid of the gift, Tolver thought as he tossed and turned, trying to get comfortable, *he could take it apart and learn how it worked. Then he could build something similar. Unless his Nana taught him magic first.*

Eventually, Tolver gave up on sleeping. He roused himself from the cottage loft and went outside to watch the sun rise over the island and start the next round of chores. Those were never really done out here on the marsh.

By the time Nan woke, Tolver had realized they needed more words to fix the converter. And eventually to buy the island. Just a few more was all.

"Please, Nan, just this once?" He asked over breakfast. "I've already asked Starflake, and she doesn't mind."

Nana frowned but didn't say no. She knew they needed more words too.

Chapter Three

Sam

"I don't understand," Sam said over the creak of Ms. Malloy's porch swing.

His fifth-grade teacher swung back and forth, sipping a lemonade she'd gotten from the kitchen. Sam's glass of lemonade sweated on the table next to the swing, untouched. Anita made hers a lot sweeter. "What are they?"

"Maybe goblins?" Ms. Malloy said. "Or fairies. I've never been sure."

Sam swallowed. "Why are they here?"

"In Mount Cloud?" Ms. Malloy mused. "They took something from me a long time ago. Now I guess they're back for more." She looked pale and sad. Her hand was shaking so hard the ice clinked in her glass.

Sam scooted to the edge of the porch swing to see the Little Free Library better.

The box was tilted, the door hung open, dangling from one hinge, and Mrs. Lockheart's hedge looked like hogs had trampled it.

Which was kind of what had happened.

Ms. Malloy and Sam had pulled all the books out and pounded at the sides of the library, but they hadn't found a single silver hair. They'd tried to put it all back in order, but the box wobbled on its post. Sam promised himself that he'd come back to fix it later.

He would much rather have been playing baseball.

Down the street, Anita's car pulled up to the curb, home from picking Bella up at prekindergarten.

Now was his chance to explain what had happened with Mason before Ms. Malloy talked to his stepmom. Maybe now he could get out of trouble—or at least not have to go back to school on Monday to meet with Principal Vane. Ms. Malloy couldn't deny she'd seen *something*.

"I think whoever they are stole my words too."

Ms. Malloy looked at Sam hard. "Which words?"

"The ones you wanted me to say today." He held his breath and waited.

"Oh, Sam, oh no. I'm so sorry." Ms. Malloy looked downright embarrassed. "I thought you were just being stubborn. I never thought—" She drew a breath. "I'd stopped thinking they were real."

She meant the creatures. Sam knew it. He inspected the scrapes on his arms from the bushes. "We both saw them, though?" He had to be sure. Adults might be unreliable about this kind of thing.

She rubbed her temples. Her hair, escaped from its bun, had fallen into her eyes. She brushed it away. "I saw them. But, Sam . . ." She paled. She'd been about to say something else; he was certain. Instead, she sipped her lemonade until the ice clinked in the glass, then took a deep breath. "Sam, you need to get those words back! Not being able to apologize? I know how difficult a life that could make for you."

What did she mean? Sam stared at her. The porch swing creaked. "So I don't have to go back to school on Monday? Because you believe me? And you understand? And you'll tell Dr. Vane?"

Ms. Malloy blinked. She shook her head slowly, side to side. "Unfortunately, Principal Vane expects you, and he's very strict. You'll have to come back until you can apologize. There's no way around that. And if I tried to tell Dr. Vane what we saw . . ." She sighed. "Sam, I wish I could, but I just can't. Dr. Vane's so new. I could lose my job. And I love teaching."

She was a really good teacher. Sam didn't want her to lose her job either. "Maybe you could just tell him I *did* say ____?" He tried to smile, hopefully.

She shook her head. "I'm not going to say you did work that you didn't do, Sam. Perhaps you can think of another way around the situation, however. Did the–goblins–say anything this morning? Before they took your words?"

She *did* believe him.

He nodded. "The old woman said I was careless. Then she shook that stick at me."

"Sam, the times you've said you're sorry, did you truly mean it?"

He concentrated on his sneakers. "Not always."

"But sometimes?"

Sam nodded. "Of course." When he'd fought with his friends when he was really young, he'd meant it when he'd said ____. When he'd hurt his stepmom's feelings, or Bella's. Those times. "But maybe not this morning."

"I tried to read everything I could about magic creatures once. All the different kinds. Did you know there were different kinds? Some nicer than others. They used to steal things people were careless about. But then they disappeared—except for in stories. And now they're back in Mount Cloud!" Ms. Malloy said. She stared at the Little Free Library. "That's a problem."

"What did they take from you?" Sam asked.

And that was when Ms. Malloy began telling Sam the strangest story he'd ever heard.

"There was a brown-and-white pig," she began. "Right here in the village—you know I grew up in this house, right?"

Sam shook his head. He hadn't known that.

"I bent down to scratch the pig's ears. And I think I said ____. Well, I said those words a lot, whenever someone was kind, or even if they were mean. I didn't think about them, I just said them. And there was a lady with the pig. She waved a stick at me, and I could almost feel the word being pulled from my mouth. And suddenly, I couldn't say it anymore. My parents sent me to all kinds of doctors, and I learned quickly *not* to mention goblins or fairies."

What were the words? She couldn't even tell him. Just like what had happened to Sam.

She tipped the lemonade glass to her lips and, when there wasn't anything to drink, crunched one of the ice cubes between her teeth. It made an awful sound.

"So, after a while, I didn't believe the goblins were real any more than the doctors and my teachers did."

Ms. Malloy pushed at the porch floor with her cane, and the swing moved back and forth in the hot summer air.

Across the street, Anita set out the lemonade pitcher and a plate of cookies. Her head turned as if she was looking for Sam. Then she checked her watch.

"I should go home soon," he said.

That broke the storytelling spell. Ms. Malloy stopped the swing. "Of course, Sam. I'll go over with you and explain everything. Well, some things. Just—I mean, it's up to you, but I can't... I'll lose my job if people thought I'm seeing goblins."

She looked so upset, and Sam patted her arm like he'd seen his stepmom do when Bella or his dad was worried. "It will be okay, Ms. Malloy. I'll figure something out."

"Thank you, Sam." She walked slowly down the steps of her porch and Sam followed her. She didn't sound convinced. They were almost all the way across the street when Ms. Malloy said, "Starting next Monday, at school."

Sam couldn't help it. He groaned. But then his stepmom was there with cookies and lemonade, and Bella came running at him and gave him a hug. She jostled the lemonade, and it splashed cold on his shirt. "Thorry!" Bella said through her two missing top teeth.

And for a moment, it was just like a normal first day of summer. But Sam knew, if he was going to get out of trouble, that he needed to catch those goblins-or-fairies and get his words back. As soon as possible. Like today.

As Ms. Malloy talked quietly with his stepmom, he watched the Little Free Library carefully and sipped his lemonade.

⌒⊃

"What are you doing, Tham?" Bella asked. "Can I help?"

Sam's half sister stood in the doorway of his room, staring at the mess he'd made on the floor.

The mess would eventually be a goblin trap. His own design: shoebox, pocket dictionary, string, and a stick. But for now, it was a frustrating heap.

Bella, at five, was his favorite person in the world, but she was too little to help with this. "No. It's too dangerous."

"What is?" Bella was also the most curious person in the world.

While Ms. Malloy had explained to Anita some of the situation, keeping the goblins out of it, Bella had curled up beside Sam at the porch table and sucked her thumb. She'd listened wide-eyed while Anita had asked Sam careful, concerned questions.

Now she touched one purple, sparkly sneaker to the edge of the goblin trap. "Why are you building that? Why don't you just say thorry?"

Since Bella's front teeth had both fallen out a few weeks before, most everything she said that began with an *s* sounded fuzzy.

"I want to say it, Bell. I have to go back to Ms. Malloy's classroom every day until I can."

"But Ms. Malloy lives across the street. Why do you have to go all the way to school?" Bella worked hard on the *s* sound for each word.

Sam winced. He had to go all the way to school because Ms. Malloy had talked to Dr. Vane. And Dr. Vane was a stickler for rules. And because an old woman and a pig had stolen his words. Thinking about it made the back of Sam's throat itch and his eyes prickle. To make the feeling go away, he kicked the goblin trap. Hard enough so that it came apart with a clatter.

"Sam!" Anita called from downstairs.

"____" Sam replied, his mouth opening and shutting around the space where the word was supposed to be. Then, "Won't do it again!"

Bella's eyes widened. "You really can't thay it?"

Sam's breath caught. He shook his head, ashamed and frightened. And Bella, thinking he was still joking, giggled nervously. "Tham, maybe if I thay it with you?"

That was it, the last straw. It had been a very long, terrible, hot day.

"Bella," Sam said. "Practice isn't going to help. I can't THAY it. Period." His heart raced, and he immediately felt terrible.

Bella's eyes glittered and then the tears came. She disappeared with a wail that carried all the way to the kitchen.

Sam wanted to go after her, but he was also so embarrassed and angry. Instead, he sat there on the floor, staring at the goblin trap.

Why couldn't Ms. Malloy have just told his parents about the goblins or fairies— No. No adult would have believed her, either. At least this way, he'd maybe have an ally when he needed to stake out the Little Free Library. That's where it seemed like the goblins were congregating. And if he could catch one of them, he'd have proof.

A moment later, Anita stomped upstairs, holding his sobbing sister. "Sam! Really?"

From his stepmom's expression, Sam was pretty sure that when his dad got home, he'd be one hundred percent grounded. He was a nice dad and pretty patient as things went, but the call from school and a sobbing sister all in one day were a lot for anybody.

And Sam hadn't even done anything—well, he hadn't done all that much—wrong.

Anita went back downstairs. He climbed into bed and pulled all the covers over his head.

Soon enough, he heard his dad come home. The front door squeaked as it swung wide and closed with a heavy *thunk*. Then Anita spoke quietly to Sam's dad at the door. And once the door shut, Sam's dad came upstairs and into Sam's room. He was still wearing his summer suit—one he'd once said was kind of like a knight's armor for his job at the design and PR agency—plus his T. rex tie. He wore the suit because he had to. He wore the tie because it made Bella and Sam laugh.

But this afternoon, Sam's dad took one long look at the goblin trap splayed across the floor and then sat down on the corner of Sam's bed.

"Hey, kid. Rough end to the school year?" Sam's dad's voice was quietly curious. Sam nodded furiously, and the blanket rustled. His dad's compassion made the anger evaporate; he could feel it shimmering away, like heat from the playground.

But when his eyes began filling with tears again, he knuckled them away and pressed his face into his pillow.

"I don't know what's happening. But it's NOT my fault."

Muffled by the fabric, Sam's voice sounded thick and muted, even to his own ears. He turned his head to the side, facing the wall, so his dad couldn't see the tears still flowing down his cheeks. He knew he couldn't tell his dad about the goblins, either.

"That sounds really frustrating." Mr. Culver didn't push further. "Especially when everyone's thinking you're in the wrong."

Sam nodded but didn't turn over. His dad always got him. Ever since his mom had left—a letter on the table for his dad, a postcard for Sam, because he'd been a baby—they'd been a really good team. And summer was their best season because of baseball. They both loved the game.

Sam remembered then that next Sunday dad's company had seats at the stadium—the Phillies versus the Mets. *Please*, he begged himself. *Please let this be fixed by then. Please let me have caught the goblins by then and made them give me my words back.* "It's not a very fun time," he whispered.

"Not fun for Bella, either. She worships you. And you hurt her feelings. And Mason's. Things will be rough until you apologize." His dad's voice was still calm, but with each word, Sam felt himself shrinking. He wished he could turn invisible too.

"I want to make it better. I just don't have the right words," Sam finally whispered.

His dad sat for a few more minutes, quietly, and then patted Sam on the leg. "You'll figure it out. Sometimes it's not what you say; what you do matters more."

The bed creaked as Sam's dad got up, then the stairs creaked, each tread like an old keyboard made of groans, as he descended them.

Just like the Lockhearts and Ms. Malloy, the Culvers lived in an old Victorian house; the kind with a lot of woodwork and shadows in strange places. It had secret doors and built-in closets, and Bella and Sam had opened all of them, hoping for one like in *The Lion, the Witch and the Wardrobe*. So far, they hadn't found any secret doors that led anywhere good, like a Mets game, or spring training, or the World Series.

Instead, sometimes they thought they saw mice, and Bella had sworn a couple times lately she'd seen fairies.

"Hey, Bella?" Sam knocked on her door. Then he pushed it open. She wasn't there.

Out her window, he saw his sister standing on the porch, a lightning bug jar in her hands.

He walked back down the curving stairs, looking out the old glass windows that made tiny patterns on the lawn as the sky turned a purplish blue outside. The evening was warm, fireflies pricked the grass, and cicadas hummed. Bella ran through it all, trying to catch the lights and put them in a special jar.

He went to help her.

As he knelt and gently cupped a firefly so she could sweep it into her lighting bug container, one Anita had punched a few holes into and laced with leaves, Bella whispered, "Thank you, Tham."

"You're welcome," Sam replied, and he meant it. And the word didn't get stolen. He breathed a sigh of relief.

At the edge of the yard, though, Sam saw a glimmer of white. Then, in the moonlight, a silver-haired boy riding a white pig crossed the street toward Mrs. Lockheart's house. "Bella, are those the fairies you said you saw? Can you help me catch them?"

Bella stared into her glass jar, watching the small lights turn on and off. "What, Tham?" By the time he drew her attention away from her fireflies, the creatures across the street were gone.

"You all right now, Sam?" Their dad came out and put his hand on Sam's shoulder.

"It's been a really strange day," Sam replied. "I'm ____." He shook his head. Still couldn't say it. "I'm glad it's over."

～⊃

But the evening wasn't over, of course.

Once Bella was asleep, and the lights had turned on upstairs at Ms. Malloy's and at the Lockhearts, Sam gathered up his goblin trap and rebuilt it on the sidewalk below Mrs. Lockheart's Little Free Library.

If those creatures liked words so much, Sam had a whole book full of them.

He trailed the string along beside him, set up to watch from behind the oak tree, and, with the cicadas singing, watched the stars come out in between the branches.

If Mason hadn't been so mad, Sam might have asked if she'd set goblin traps with him.

He kind of wished he had. It was too quiet, sitting out here alone.

He checked his watch, which had glow-in-the-dark numbers. Eight thirty. He couldn't help it. He yawned.

He must have fallen asleep, because the next thing he knew, Mason and her friend Gina stood beside the Little Free Library. He hadn't seen or heard them arrive. And they'd been there long enough to pull apart the goblin trap. Mason held the dictionary spine-out as if she was about to put it inside the library.

Was she peering at something in the box? Sam couldn't tell. His muscles tensed like right before trying to steal a base.

He didn't want to scare Mason and Gina, but he didn't want any goblins hiding in the Little Free Library to jump out and steal their words, either.

Worse, Sam *really* didn't want the two girls to see him sitting here holding the string end of a homemade goblin trap. He was caught.

For a minute, Mason's glow-in-the-dark nail stickers winked like fireflies against the box. Then she pushed the dictionary inside and closed the door as best she could with its broken hinge.

"Why do you even bother? He was so mean." Gina cracked her gum.

"We're doing a summer project together, is all," Mason said. "And we've been friends a long time. I wanted to try and help him get out of trouble with Ms. Malloy, at least."

"It's your summer, I guess." Gina shook her head. She headed down the street to her own house and went inside.

Mason paused, looking up at the stars. Listening to the cicadas. Sam didn't move.

Then, without turning toward the tree he sat behind, Mason said, "Sam."

Sam gulped. How long had she known he was there, listening? He wanted to melt into the grass with embarrassment.

"What are you doing out here?"

"What are *you* doing out here?" Sam said back, and then scrambled for the first thing that came to mind. "Me, I thought I'd study who uses the library and when." The words came out jumbled, but kind of made sense. Still, Sam's skin felt red-hot.

"At night?" Mason looked back down at the shoebox and then up at the oak tree. She narrowed her eyes. "With a trap?" She waited a minute more. "I was trying to help you. But you're getting really weird, Sam."

He sat silent, embarrassed again, and also kind of mad. Mason sighed and walked down the sidewalk, heading home. "See you later, I guess."

Maybe Mason and I aren't friends like that anymore, anyway,

Sam thought. *Which might be at least partly my fault, but I can't fix it until I get my words back.*

So Sam waited until she'd disappeared into her house and then he set up the goblin trap again. He pulled the dictionary from the library—checking to see if he saw anything (or anyone) strange inside first—and set it open this time to the *S*s, and one of the words the creatures had stolen from him. He could read it but not say it, which was so frustrating. And then he waited some more.

His stepmom called from the front porch. "Sam? Time for bed."

Sam didn't answer because right then, he saw the two goblin-fairy-creatures, heading for the library. The silver-haired people walked close to the hedge, beside the white pig. The pig itself was snuffling wetly along the sidewalk and limping a little.

The pair spoke to each other, their voices low and musical. Sam could barely make out what they were saying. He thought he heard the boy saying, "I almost had that old man's word. I would have, if I had a spell! Show me how the magic works, Nana, please."

Quiet as crickets, the old woman answered, "Not just yet, Tolver. I want to make sure we do this right or not at all."

Their words confused Sam, along with what happened next.

The old woman climbed into the Little Free Library. The boy lifted the pig up as she waved her willow branch around, and the pig also disappeared inside the box. Then, holding the pig's leash, the boy began to pull himself inside.

How did they all fit? Them and all the books too? Sam was baffled.

But if I caught them, Sam realized, *they'd have to tell me how and give my words back.*

He left his hiding spot and grabbed the silver-haired boy's boot, then his canvas pant leg, the cuff of which was just then disappearing inside the library, and, finally, the pig.

"Get off!" Kicking and struggling, the boy turned to look at Sam, and he started becoming transparent.

"No you don't!" Sam yelled for the second time that day, and tried to hold on.

As he did, Sam realized he was shrinking, growing small while the library loomed large.

But when the boy kicked free, Sam fell back and stopped shrinking. As he struggled to his feet, the old woman, the boy, and their pig crawled over books toward the back of the library, which seemed to have a hole in it. There was a star-filled sky on the other side, and Sam imagined he could smell the sea. The old woman had already disappeared, and the boy was about to. Sam reached out fast and caught the pig's trailing leash once more. This time, he refused to let go.

The pig squeaked, surprised, as the hole at the back of the library closed. Sam grasped the tiny leash with his fingers and pulled gently until the miniature pig sat in his hand. Very carefully, he put the pig in the goblin-trap shoebox and closed the lid.

Then he brushed Little Free Library splinters off his sleeve and listened to the pig grunting and snuffling in the shoebox. He walked home, shaking.

Whatever was going on inside the Little Free Library had something to do with his words disappearing, and Sam would figure it out. He had the whole weekend to work on it.

Just as soon as he figured out what miniature goblin-fairy pigs ate.

And how to hide one from his parents. And his sister.

He let himself back into his house, the shoebox grumbling and grunting quietly under his arm.

Once he got the pig situated—air holes in the shoebox, some vegetable peelings and a piece of felt from Bella's craft room as a bed, and a small bandage for the pig's scraped hoof—Sam tried to sleep.

He wished, as he pulled the covers up and thought of the strange hole at the back of the Little Free Library, that he had friends who could help him figure out what had happened tonight. Ms. Malloy was great, but she couldn't possibly fit in a Little Free Library, and Mason was out of the question. There was Suyi from baseball, but he was a year older and might make fun of Sam when he heard what Sam was doing. It really should've been Mason.

The Culvers had moved to Mount Cloud a couple of years after Bella was born. Most of the kids on the street were Bella's age or in high school, and, though Sam knew a few others from the neighborhood baseball league for the longest time, Mason had been his best friend. He'd met Mason walking to the Fourth of July picnic the year they moved in.

Mason had been a perfect partner for games and elementary-school pranks. She knew he was afraid of spiders, which no one else did. She loved graphic novels as much as he did, even if everything else she read was different. They watched all the same movies. She would be perfect for this.

But that first time he'd teased her this year, he'd called her Mason McGarPEE in front of Ben and Suyi—sixth graders—and she'd started to drift away. Sam had said ___ then, but she'd yelled, "You always say 'sorry,' but you don't mean it." And though they'd teased each other off and on ever since, it wasn't always in a nice way when they *were* on. And she was a master at the silent treatment when they were off.

The shoebox sat on Sam's desk, drenched in moonlight. He'd taped the lid down and made sure the air holes were clear.

Now, thanks to that pig and its goblins-or-fairies-or-whatever, Sam couldn't say ___ at all.

At least, not yet.

Chapter Four

Tolver

"That boy is dangerous!" Tolver grumbled from the mud puddle where he'd landed beside the cottage. The world beyond the portal seemed much less fun than it had a few days ago. "Probably the whole neighborhood is dangerous!" He stood up and helped Nana from the reeds. She was damp but not injured. "We should gather words somewhere else!"

"Mount Cloud's my territory." She pulled a twig from her hair. "I grew up there. Someday, it will be yours. *After* you learn all the ropes. But we should have waited, at least until those two forgot about us. Starflake can blend in and be all right for a little while, but it was too risky."

"But we needed the words. And now we have them!"

His grandmother patted his arm. "Patience." Then she went to the cottage and rustled though the pantry. "You are so much like your parents, always wanting to find new ways to do things. But Tolver, too much too fast is riskier than any human boy."

But now we've lost Starflake, Tolver wanted to shout. *How will we get her back?*

The thought of the white pookah wandering that neighborhood, hurt, made Tolver want to break the promise he'd given Nana that he'd listen to her in all things. Even if Nana seemed calm about it, Tolver figured she was worried.

*And if we had the proper equipment, maybe it would be safer and faster, like—*Tolver thought of the "gift" from the prospectors that he'd hidden under his pillow in the loft.

Nana stopped him. "You know it's good to learn how to gather words yourself first, so that if any of those newfangled machines break down, you can still get what you need," she said.

Tolver knew. That didn't mean he had to like it. Not when it meant Starflake was all by herself on the other side.

"We boglins," Nana added, "only take what we need. Prospectors..." she cast a long look at a distant island in the marshbogs. Brightside gleamed from work that continued on through the night. Nana rustled through a bag, then handed Tolver a sand-wich. "We'll feel better after we eat. You need food to keep row-ing. Machines take a lot of goblins to keep going. And the bigger a machine gets, the more workers it needs. We just need us and the pookahs. Patience."

Tolver had been hearing *patience* for a long time. He loved his nana and the cottage. But he wanted things to go faster. And now? Now that one of the pookahs was lost—had been *stolen*—Tolver won-dered if maybe Nana was missing an opportunity.

The metal gift from the prospectors weighed heavy on his mind. He could make a portal with it, they'd said. And that could take him to Starflake. But how?

A marsh bug dove at Tolver's cheek. He swatted at it. Then he heard a deeper buzzing: a thrum in the air.

"Shhh," Nana said. She hunkered against the cottage wall, pointing at the horizon. "Prospectors on the wind."

Tolver pulled a set of binoculars from the jumble of tools that he wore on his belt. The prospector's ship was a large, dark shadow in the moonlight. An airbag haloed the hull. He watched the ship glide through the air, his heart keeping pace with the thrumming of its pumps and baffles.

When it turned, he sighed in relief. "They're heading back toward the city, not this way. Don't worry, Nana."

She watched the sky until the dark shadow shrank behind Felicity. "I'm not sure about that."

Through the lenses, Tolver could see the city's elevated glass buildings, all supported by an even bigger pillow of gas than the prospector's ship.

"How do they make such big machines go by themselves? When we cross over, we have to ask the pookahs for help." Tolver understood that boglins did things in traditional ways while modern goblins like the prospectors loved the newest things. That didn't stop Tolver from wanting to know *how they worked*.

"They use word magic, just like us," Nana said, still distracted. "But a lot more of it, all fed into the machines. And a lot more hot air."

"But—" It dawned on Tolver that if he knew the right things to say, he might use the prospectors' gift. "What kinds of words?"

"Words that mean what you want to do, or close enough to it. When I open a portal, I'll use the lens and an opening word. Why do you ask?" She didn't sound suspicious. She was used to Tolver being curious about magic.

"So why don't we use a word to call Starflake back, then? I mean, couldn't we, if we had the right tools?"

Nana shook her head. "It doesn't quite work. Pookahs are made of more magic than you and I, so our words won't work directly on them. Just around them. Shape-shifting goblins have always been like that. Even now they can change shape, and—if we're connected to them—it affects us. But when we change shape—growing up, for instance—it doesn't affect *them*."

"Growing up isn't magic, Nan," Tolver said.

She ruffled his hair fondly. "Isn't it?" Then she gazed at the sky. "We'll get Starflake back. It may just take some time."

Always time. When they were running right out of it. The more Tolver thought about it, the more upset he got about losing the pookah to the boy. They'd only gone over again so soon because he'd pressured Nana into getting more words. Tolver kicked at the mud.

Inside the pen, the small pookahs rooted around, looking for Starflake. "What if we asked for help to get Starflake back? Or . . . borrowed something that could help?" He began walking toward the cottage to get the compass from the loft.

"We won't use prospector machines, if that's what you're

thinking. Use those without paying? Means you'll owe them some-day, Tolver. We don't want to do that." The old woman shook her head regretfully. "They've gained control of enough already in this world."

Tolver slowly took his hand off the cottage door. He'd hoped to show her the gift Julius had sent him. He scuffed his foot on the stoop. It wasn't like he knew they were prospectors. The goblins who gave it to him had never *said* they were prospectors. They might have just been being nice.

"We'll get her the old-fashioned way. Tomorrow, once we're rested," Nana said. "And then we're leaving Mount Cloud alone again for a long time. We survived for many years without being able to go there. We'll stay away for long enough that those humans will forget they've ever seen us. Promise?"

Tolver nodded, his heart sinking. "I promise."

For the second night in a row, Tolver barely got any sleep.

For one, Nana snored. The cottage fairly rattled with it, goblin snores being serious business. Tolver lay awake, staring out the window. All he wanted to do was help.

He took out the metal compass and practiced saying words at it. None made the machine do more than glow slightly, then shut off.

Finally he fell asleep, his face pressed against the glass dome of the mysterious gift.

As the sun came up the next day, Tolver slipped the compass into his pocket, then finished his chores with a guilty twinge. There were fewer chores without Starflake on the island.

By the time he returned to the cottage, another cloud-shaped ship had appeared in the sky. One that loomed ever closer instead of sailing away.

They'll turn, Tolver thought. *Soon they'll head for the city.*

But the ship didn't turn. It didn't head for another distant city floating far away. It kept coming toward the islands, until its engines grew loud enough for Nana to hear.

Nana peeked from the cottage as the prospector's enormous airship, with its great cloud of an airbag suspended above it, hovered over the small island. The pummeling of the ship's rotors started to push the marsh grasses down near where Tolver stood. Tolver could see the ship's name on the stern: *The Colophon.*

"They must have heard we visited Brightside, or someone

told them about our windfall in Mount Cloud," Nana said. "I know they're wanting to do all the word-gathering themselves. Or perhaps they've figured out you're twelve and have finished school. So they'll want you to do it for them. Typical prospectors." With the sun higher in the sky, the ship cast an enormous shadow. The little bog cottage seemed to shrink beneath it. Gilfillan squealed, outraged.

"Let's send them on their way, then." Nana stepped out of the cottage. She'd removed her apron and rolled down her sleeves. She held the willow switch in her hand.

"The city is ready to begin converting your island to factory work." A voice boomed from the ship. "We've been told to let you know that you and your grandson may stay here and build ships or we'll take you to Felicity."

Oh no. Tolver glared at the sky. *They'd been too slow.*

"Our rent is paid through the summer," Nana cried defiantly. "You can't force us to leave, no matter who you are." Her voice shook with anger.

The Colophon finished dropping its anchors, and goblins readied to descend the ladders. "Hoy, Tolver Boglin!" one of them called. "Good to see you again!"

Tolver began to stand in greeting, but Nana gripped his shoulder. "You can't dock here," she said, voice steady. "This is still my home!"

"It's city property. Now that we're helping the city expand, we can dock anywhere in the city we wish. Besides, no matter what your rent, your boy accepted something from us." A voice boomed from the ship. "We're allowed here to get him to pay for it."

"That's a lie!" Nana said. "My Tolver would never."

Tolver flinched, his face turned away so she couldn't see his eyes. He wanted to fling the compass into the water. But that would give everything away.

Nana's eyes turned dark and angry. She lifted the switch in the air and shook it. "Begone!"

Oh no. Tolver thought. He knew that word. She'd had it forever, and it was so old. *Nana must be running out of words to use that one. How could she fight off a ship like this with something so old?* And he was right. The ship didn't go. More anchors dropped, the heavy lines weighted by pieces of old gears. Tolver's heart sank as each object pressed deep into the soft sides of the island.

But Nana's ancient word? That "begone!" passed up the willow stick like bright lightning, and moments later a small hole appeared in the ship's airbag. There was a tiny puff of smoke.

Unaware, the crew kept dropping anchors, and the first ladder struck the ground.

"Say it again!" Tolver said as he made his way toward Nana.

"I won't! That's a special spell," Nana whispered. "My oldest one. The woman on the island who traded it to me said it takes time to work. She wanted a week's worth of mis-used words. I traded so much hot air for that, before I learned to put the rest in the Depository." Her eyes narrowed. "Wait for it, and keep out of the way, Tolver. They're not taking anything from us today."

By her tone, he knew she meant for *him* never to be taken by the prospectors, nor the island. It stung that she wouldn't let him help defend their home.

As they watched, the small hole in the sail grew and began to flutter at the edges. A blur of tiny wings lifted and tore at the airbag, and the ship began to list in the wind.

The wings multiplied into a cloud that ate away at the channeled canvas. Soon there was a serious dent in the structures holding the great ship aloft. The crew began to lift its anchors as goblins struggled to beat back the destructive moths. The ship's engines began to churn in reverse.

Soon the ship slumped back toward Felicity.

When the prospectors were gone, Tolver helped Nana clean up the mess on their shore. "They think they can just come here!" Tolver's voice wobbled with panic.

Nana brushed the hair out of her eyes and nudged back tears. "Well, if they're helping the city expand, they can. Otherwise, they're just trying to scare you and me into doing what they want. Imagine, making me think you'd taken one of their gifts. Honestly."

"But what was that spell you did?" Tolver asked, brushing past the mention of their gift and thinking instead of the gas bag being devoured. *Teach me,* he almost said. *Teach me how to do that. I need that.*

Nana's smile bloomed slow. "Yes, it's time you learned a *few* more things about magic. But! Ideas first, *before* practice. That was a bedevilment. Silverfish variety. They're made out of old words that have gone astray or out of common use. They're not as well-known as curses. I won't risk curses, of course; those can get away from a person. But a good bedevilment? Boglins have been using those for generations." His grandmother tapped at her smoking willow switch. "Knew it would work. Worth every ounce of hot air."

She sounded pleased with herself and with the spell.

"But what if they come back? They'll be even more determined! Teach me how to do one so I can help next time instead of standing around!"

"Tolver," Nana said. "I'm old enough to remember when things weren't like this here. Before the prospectors started building their big machines, we weren't always struggling to pay for fuel or land. We weren't exactly peaceful, but we made glorious objects. We kept to our own territories. We did a little magic. We weren't constantly pursuing 'bigger' and 'faster' and 'more.'"

She eyed a piece of airbag that had fallen on the island. Poked at it with her switch. "There are wonders nowadays, it's true. But maybe it's time to slow down again. To use our own hands to do the work the slower way, not rely on the wasted words of others."

Tolver picked up the airship's fallen canvas and put it in the trash. The weight of the inventor's compass in his pocket was almost too much to bear. "All that stuff you're talking about—the old ways—that won't change now. The prospectors are powerful. You heard what the kobolds said last night. Everyone in the city is too invested. Other cities will be too. So teach me how to use a switch now, and then we'll get Starflake and more words, and we'll be able to fight them off. Please."

Nana moved the canvas from the trash to her rag bag. Then she returned to watch the sun rise with Tolver. "I won't let them take you, Tolver. But I won't teach you more magic, either. Not until I know you'll take it slow."

When would that be? Tolver wondered. *When it was too late?*

She still looked so angry, he was afraid to ask. But with the prospector's ship gone and everything around them turning gold and bright in the high morning, it was hard to believe he'd been scared. Dew prickled the marsh grass and reflected the sun in each tiny bead of water. The pookalets began to squeak hungrily until Gilfillan nuzzled them quiet.

Nana lifted her willow switch and sighed. It was singed and bent from the silverfish. "We'll show them we're willing to fight for the marshbogs, Tolver, I promise. But first I'll need a new switch. And more words. And we'll need Starflake." She pulled the box and magnifying lens from its safe spot in the cottage. "Get ready, Tolver, Gilfillan. We're going back."

Finally, Tolver thought. *Now we're getting somewhere.*

Chapter Five

Sam

"Dad, what do you do when you can't find the right word?" Sam asked at breakfast. "When the one you want is just *gone*?"

Mr. Culver poured more batter on the griddle as he thought about Sam's question. He was making their traditional Saturday-morning chocolate-chip pancakes. The batter was two parts pancake mix, one part chocolate, and the pancakes would be gooey and messy, exactly the way Sam liked them.

As his dad mulled the question and cooked, Sam relaxed a little. *If we're still having the good pancakes, maybe they're not still mad about what happened at school.*

"A dictionary is a good place to start." His dad slid two thick pancakes onto Sam's plate, then two onto Bella's. Anita passed Bella her juice and sat down next to her to cut the pancakes up into squares, the way Bella liked it.

Sam felt a little guilty. He'd left his dictionary at the foot of the Little Free Library, and it had rained overnight. Would that qualify as "careless" enough to attract the goblin's attention or just make the book smell moldy?

No matter what, the silver-haired creatures would want their tiny pig. And when they came back, he'd hold on to *them* this time instead. And then they'd give Sam his words back.

That morning, he'd made sure the white pig had water and some vegetable scraps from the compost, and he'd left it happily curled up in the shoebox on top of his desk. Then, before breakfast, Bella had helped Sam cut out letters and paste them on two plain pieces of paper. Folded, the paper made cards. One card for Ms. Malloy. One for Mason. Both cards said the word Sam couldn't say. The one he couldn't even write. Bella could say them, though. And she could spell them. Barely.

Even if the cards looked a little like a five-year-old did them instead of an eleven-and-a-half-year-old, he'd found a solution. Sam felt pretty proud of that.

"A dictionary's not exactly what I need," Sam said, trying

not to argue. He put a slab of butter on top of his pancakes, then poured syrup over everything. It sloshed off the plate and onto the table.

"Oh no," said his stepmom.

"___!" Sam said—or tried to.

His stepmother's expression, as Sam sopped up the sticky mess, was two parts frustration, one part puzzlement.

"Sam," his dad said, bringing a mug of coffee to the table. "We talked about this with Ms. Malloy, and if your stubbornness about saying sorry continues through the weekend, we'll all have to go meet with Dr. Vane on Monday. You said you have a plan? Good. Until you've sorted yourself out, no movies. No baseball." He turned to Anita and she nodded grimly.

Pancakes or not, they were still mad.

Sam pushed his fork around in the syrup, glum. How could summer turn this awful? "I'll make things better, I promise. But—haven't you ever heard of someone losing their words? Isn't it possible?"

His parents looked skeptical. He wasn't off to a good start. Still, Sam was sure that once he gave Mason and Ms. Malloy the cards, things would get better.

"I'm sorry you still can't say it, Tham," Bella said. "Sorry I made you mad too."

"Bella, you don't need to apologize for that," their dad said. "You didn't do anything wrong."

"Sometimes a word can mean a lot of different things, right Bella?" Anita sipped her coffee. "Words like 'sorry' especially. I say it sometimes when I'm mad or when someone's sick and I wish I could make them feel better. It's a way to reach out to someone else, to empathize with them. It's one of those really special words that can mean a lot of things."

She turned and whispered to Sam, "Even if it sometimes gets taken for granted."

Sam blushed. Was his stepmom right? He didn't think he'd been taking the word for granted. He *loved* that word. He stared at his plate, grumpily pushing at a bite with his fork.

Everyone else at the table can say it except me. How is that fair? Lots of people are careless with words. So why is it just me who has to miss out on baseball?

Sam's pancakes didn't have any answers. They got mushier while he moved them around on the plate. He took a bite. They still tasted really good.

"Mmmmm." Bella nodded agreement while chewing. She had chocolate at the corner of her mouth. Bella's hair—dark and glossy like her mom's—got caught in her mouth and tangled in the chocolate. She wiped at it, smearing everything. Sam handed her a napkin.

"Thorry."

"Bella...," Dad groaned.

As Sam chewed, he saw a nimbus of silver hair right outside the window. He coughed as the top of a baseball bat—one of his dad's old bats!—waved back and forth.

Then a small, glittery ribbon fell from Bella's lips, to the floor.

Was it happening again? Sam shook his head, trying to make sense of what he was seeing.

While his parents' backs were turned, a black pig, smaller than the white one had once been (but much bigger than the white one was now), pushed through the dog door and grabbed the word, then ran back out.

Another pig! Sam stared as the dog door flap swung back and forth loudly. "Hey!"

"We need to get that door fixed," his dad muttered.

"Or get a dog," his stepmom added.

Normally, Sam loved conversations like that—he really wanted a dog—but what he had right now was a pig problem. A word-stealing pig problem.

He slid around the breakfast nook and jostled the table hard, trying to see where the pig went. Bella's juice spilled, making a pink puddle.

Sam's dad sopped up Bella's juice with a rag and raised his eyebrows at both of them. "Guys, the weekend's just started, can we have a nice breakfast at least?"

Bella looked up at her dad, then back down at the juice. "_____," she said. Or tried to say.

Sam froze, watching her try. *Oh no.*

Her mouth opened and closed like a fish. "I can't thay it. Maybe I caught your cold, Sam."

Sam stomped his foot. "Thieves!" he shouted out the door. Whoever the creatures were, they were not going to steal his sister's words too. Or his dad's bat.

"Bella," his dad said. "Stop teasing Sam. And Sam, knock it off. You can say sorry— It's all right to stop pretending. Look how Bella's following your example."

"I'm not trying to set a bad example!" Sam had just watched a black pig steal a word right off his little sister's plate, and now his dad was talking to him like a little kid. "I'm trying to help fix everything. We made cards this morning! Remember, Bella?"

He held up the card Bella had helped him make. Multi-colored letters, cut out of magazines. His dad nodded approvingly. "Good."

"Bella, what does this say?" Sam continued. She studied the magazine letters she'd cut out and helped Sam stick on the cards and shook her head. "_____." She started to cry.

That's when Sam knew. His Saturday was only going to have one goal. *Catching the word thieves. And, after that, making* them *say they were* _____. "Dad, they got Bella too!"

"'They,' who?" Anita looked between them both, concerned.

Sam's dad shrugged. "Sam, buddy, this isn't how you sort things out. I don't know what else to say to you."

Sam froze. His dad always knew what to say. Even when it was hard. And he'd always tried to listen to Sam. He was really good at that, because that was his job. When he'd met Anita, he'd known what to say and he'd listened. Why not now?

Back then, for Sam's fifth birthday, his dad had invited *him* to the office for lunch, which he thought was really cool. He'd asked his babysitter to let him go up the elevator to the office by himself. They'd lived in the city, and his babysitter was all about independence. Until Sam got to the office, he'd felt very important and grown up. Sam had held his breath, waiting for his father's secretary to tell him to go away, that little kids didn't belong there. But she hadn't. In his dad's office, where a whole wall glittered with awards, his dad had taken a big, nervous sip of water, and said, "Okay, buddy. I'm going to ask you a question, because what you think matters a lot."

That had made Sam feel really important again, and he'd nodded.

"You like Anita, don't you?" His dad had asked. And Sam had nodded, because he really did. Anita Vasquez was an architect who sometimes came over for dinner, and sometimes she and Sam's dad went out. She was really nice. And Sam was pretty sure he knew what was coming next. Knowing had made him feel better and bigger.

Mr. Culver hugged Sam. "I'm glad. Do you think you'd like to try to be a family? You don't have to call her Mom or anything like that, unless you want to, okay?"

That was the beginning of the next part of Sam's life, where his dad married Anita, and it felt like all he had left of his real mom was the postcard she'd left in his crib with one word—"Sorry"—on it, before she disappeared. She'd gotten really bad depression, his dad said, after Sam was born, but it wasn't his fault. And now with Anita they were going to be a new family. And then Bella came, and they were.

So now, Sam knew it was very important for him to help his sister. Then, afterward, he'd make things right with Mason and finally Get Out of Trouble. "Don't worry, Dad. I know what I need to do." He was in the middle of saying this when the black pig and the old woman crossed the lawn, heading for the Lockhearts'. The woman carried his dad's baseball bat over her shoulder.

"Mayibeescusedplease?" Without waiting to hear the answer, Sam bolted from the kitchen, chasing the pig and the silver-haired woman down the sidewalk.

"Sam!" His dad's voice followed behind him.

He would get the words back, *then* he'd talk to his parents. *I'm doing it for Bella. And for me. And for Ms. Malloy too.*

He chased the pig all the way to the Little Free Library. Sam heard the old woman talking with the boy beside the library as they tightened the leash and saddle on the pig.

"What did you get?" The boy sounded like they planned to steal all the words in the world.

"Another 'sorry'! From the boy's sister." The old woman said. "And a lead on a few more in the neighborhood! What did you find?"

"Three 'awesome's and one 'amazing' that were lying around."

"Tolver—you know we can't use those. We don't have the right converter," the old woman said.

"Maybe we could rent one? Or borrow—"

"Tolver, no."

As the two of them bickered like umpires and coaches, Sam edged closer to the Little Free Library. All he had to do was grab Bella's word and then the goblin-fairy-creature.

He wasn't sure what he'd do then. Maybe they'd have to give back his word when he caught them, like in Bella's fairy tales.

"I know," the boy continued, as Sam drew closer, "but the kids were so careless, and you hate seeing words like that just lying there, poorly used. Besides—" He wiped his hands on his shirt. "You said we can't come back here for a long time. This will be enough to help us against the prospectors."

The old woman said, "I hope you're right," and then the pig bent its knees and prepared to leap inside the library.

"Oh no you don't," Sam yelled, and slammed the broken plexiglass door shut.

The pig crashed into it nosefirst and lay stunned on the ground. The silver-haired woman fell from its back. In seconds, they shook themselves. Stunned, but waking up. Sam took the opportunity to grab at the pig's leash.

The broken door squeaked open on its hinge.

The leather strap wrapped around his wrist, trapping him. Sam tried to snatch back his sister's word, which was dangling from the pig's mouth, but as soon as he did, the pig startled from its daze.

Snorting, the pig rolled to its hooves, and, caught in the kind of panic that comes from being suddenly awake, it leapt again, crashing past the doorframe. This time, it left the old woman behind and pulled Sam into the Little Free Library instead.

The corner of Sam's favorite Ponyo shirt tore on a hinge. His knees and elbows burned from paper cuts and splinters. "OW!" Being dragged through a Little Free Library—even a really big one—by a miniature black pig on a leash really hurt.

The pig didn't care about Sam's yelling. Sam bumped along behind as it shoved aside the books with its snout, barreling through the library, all the way to the back. Sam saw a blue sky and one puffy cloud where he'd once helped build a back wall.

He would have been absolutely certain that it was a blue sky, except that the pig jostling—and with its backside blocking the view—and the leash tightening around his wrist and the experience of being pulled over and through the books, and somehow him fitting into the library at all, had him really shaken up.

In the summer heat, the wooden box—stamped MOUNT CLOUD HARDWARE in green ink on the unpainted inside—smelled like books and the memory of trees.

Except it also began to smell damp and breezy, like the ocean. Sam didn't recall it smelling this way when he'd helped Mr. Lockheart and his stepmom build the Little Free Library.

A salty wave of air hit his face, even as the books got denser and he kept getting pulled through them. And though Sam somehow—*Magically?* he wondered—fit inside, he wasn't *that* little. Everything felt very squished and uncomfortable.

Sam held the strap tighter.

He'd promised himself he wouldn't let go of the word thief, and that meant the pig too. He kicked a lot of books as he struggled to hold fast. They tumbled from the Little Free Library with a clatter that was louder than the old woman's voice. She was yelling—at Sam, at the pig, at everyone.

And then there was a loud scraping sound and a pop. The pig disappeared, and Sam felt like he was being stretched and pulled a lot like the homemade spaghetti he sometimes helped Anita and his dad cook. He was growing longer from head to toe, and skinnier too, and then there was another pop and he fell out the back of the Little Free Library into a sky as blue as anything.

Sam lost his grip on the pig's leash. And as he fell, he saw the ocean below, and a bright pink bird flying upside down.

Wait—it's me who's upside down! Sam realized. When he windmilled his arms and flipped right side up, he discovered that the bird wasn't pink. That had been the sunset reflecting on its belly. Then the bird—a seagull, Sam thought—flew away, and Sam kept falling.

Falling felt as uncomfortable as being pulled through a Little Free Library, except with fewer books.

After a few seconds, Sam landed in the mud, right next to the black pig and a white cottage with a thatched roof and a blue door.

The pig snorted at Sam as if to say, *I hadn't expected to see you on the other side of a Little Free Library.*

"Same here, pig." Sam coughed. He sat in the mud for a minute, catching his breath. Sea air filled his lungs.

Mount Cloud, where Sam lived, wasn't anywhere near the sea.

The mud began to soak through Sam's jeans, making them heavier. Wet too. He shivered and pulled one leg up with a loud squelch.

"What are *you* doing *here*?" The strange boy's voice held a sharp edge, right by Sam's ear. "Where's my nana?" Green fingers curled over Sam's shoulder. He looked up into black eyes and at silver hair.

"Your nana hit me with a stick!" Sam said. *That's probably the worst way to start out a conversation with a magical creature,* he realized, too late. "What was that? Some kind of witch's wand?"

The boy blinked. "My nana's not a witch. She's a goblin. And you? *You're* terrible." He said this, Sam thought, with the kind of scorn people used about new batters who struck out on the farm team. "And you're on the wrong side of the worlds."

With his heart pounding in his ears and his mind trying to process so much strangeness at once, Sam panicked. He shouted at the boy. "That's your doing! I wouldn't be here if *you* hadn't taken…" He trailed off, finally losing steam. The shock of falling and landing–*here*? It was too much.

The goblin boy balled up his fist, and Sam put up his hands and shut his mouth, deeply shaken. "I'm ___." Sam knew from lots of playground experience when he'd first started school in Mount Cloud that he was on this strange kid's turf. He needed to make amends fast or the fight might get much worse.

But Sam couldn't say the right words.

"It's all a big accident," he finally said. "I'll fix that—tell me how to go home."

"I wish I knew," the boy said. "Humans can't be in the marsh-bogs. This is our side. No one wants you here. If the city finds out..." Sam thought the boy looked even greener at the possibility.

Well, you shouldn't have stolen my words, then, Sam thought. *Serves you right.* But he didn't say so. "Who are prospectors?"

The boy didn't answer. Sam shivered as a breeze kicked up over the water. He sat in the mud near a small cottage, looking up at a shrinking hole in the sky where the Little Free Library had been. Stranded with these green–goblins–who had taken his sister's word, plus several of his.

The black pig beside Sam snorted and rammed its snout into Sam's hand until he absently scratched its ears. At first, the pig grumbled. Then it sighed happily.

Sam kept scratching, even though he felt like yelling.

"Gilfillan likes you," the silver-haired boy said. He'd unclenched his fists. "You can't be *all* bad. But you have to go back. You being here might attract the prospectors' attention. They'll take all the words you have and then Nana and I can't–" The boy stopped short.

"Prospectors steal words?" Sam asked. "Just like you do?"

"They take a lot of things." The boy looked so upset and pale that Sam didn't press. "Not like us. Boglins are better than that."

Sam wanted to ask better how, but questions only seemed to make the boy more upset. He bet his dad would have known what to say. "Okay." He stood up. "We have two problems: first—you want me to leave. So let's start there. How do I go back up?" He pointed at the sky, showing the way he'd come.

The boy shook his head. "It's hard. Someone has to make you a portal—and then you have to be small enough to get through. And that takes a pookah—they're shape-shifters. And we've got only one pookah right now, and I need him to go get my nana, right, Gilfillan?"

Gilfillan snorted and leaned in for more ear scratches. Then, as Sam kept scratching behind its ears, wondering what a pookah was, it lay down and went to sleep.

The boy groaned. "I wish I could magic us out of this." He looked for a moment as if he were going to cry. But then the boy shook his head at the pig and at Sam. "Come on. We can't get Nan across without you." He nudged Gilfillan, who snored louder. "Get UP."

"Why are you talking to a pig like that?"

The goblin boy blustered at Sam. "This is a pookah. They only look like pigs." He nudged Gilfillan with his foot. "They're goblin shape-shifters. You hold on to one, even just the leash, they can change you too—that's how you fit through the portal."

The pig snorted in agreement and closed its eyes again.

"Are you—polkas also?" Boy, how Sam wished he'd paid attention to Bella's books.

"POOKAH, not polka. They're not dances. Be careful how you say it. And no, I'm a boglin, from the hobgob family. My nan's a kobold, I think. It doesn't really matter so much over here though. Goblins are goblins. We just want to be left alone."

Goblins. Not witches or fairies. He couldn't wait to tell Ms. Malloy. "You can't come to my neighborhood, take what's not yours, and then say you want to be left alone. So I'm leaving, but not without our words. My sister's and mine. And whatever else you've taken."

It was a brave thing to say, given that Sam was covered in the mud of what looked like half the small island, near a strange white cottage with a low, thatched roof, and arguing with a goblin.

If Mason and Gina called me weird before, this is even weirder.

The goblin boy grew quiet. "I want to send you right back,

and your words too. Your town's getting to be bad luck for my nan and me."

"Then why don't you find a better town?" Sam said.

"My nan's been using ill-used and taken-for-granted Mount Cloud words to power our boat for years. Your town has so many—they're all just lying around for the gathering." He walked around Sam, nervously flexing his fingers near his pockets. "That's our second problem, isn't it? My nana's stuck over there, and Starflake too. And she's the one who knows how to open the portal, not me. Why did you leave Nan behind, Gilfillan?"

This last question was directed at the pig. The pookah, Sam reminded himself.

Instead of an answer, Gilfillan got up and waddled away behind the cottage. The boy followed, muttering, looking all around the cottage and out to the water's edge, as if he thought he'd find his Nana hanging there by her fingertips.

Sam knew that wouldn't happen. "It's not Gilfillan's fault. I was trying to get my sister's word back when *you* dragged me through our neighbor's Little Free Library. And *your* nana fell off the pig. I don't know what happened to her then, but she didn't come through with me to—wherever we are."

"You," the boy said, his voice wavering, "are in the marshbogs. My home. I'm Tolver Boglin, master of this island until my nana gets back. So you have to do what I say."

Sam bristled a little at that, but then Tolver began to pace again. "Nana might be okay for a little while over there. Maybe. At least she's got a new switch. And if we're lucky, she'll find someplace to hide, or find Starflake and come back on her own. Meantime, I can figure out how to–"

"A new switch? Is that my dad's old baseball bat? Is Starflake the white pig?" Sam guessed. That was the pig he'd seen first, when he lost his words. The one that he'd trapped in a shoebox in his room.

Tolver turned and stared at him, then took a step forward, backing Sam nearly into the water. "You've seen her? Is she okay?" Worry edged the boy's voice as he looked at the sky again. "I really wish both of them were here. Then I'd know what to do."

Gilfillan grunted in agreement.

Sam felt a tug of familiarity in Tolver's frayed words. "She's okay. I put a Band-Aid on her scraped hoof. I wanted to help. I still do," he added.

"If you really did help Starflake, that means I should help you too. But I'll need you to do me a favor." When Sam agreed, Tolver went inside the cottage. Sam heard him rummaging around.

When the goblin emerged, he carried something metal, wrapped in a cloth. "I've watched Nan do this. Now it's my turn," he muttered. The boglin's forehead creased in dark green wrinkles. "You can't do any magic, can you?"

"No," Sam said. "No magic. I can play baseball. And I'm pretty good at fixing things. But that's it. Can *you* do magic?" With all the strange things he'd seen so far this week, Sam wouldn't have been surprised if Tolver said yes.

"Not yet," Tolver said. "Unfortunately." He kicked a clump of grass with his foot. Sam understood so well how he felt. "But..." he stared for a long time at the cloth-wrapped object in his hands. "I think I know how I might change that."

Chapter Six

Tolver

Tolver knew he shouldn't try to use the prospectors' gift. The only reason he'd kept it was to sell it at the Depository, as soon as he and Nana went there with the words they'd gathered for safekeeping.

With the money from a good sale, he'd have enough to fix the compressor, and then maybe he and Nana could make everything all right again.

Besides, the last time he'd even *thought* about the compass, terrible things had happened, including the prospectors coming. And now his grandmother was on the other side of the worlds and Tolver was here, without even a good switch, not to mention any magic. Plus, Starflake was still gone. And in their places, he had only a human boy. One worth more to Tolver on the other side of the worlds, as far away from the prospectors as possible.

He had to get Nana back and fast. And send the boy–Sam–home.

There's only one thing I can do. He took out the compass. The metal gleamed in the sunlight.

Sam's eyes widened when he caught sight of the inscriptions and gears inside the compass. "What's that?"

"Nothing," Tolver said, turning slightly away. The boy had taken so much of what was Tolver's already.

But the compass wasn't glowing. Tolver tapped it. Then he shook it. "Aperture," he said carefully, as Nana had. Just in case that would wake the thing up. Nothing happened. So he pried at Nana's safe box, whispering "unprotect," as he'd seen her do many times. The box clicked open.

Tolver pushed a few scraps around in Nana's safe, searching, trying not to think about what he'd done. Finally, he lifted up a piece of paper, torn from a book on the other side.

"I can do this," Tolver muttered again. He didn't feel too certain. Then he tilted the compass into the sun and held up the paper. "Throughway," he said.

Nothing happened.

"Throughway!" Tolver said, louder this time. A seagull cack-led nearby.

"What's supposed to happen?" Sam asked. "Maybe I can help?"

"My nan says a word, and her lens uses it to open a portal. But this compass doesn't work like that." Tolver frowned.

"If it's a compass, why not tell it where you want to go? Say 'Little Fre—'"

Tolver clapped a hand over Sam's mouth. "Write it down instead."

He handed Sam a pen from his tool belt and a piece of paper from Nana's box, and Sam wrote LITTLE FREE LIBRARY in neat block letters. "Why?"

"Because I don't want to take it from you forever. Written ones? They're not as magic, but you can keep using them." Tolver explained as he placed the strip of paper on top of the compass and held it up to the sun. "Little Free Library!"

The sun caught the lens of the compass and the rays bounced off the clouds above Tolver's head. A hole formed, tiny and dark, through the very sky. Sam pointed. "Are those books? It worked! It's working!"

Tolver pulled his binoculars off his tool belt and studied the portal. Sure enough, he could see the books in the Little Free Library and the Mount Cloud Hardware stencil. *He'd done it!* But he couldn't see his grandmother anywhere.

And when he lowered the binoculars, he caught Sam trying to climb up the cottage roof to reach the portal. "Get down!" *The boy needed a pookah to get through such a small hole.* Sam tumbled into the mud once again and jostled Tolver so much that the compass fell from his hands and landed on the ground.

The portal shimmered and closed up, leaving only clouds and sky. It had almost worked. Tolver sat down hard on the cottage stoop. Cautiously, he raised his eyes to the sky, looking for prospectors. The sky was clear.

"I thought you said you didn't have any magic," Sam said from the mud puddle.

"I don't. Pretty much only this one thing." Tolver pushed at the mud until he found the compass. He lifted it to the sun. The glass was intact, but something rattled deep inside. "And now it's broken."

The last time he'd taken apart one of Julius's inventions, he'd never gotten it back together.

"Maybe I can help fix it?" Sam offered.

Tolver looked up at the boy and rubbed his eyes. Then he laughed a little. "Why not. What else could go wrong? How much do you want?"

Sam hesitated. "Like payment?"

Tolver nodded. "Boglin ethics. You do work, you get paid."

Sam didn't hesitate. "I want my sister's word."

Tolver opened Nana's safe box again. Inside, he saw Sam's words, the curses, and the *amazing*s his Nana had picked up lately. He slipped Sam's "sorry," "regret," and "apologize" into his pocket. *My first words,* Tolver thought. He couldn't afford to lose those.

The other "sorry"—the one from the boy's sister—felt far too light to be of any use anyway. He lifted that from the box. The ribbon gleamed silver in the daylight.

Sam stretched his hand out to touch his sister's word.

Tolver pushed his hand away. "First, show me you can fix the compass. Then this one's yours. If you can't fix the compass, I'll take the words and you to the Depository tomorrow. The city can decide what to do with you. And we'll store these with your other words, which are already in the Depository, of course." Tolver bit his lip, hoping Sam would believe him.

Sam held his hand out again, but this time for the magical compass. "Okay. Let me try." He put the compass on the stoop and very carefully lifted its lid, then smiled. "It's just a loose gear," he said.

Tolver gave him the tools from his belt and listened to Sam tinkering for a few moments. Then Sam looked up, satisfied. "I think that's it." He handed back the compass.

"Thanks." Tolver bit his lip.

"What's wrong?" Sam was already standing, holding out his hand for his sister's word. "I'm ready to go home."

"It's just—everything I've tried to do has worked out so badly. What if this also goes wrong?" Tolver's faith in himself hardly ever wavered, but the past few days had been a test of it. And now his confidence was buckling.

"Hey, I know what you mean," Sam said, sitting back down next to him. "I keep trying to fix things and they keep getting worse too. I'm probably missing the first baseball game of the season right now."

Tolver nodded. "You're in trouble also?"

Sam kicked the dirt. "Yeah. My teacher's mad at me, because I couldn't say _____." Sam gestured. Then he frowned. "Because you took my words. I don't want my sister to get in trouble like that."

Tolver handed him the girl's ribbon. "It wouldn't have made much hot air, I don't think. She really meant it every time she said it. But tell her to be careful. Words can be taken more than once, and it weakens them."

"Do you ever wonder what happens if you take the wrong words from the wrong people?" Sam asked quietly. "Or words someone really needs?"

"They're not easy to take if they're used carefully. Words are only easy to gather when they're overused or taken for granted. What's wrong with that?"

"I think…" Sam looked like he was mulling his next words carefully. "I think if you're taking words from people—kids—who are just learning how to use them, that might be a mistake."

Tolver remembered Nana saying she'd made a mistake long ago. Had she taken the wrong word? No, he couldn't think like that. "We know what we're doing."

"Maybe. But maybe not. I think you should let me earn back my words too, and a word you took from my teacher a long time ago."

Tolver tensed. He didn't want to give the boy any more words. He very carefully didn't look at the broken converter by the cottage. "We don't need anything more from you, thank you. And your words are in the Depository. Far away."

"What's that?" Sam asked. "You mentioned it earlier."

"The Depository? It's storage, kind of. Part of an old system that used to hold words, from before your world wars. We borrowed some of it when we crossed from your world to ours. And in the marshbogs, it went magical, all boxes and locks and tubes, a perfect place to keep things. It's over there." Tolver passed over the binoculars so Sam could see Felicity.

In the distance, a slim train circled the cloud, slipping between glass and brass towers connected by gardens and tunnels. Above all of it, thin walls arched like a book splayed on its spine. More ships passed beside the walls. "Wow," Sam breathed.

Tolver chuckled. "Felicity's the first of the floating cities. The Depository's that arched bit at the center. Too bad you won't get to see it up close since you're leaving, before the prospectors catch wind you're here." Tolver ran his fingers through his silver hair, then smoothed them against his jacket.

Sam squinted at him. "That really bothers you? The idea that the prospectors might get me?"

No, Tolver thought, *it bothers me that they might get* me. "Of course. No one should be taken against their will. You should get back to your baseball games."

Sam stood slowly. "You're right. The white pig probably needs food. The pookah, I mean."

Tolver froze. The nerve of this human boy. "You didn't just *help* Starflake? You kept her? You weren't telling me the whole truth!" Tolver gestured at Gilfillan and the piglets. "They need their family."

Sam frowned at that but crossed his arms, keeping his grip tight around his sister's word. "When you give me the rest of my words back and get me home, I'll give you the pookah."

Tolver's mind spun. "Is Starflake all right?" he asked in a small voice.

"She was fine when I left. Tiny."

"That won't last. Pookahs are a bit unpredictable, but she'll be back to full size soon. We'd best get her home before that happens. You do that, and I'll give you all your words once I get them from the Depository." He lied to buy time, until he could get Nana's help. "But I need you to do something more too," he finally admitted to Sam.

"Anything. What do you need?"

He held up one of the paper scraps. "When you get back home, you have to bring me more words, for fuel and for magic." Tolver knew that he'd used too many words in Nana's book, and she'd already needed more from the other side. "Dictionary pages, for one. From a really good dictionary. Lots of them, and not wet or moldy ones. Quality words, for all the trouble I'm going through getting you back to the other side. And also Starflake."

Sam considered this. "And you swear you'll give me my words back?"

Tolver wanted to growl. He'd said so, hadn't he? He caught himself baring his teeth, and goblin teeth are sharp. If Sam helped him, then maybe Tolver could avoid getting conscripted by or losing the island to the prospectors. He forced himself to nod.

Sam took a deep breath. "I'll get what you need. You'll give me my words. And maybe Ms. Malloy's too. And then you'll leave Mount Cloud alone."

Tolver had to smile. It was the kind of thing he might say himself. "Deal."

"What if the pig grows before I can get it back through the library—the pookah?" Sam asked. "A full-size pig in my house will be a disaster."

"Then you'll have to hurry, won't you," Tolver said, very seriously.

And then Sam held out a pale hand. "Deal."

Tolver had Sam write where they wanted to go on a scrap of paper. He held the repaired compass up to the sunlight. "Little Free Library," he whispered.

The portal opened and stayed that way. After a moment, Nana's silver head appeared close to the edge. She was too big to pass through. "Tolver! You did it!"

Groaning, Tolver and Sam lifted the pookah up as high as they could. Gilfillan scrambled and climbed into the portal. There was a scuffling sound, and several books fluttered from the library into the sea. Then the pookah's snout reappeared, pushing the old woman forward.

Sam tried to jump for the pookah's dangling leash at the same time Nana fell into the water. *Splash!* The wooden bat she carried and her basket landed in the marsh, loud in the quiet morning. And Sam fell back to the ground. The portal was too high.

"Hey! You have to help me!" the boy said. "You said you would."

Tolver gave him a boost so that Sam could grasp the leash. "Thanks," Sam said. "You're not terrible for a goblin."

"You're not bad for a human," Tolver agreed. He waved. "Remember your promise." He waved to Gilfillan. "One more time, friend."

"I will." Sam climbed on the pookah's back even as the portal began to close. He took one more long look at the marshbog, finally focusing on Nana, who was fishing her things from the water. "That's my bat!"

"Jump, Gilfillan!" Tolver shouted. "Now!"

The pookah jumped. A few long moments later, Gilfillan reappeared, without Sam.

The portal snapped shut as Nana pulled herself out of the shallows. "What a mess! What a bother. Really, Gilfillan, if you're going to leave me behind, do it when I'm not carrying a bag of words."

Tolver stuffed the prospectors' compass in his pocket before she could see.

Nana huffed after she'd pulled herself to shore, then hugged him tight. "My goodness, you are a sight for sore eyes. And what a surprise too! Magic! All on your own!"

Tolver bore Nana's praise cheerfully because he was glad to have her back. But he arranged his face as if to say, *Like I'd had any choice in the whole mess*, so Nana wouldn't wonder why he looked so nervous.

Chapter Seven

Sam

When Tolver yelled "Jump!" Sam and the pig had lurched toward the portal and then through. As the portal narrowed behind them, Sam felt like he was getting longer and stringier. It itched.

This time, he knew it was the pookah's shape-changing magic, and that made it less frightening. But he still closed his eyes.

When Gilfillan shook him off and backed away, Sam didn't try to grab the pookah's leash. He crawled forward as the pookah disappeared back through the portal. Sam smelled damp paper and opened his eyes to find himself crammed back into the Little Free Library. His idea had worked!

A piece of marsh grass dangled from his T-shirt. His cheek, crusted with salt, pressed against a copy of *The Vanderbeekers of 141st Street*.

Morning sunlight sparkled through the broken plexiglass door. To Sam's dismay, the light took on an especially bright edge around the easily recognizable silhouette of Mason McGargee looking at him curiously from the other side.

Part Two

Chapter Eight

Sam

"How did you get in *there*, Sam?" Mason asked. The Little Free Library door muffled her voice, but Sam could still hear her confusion and frustration. "And WHY?"

Water speckled the outside of the plexiglass, and a few drips streaked the inside. The muggy scent of damp books and unfinished wood made Sam sniffle. He had no answers for Mason.

He pushed the door open with his foot as gently as he could. But his chest and face contorted as a sneeze jolted him, and he kicked. The hinge he'd pushed so carefully back into place the day before gave way. The wood-and-plexiglass door clattered onto the tulips.

"Are you okay?" Now Mason sounded concerned. Nearby, a Weedwhacker roared.

Last fall, Mason would have held out a hand as she asked the question. Then she might have helped free Sam, shaking her head and laughing at his predicament. They would have made it into a big prank to play on others later. Sam might have even told her about the goblins.

But today, Mason didn't bend to pick up the door from the tulips or offer Sam a hand.

Sam began squirming his way out of the library without her help, relaxing his shoulder where it was wedged by his ear, then wriggling forward.

"I was doing a structural check," he explained. Anita used phrases like that a lot. "Making sure it's stable." He unbent his elbows and knees, then squeezed himself from the library. When his feet were firmly on the ground, he replaced the books that had fallen out with him and picked up the library door.

Mason watched Sam brush tulip pollen off the hinges. "That structure looks even *less* stable than before. And yesterday, you said you were checking usage patterns." She scuffed the ground with her shoe. "Something's weird."

Couldn't agree with you more, Mason. "It's complicated. Why are you spying on me?" Sam didn't want to give her any reasons to complain to her dad or anyone else.

"I'm not!" Mason growled. "I'm taking care of the Little Free Library. And I was worried about you. Remember our summer assignment?" Mason's voice pitched higher with the question. "We're partners? Which I thought might be okay eventually, but if you keep breaking the library, we're probably going to fail."

Sam had nearly forgotten their summer project. He pressed the library's door back into place again. The screws held, mostly, but he'd need nails and wood glue from his stepmom's toolbox to really fix the hinges.

"You don't have to worry. I'm not breaking it. I'm making sure it doesn't fall down. I'd say that's a major part of taking care of the library."

Mason watched Sam doubtfully as he swung the purple door with its gingerbread trim open and shut.

"See? Fixed." He turned to look at her, hoping she believed him.

From her expression, it was clear she didn't. He looked away—down to the pile of books in her arms. Sam saw *Easy Algebra* on one spine. *The Lion, the Witch and the Wardrobe*, and *Sal and Gabi Break the Universe*. And a Star Wars book. The whole pile was topped with green and yellow three-by-five cards. She'd lettered her recommendations neatly in silver pen and outlined the titles with star stickers.

He was glad she was holding up her part of the assignment, but he wished she'd do it far away from the goblin portal. He made a face without thinking. "A *math* book?"

Mason shifted her gaze to the books in her arms, frowning. "I brought these because I liked them. I thought someone else would too." She didn't look at him when she asked, "Sam, are you feeling okay? You seem—I don't know, maybe…smaller."

The Weedwhacker started up again and Sam jumped. She was asking too many questions. He had to distract her, at least until he uncompressed from the pookah magic. But he wasn't about to tell her about the world on the other side of the library.

The best way to proceed, Sam decided, was to make Mason mad again. "*You* might like math books, but who else will?"

Even though this was for a good cause—getting the rest of his words back—Sam felt terrible when Mason's expression knotted up. "Hey, Mason, I'm _____" *Ugghhhh.* He still couldn't say it.

This made her even madder. "You're what, Sam? You're wrecking our summer project and the library. Mrs. Lockheart's going to be furious. Ms. Malloy too. And no half-hearted apology is going to fix it."

Sam remembered what Mason had said months ago. *You always say __, but you don't mean it.* He had been using apology words pretty recklessly, especially with his friend. And now one wasn't there when he really needed it.

"I'm not—it's not me—Mason, wait—I'm __."

But she didn't wait. She stomped down the sidewalk toward her house, with most of her books still in her arms. Sam sat down in the grass next to the tulips, a lump in his throat, and stared up at the oak tree.

The big, cement-filled knot on the tree trunk stared back. It held no answers. Had the marshbogs and Tolver and the magic compass really happened? Sam stared at the purple library, then at the oak tree, trying to convince himself that he'd imagined it. If he had, he wouldn't have to get the dictionary pages for Tolver.

But his arms ached from being pulled through the library, and he still held Bella's word ribbon. His pants were muddy, and he had a corner of the paper cover from *The Vanderbeekers* stuck to his shirt. And he was still a little smaller than usual, having just ridden a pookah through a Little Free Library, where he normally wouldn't fit at all.

How long had he been gone? The sun sparkled morning light through the leaves of the big oak. Mason had been dressed for baseball practice. It was definitely the weekend from the sound of the Weedwhackers. The hours Sam had spent in the marshbogs seemed to have gotten compressed just like he had.

But it *had* to have happened.

Mason was a long way down the sidewalk now, her brown legs moving fast, her curly hair swinging furiously in its ponytail. She slowed only when the door to her house opened and her dad came out, followed by Coach Lockheart. The two carried a large, gray canvas bag between them marked MT. CLOUD ATHLETICS. There were so many bats, balls, and gloves inside the bag that it took two people to carry it.

Mason gave her dad a hug, spoke for a moment, then went inside. Dr. McGargee waved at Sam.

Had she told him how mean I'd been to her? Or that I was acting weird? Sam really hoped not. It wasn't so much that he wanted to get out of trouble, though he did. It was that he wished he hadn't said all those things.

Dr. McGargee wore a blue-and-white Mount Cloud team shirt. As he and Coach Lockheart got closer to where he was sitting, Sam could hear them talking, even over the sound of his heart, which was pounding pretty hard.

"Catcher, definitely," Coach Lockheart said. Followed by a name Sam couldn't hear.

Dr. McGargee asked, "What about infield?" They were discussing player assignments, not Sam's behavior. Mason was hoping to play catcher this year. Maybe Mason had asked what she'd be playing.

Sam got to his feet, picking purple paint chips from his shirt. He tried to position himself in front of the Little Free Library in a way that kept Coach Lockheart from seeing the loose, badly repaired door.

For a moment, being in trouble and not allowed to play baseball at the start of summer felt like the most unfair thing in the world to Sam. But then he remembered what Tolver had told him about the prospectors and about them forcing boglins and city goblins to work on their ships. Some things were much more unfair than others.

He'd take his punishment and do what was needed to fix things. Even if that meant helping Tolver with his goblin shopping list. Then he'd have his words back and his parents would let him play.

"Hello, Sam," Mrs. Lockheart strolled past, eyeing her tulips. Sam jumped. He'd been so focused on his coaches, who were still far down the sidewalk. "What are you up to?" She was carrying a pitcher of iced tea.

"Ms. Malloy asked the class to take care of Mount Cloud's Little Free Libraries this summer and make sure they're well stocked," Sam replied.

She squinted at him, glanced at her tulips, which he was *not* stepping on, and then smiled. "What a good idea! I'll admit, I was worried you were bothering my flowers again, Sam. Someone certainly is. But helping care for the community is exactly what neighbors should be doing. Now, I'm going to bring Ms. Malloy this tea because she said she wasn't feeling well. It's been so hot."

Sam worried. Ms. Malloy had seemed very upset yesterday.

He really wanted to talk to her too. But he couldn't, not with Mrs. Lockheart right there. So Sam nodded hearty agreement. "That's really nice, Mrs. Lockheart." Then he eased the door open and began rearranging the books. He added the one Mason had left on the sidewalk, *Easy Algebra*, while watching Mrs. Lockheart out of the corner of his eye. Mrs. Lockheart carried the iced tea up to Ms. Malloy's front door, then disappeared inside.

Sam breathed a sigh of relief once she was gone.

"Coming to practice, Sam?" Dr. McGargee said, right behind him. Sam turned and the library door nearly fell off again. "My parents say I can't, not until I _____. Fix some things." Mason hadn't told them anything.

Coach Lockheart frowned. "We have our first game tomorrow, Sam."

Boy, do I ever know that, Sam thought. The game was against Blue Lake, and afterward, there would be a picnic to kick off the season. His stomach growled just thinking about barbecue and burgers. Sam kicked at the dirt nervously, still avoiding the tulips. Why hadn't Nana and Tolver just left him and his words alone? But then Sam wouldn't know about the whole world inside the Little Free Library.

And he wouldn't be able to help return Ms. Malloy's words or stop the goblins from stealing more. And he couldn't have gotten Bella's word back, either.

No, Sam was right where he needed to be. He straightened up. "Once I do fix things, I'm looking forward to playing," he finally told his coaches.

Dr. McGargee smiled. "That's the right attitude! How about you come help pick up practice bats and retrieve balls when you can? We'd hate to lose you."

"If you help out at practice today, you can come to the picnic tomorrow." Coach Lockheart grinned. "Maybe we can convince your parents it's community service. You were a big help getting the cotton candy machine working last year." His eyes twinkled. He knew Sam's parents well.

Helping out at the field was the perfect opportunity to get most of the items on Tolver's list: the dictionary pages. The school had dictionaries. And it was right next to the baseball field.

All of Sam's problems were about to be solved. "Thanks, Coach! I'll ask my parents." He might have said that a little too brightly. Coach Lockheart raised his eyebrows. "After I finish taking care of the library," he added.

"Good job, Sam. Mason's excited about the summer project too," Dr. McGargee said.

"And we're grateful to have the help." Coach Lockheart patted Sam on the shoulder. "The library's important for the neighborhood. And lately, someone's been coming through at night and knocking it around."

"I'll keep an eye on it for you, Coach," Sam said, still gripping the plexiglass-and-wood door tightly.

As soon as his coaches had crossed the street, Sam let out a huge sigh of relief and closed the Little Free Library door. It wobbled on its hinges. Good thing Mrs. Lockheart was still at Ms. Malloy's.

What he wouldn't give for a tool belt like Tolver's. Or even some tape. Sam pressed harder. Finally the hinges bit, and the door looked steadier for now. Then he ran across the street to his house, shouting, "Bella!"

Sam couldn't wait to give Bella her word back.

As he climbed the stairs to the porch, Sam recited Tolver's list in his head: dictionary pages and the pig.

Oh no. The pig.

Sam slammed through the porch door, sped past Bella—who was at the breakfast nook drawing fat horses in pink and yellow crayon—and hit the stairs two at a time.

It seemed like there were a lot of stairs this morning. Finally Sam got to the top and pushed his door open. Or, at least, he tried to push his door open.

The door oinked at him.

"Tham." Bella stood right behind him, holding out the horse drawing. "I drew you this." Sam could see very well now that those weren't horses at all. They were pigs.

"Hi, Bell, what a great picture! Where'd you learn how to draw these?" He forced himself to wait to give her word back until he'd dealt with the pig.

His door wouldn't open, and the more he pushed, the more high-pitched squealing came from the other side. Sam's sister tilted her head at his door and then down at her shoes.

"I peeked. It's so cute. What's its name?"

By now, Sam was pretty sure the regular-size pookah behind his door wasn't as cute as it used to be. He groaned. "Bellaaaaa."

"Sam? Everything all right?" His stepmom called from the other bedroom.

Bella's lower lip wobbled, so Sam waved her closer. "Shhhh, Bell, please."

"Can I pet it?"

"Bella, it's ... for school. I'm watching it for Ms. Malloy. It can't get too excited or bothered. And it has to calm down so I can go to baseball practice this afternoon. Coach asked me special. Can you help me?"

Slowly, Bella nodded. "Did you catch the fairies?"

"Yeah. But they're—"

Her face lit up. "I knew you would."

Sam was about to give Bella the ribbon when his stepmom called him again. "Sam?"

"Just finishing a project! Once we're done, can I—" Sam tried to figure out the best way to ask his stepmom if he could go to the baseball practice. His door rattled once in its frame and then stilled. He panicked. What was he going to say?

Then Bella's voice carried over the soft snuffling of the pig trying to get its snout under the door. "Tham wants to go watch the practice today, Mom. Dr. McGargee asked him to help. I want to go too."

Sam's dad came to the foot of the stairs. "But what about Ms. Malloy? Did you deliver the cards?"

Sam leaned against his bedroom door. "Not yet. I've been out working on the Little Free Library. But I'll do that on my way to the field."

Bella nodded. "I'll help."

Sam and Bella stared down the stairs, and his stepmom squeezed his dad's hand.

"All right. But just help. No playing," Mr. Culver said.

"And you'll keep an eye on Bella," Anita added.

Bella looked up at Sam expectantly. "I bet they want to have a lunch date," she giggled.

Anita laughed. "That's not a bad idea!"

Sam didn't mind helping watch Bella. Especially if it got him to the baseball field *and* distracted everyone away from his bedroom door and the white pig right behind it.

They would go to the field, find the things on Tolver's list, and then he'd drop everything off at the Little Free Library tonight. The pookah would go back to the marshbogs, and he'd have his words back. And maybe Ms. Malloy's words too. Then he wouldn't have to go back to school on Monday. He could play baseball for the rest of the summer. "Sounds like a perfect plan!" Sam said as cheerfully as possible.

"While you're there, check if the McGargees are planning on coming to the picnic tomorrow," his stepmom said. "Mason's grandmother passed away, Sam. You'll want to tell her you're sorry about that also. I already sent flowers."

For one really sharp breath, Sam wished he'd heard her say that two days ago. But he couldn't get upset now. "I heard. I'll tell her as soon as I can."

"Please don't tease Mason today, all right?" Anita said. "They have enough going on."

"I won't, I promise." Sam put the No Trespassing sign on his door, hoping it would keep people out. "Hey, Bella," he whispered. "Do I look smaller to you?"

She tilted her head, swaying back and forth on the balls of her feet. "Nope! You look the same as always."

That was a relief. Better still, the pookah in his room seemed to be quieting down. "Put some shoes on and we can go, okay?"

Sam grabbed a tote bag with the logo of his dad's company from the downstairs closet. The same closet he and Bella had checked for passages to Narnia last year. They'd never thought to check the Little Free Library.

How Bella would love the world he'd found. But Sam didn't want her trying to go through the library, so he couldn't tell her everything. Just a little bit about the pookah and the trade he'd made. Sam needed to be super careful.

When he came back into the kitchen, he grabbed three reusable water bottles, filled them from the fridge, and put those in the bag. Bella was taking forever to find shoes. Sam's stepmother was humming as she made cheesy meatball subs for his dad. She didn't cook a lot because she worked so much, but when she did, the whole house smelled delicious.

Jealous that he wouldn't get a submarine sandwich, Sam took a deep, flavor-filled breath. His stepmom grinned.

"Food is a great way to tell people you care about them, *right*?" She held out a piece of cheese to Sam. "Letters are too. I'm glad you're taking the ones you made to Ms. Malloy and to Mason today. May I see them?"

He'd nearly forgotten about the cards! Sam reached in the

pocket of his shorts and pulled them out. His stepmom's smile faded as she saw the crumpled papers in his hands. They were blank.

The carefully cut words Bella had helped Sam with were gone.

What had happened?

"Oh, not again." The boglins! They must have stolen the words, even as Sam was helping them. Ms. Malloy was right; they couldn't be trusted.

Goblins. Why couldn't the library have been a portal to a baseball game?

"Sam, really. You said you'd done it." His stepmom was frowning now. "This isn't some big joke. You have to fix this."

"I will. I promise."

"When?" His stepmom's frown deepened. "We'll give you a week until the Mets game at the stadium. That's it. And I'm not sure we should let you go to the practice this afternoon or tomorrow's game, either."

"Please—" At least he could still say please. "I'll have everything fixed soon. Before the game, for sure." He could sort things out fast. Sam knew he could.

But his stepmom didn't look so sure.

Bella bounced back into the kitchen. She was wearing one of Sam's old Sesame Street shirts. She handed him two ponytail holders. "Will you fix my hair?"

Sam grumbled. *Bella doesn't understand hurrying at all.* Trying to be gentle, Sam pulled her curly hair back into two pigtails, the way she liked.

His stepmom's expression softened while he did it, and she nodded when he'd finished. "That's a wonderful big brother you've got, Isabella."

"I know." Bella grinned. She took Sam's hand. "Come on Tham, let's go."

He opened the door for both of them, and as she scooted through, he whispered, "I did it, Bella. I got your word back."

Once they were in the yard, she skidded to a stop and held out her other hand expectantly.

He gave her the glittering word. It whispered softly as Bella held the ribbon up to the light. Sparkles from the fabric caught the sun and threw patterns across her cheeks. She squinted at it. "What do I do now?"

Tolver had given Sam only a few instructions. "Eat it fast, so you can't lose it."

A teenager biked past them, ringing a bell. Bella twisted back and forth on her tiptoes. "Tham?" She said after a moment of quiet. "I heard what mom said about you being out of chances. Maybe you should have it instead. You need it." She held the ribbon out to him.

Sam stopped walking. He watched light sparkle in the word ribbon. It really was magic. But he shook his head. "It's your word, Bella. Go on."

She played with it as they neared the Little Free Library, then pointed. "Sam! Look!" The box looked as if a small storm had hit it. The door hung off its hinges, worse than before, and books were toppled everywhere. Gingerbread trim ringed the post and littered what remained of the tulips.

"I just fixed this! What had happened in the past half hour?" Sam touched the door. *Did Tolver follow me through? Wasn't it enough that he'd stolen the words right off the cards? Why did he have to follow me back for more?*

He looked everywhere—in the oak tree, beneath the hedge—for the boglins, but there weren't any to find. "This is bad. So bad," he whispered. "I'm in so much trouble."

Bella waited quietly while Sam straightened the books again.

This time the door wouldn't stay on at all. He rested his head against the Little Free Library in frustration.

"This will help," his little sister said, very seriously. She held the ribbon out once more, like a promise.

That word, Sam knew, might fix things with Mason and at school too, probably. But not for Bella, or with the boglins. And if Sam couldn't fix things with the boglins, he'd never get his *own* words back. Any of them. He wouldn't be able to convince the creatures to stop stealing from his friends and teachers, or from Bella, again.

And, even more important, *this* word wasn't his. It belonged to his sister.

"No, Bella. You need it."

"Okay." She popped the ribbon in her mouth like he'd told her. "It's sweet." She laughed. The ribbon sat on her tongue, like gum.

"Bella, chew it."

She nodded and chewed very seriously, then opened her mouth again. *Gone.* "Thorr— Look! I can say it! Thorry!" She began to skip. "Thorry, thorry, tho—"

Sam stopped her right there on the street, in front of Mrs. Lockheart's perfectly manicured hedge and the wrecked Little Free

Library. "Just be careful, okay? Only say it when you really need to. That way it won't get stolen again."

"Can they do that?" She looked worried.

"I'll make sure they don't," Sam said.

"Okay." She hugged him tight, and for a moment, Sam felt like everything was right in the world.

Then there was a squawk from Ms. Malloy's front porch, like an outraged bird. Mrs. Lockheart had caught sight of the library—or what was left of it.

Chapter Nine

Tolver

The prospectors had come to the island, and a human boy had too. The moment he thought this, Tolver sat up so fast in his bed that he hit his head on the rafter. *Ow.* It was true. Their tiny cottage wasn't as safe as it had been. With so many dangerous people coming to the cottage, the words he and Nana had gathered recently would be safer locked up at the Depository. They had to go right away.

But the next morning, when Tolver told Nana his thoughts, she wouldn't hear of going. Not at first. "We are staying well away from the city. Too many prospector ships there, presently."

"We can go when they're out trading and raiding," Tolver countered. "In the daytime. As soon as we've fed the pookahs. And we'll go fast. We'll use the fan." All he wanted to do was make sure the words he'd worked so hard for would be safe.

Nana sighed and reluctantly agreed. "The Depository has withstood much turmoil—even has a bit of magic on its own. You may be right that it will be safer than our little island."

Once their chores were done, Nana opened the safe box. She put two handfuls of silvery words and the words from Sam's apology cards into her basket, clucking at the mess, "Now how did I do that?" Then she wrapped the words for safe transit. She picked up the wooden bat, then put it back down again. "Too big to bring into the city. That's a sadness." Instead, she hid it under her bed.

Tolver tucked the compass in his coat, thinking to sell or trade it when Nana was occupied at the Depository. He helped his grandmother into the mail boat and they sped toward Felicity.

The big island, with its noise and bustle, rose from the water: warehouses and factories, shipyards and smokestacks. A long tether led from the lower city straight up to the glass towers, where most goblins lived these days. Only marsh boglins stayed below.

When they reached the big island, they paid a ferry balloon to take them up. As the dirigible chugged higher, the canvas gas bags that supported Felicity's upper levels spread above them like a cloud.

At least here, beneath the city, Tolver felt safer. *Prospectors can't very well drop out of the sky and steal a boglin with the whole city looking on, now could they?* At least, he hoped they couldn't.

He and his grandmother took a small train from the dock to the Depository. Tolver had come up before, but this was the first time he'd be depositing his own gatherings. The big glass building, with its piles of metal boxes just inside the ornate doors, looked even grander than usual.

The Depository's brass and steel boxes, lockers, old cabinets, and mail bins were each inscribed with post office box numbers. The higher the numbers, the more modern the storage. Staircases and crow's nest seats wound all around the pile, and goblins crossed balconies to navigate the jumble of boxes and bins. The entire building hummed with the stored words whispering to themselves.

Nana's box was near the bottom, and once they'd passed through the doors, been examined by two very imposing kobolds wearing leather vests and big boots, and weighed their words, the bigger kobold goblin handed Nana a strip of paper. "Those are good words you got." She grinned.

Tolver blushed bright chartreuse as Nana turned to him, beaming. "My grandson's" was all she said.

As she walked on, down the ramp to the lowest floors, Tolver hung back. "Are there any people who want to sell or trade machinery?" he asked quietly.

The guard raised her eyebrows. "Prospector machinery?"

Tolver nodded, hopeful.

"I'll ask around," the guard said, hesitating. "But you should be careful, Boglin. Prospectors keep a tight watch on things. City goblins know that."

Tolver crept away to catch up with his grandmother, but not before he heard the guard mutter, "Boglins in the city, what's next?"

He turned a little invisible with embarrassment, but he recovered fast. Tolver was determined to enjoy the triumph of storing the words from his first gathering run. He'd dreamed of this for a long time. Now he was helping his nana and hopefully getting rid of the inventor's compass all at the same time. It wasn't a bad day's work at all.

At each floor, Tolver watched goblins weighing ribbons on scales and using converters. The space rustled as words were transformed into fuel.

When Tolver caught up with Nana, she turned the locking mechanism carefully on her box and the mechanism chimed. The door creaked open, and Tolver saw how empty the safe was. Only a few ribbons sparkled within the metal walls. He'd never seen it so empty. *At this rate, we'll never be able to buy the island from the city and keep it from being turned to factories.*

Toward the back, a gray ribbon curled, pale and dusty. "What's that one, Nana?"

"My first word," Nana said. "And my first mistake. I was in such a rush to get a word that I took something that wasn't being misused." She shook her head.

Tolver slowly put two and two together. "The woman we saw?"

Nana nodded.

Tolver thought about how light Sam's sister's word had felt. "So why didn't you give it back?"

Nana shook her head again and shrugged sadly. "I was too afraid to ... I didn't want to get in trouble for doing something wrong. I was very young. And then it was too late. We'd all grown up and it would have been obvious if I returned it. The humans would have noticed."

"But if it's useless, why keep it?" Tolver reached for it, but Nana swatted his hand.

"I've not found a use for it *yet*, that's for sure." Nana tilted her head, looking at the ribbon. "But it's still mine."

Tolver nodded as he put the rest of the words inside. His ribbons sparkled on top of the small pile. "But maybe there's a way to give it back, with Sam's help? If he returns with the things I've asked for."

Nana squinted. "Maybe so. Are you going to give him his words back too?"

Tolver frowned, half reaching back into the box. "They're my first words, Nana. And I still want to help you buy the island." He picked the ribbon up again. "But I promised Sam. And a goblin's only as good as his word." He'd learned that from Nana.

"I think," Nana said, "that what you're getting Sam to do is valuable too. As long as he's *also* as good as his word. If he brings us new spell words, then we'll come back here and get these for him. Besides," she wrinkled her nose and her eyes danced, "you don't think he'll be able to keep from wasting that word again, do you?"

Tolver laughed. But as a shadow fell over them both, Nana gasped and shut the box door. The kobold guard stood behind them, along with the two goblins from the other night. "This one is who's asking."

"Ah, hello again, Tolver Boglin," the goblin with the long braid said. "You," she pointed at Nana and Tolver, "did an impressive job on *The Colophon*. They'll be wanting new sails." She held out her hand to Tolver. "And you owe us for the mechanism, also. The one you're trying to sell."

"You can't bother us here." Nana glared at the goblins. "This is city property."

"We provide fuel to the city and machines. So we can do what we like. And we like to make sure we get every ounce of what we're owed, one way or another. This boy accepted a port-holer compass from us as a gift. Then used it."

"Tolver?" Nana sounded shocked.

"It was a gift from Julius!" Tolver looked between his grandmother and the prospectors. "You said!"

"The object was a gift. The use thereof? Not quite." The goblin grinned.

"Tolver, you didn't," Nana gasped.

The full weight of Tolver's actions came crashing down around his pointy ears. "I'm sorry, Nana. I didn't know what else to do. They said Julius sent it. And you were gone and—"

"That's not nearly good enough. I told you how— You get your hands off my grandson." Nana swatted at the goblins, who'd grabbed Tolver roughly.

"Tolver Boglin, you used our tools and thus owe us a term of service until you make even your debts," the prospector said. "I'm first mate on *The Declension*, and you'll be coming to serve that term with me."

"Serve a term? And what is this about Julius? Did you steal him away too? Tolver, don't you go with them," Nana shouted. The Depository echoed with her voice. But it was too late. Goblins throughout the Depository turned away as the prospectors hustled Tolver from the building and toward the port. Nana chased them up the stairways and onto the street, growing ever more breathless and distant.

"Nana!" Tolver cried.

"I'll find you. You won't have him long, you—pirates!" Nana shouted.

That slowed them. The first mate nearly dropped Tolver. "Ma'am, we resent the implication. We're businessgoblins, not riffraff."

Tolver tried to stop them by dragging his feet, but they picked up the pace. Nana ran after them all the way to the port. Her hair puffed and flowed out of its bun like a cloud escaping the pull of the wind.

Then the prospectors crammed Tolver up the gangplank of the largest prospector ship he'd ever seen. Along its stern, silver letters spelled out *The Declension*. An enormous airbag filled noisily. When they had him onboard, the ship threw its lines. They pulled away from the dock before Nana could come any closer.

"If I'd brought my bat," she shouted. She looked so tiny on the gangway.

Tears in his eyes, Tolver watched the city recede. The hull smelled of many goblins crammed into tight quarters, with very little bathing going on. Which was quite terrible, in fact, but not as awful as he felt.

He'd kept secrets from Nana and Sam. He'd hidden Sam's

words. And Nana was out of spell words—and without those, she was on her own against the prospectors and the city, with Starflake somewhere on the other side of the worlds.

As *The Declension* sailed away from Felicity, the ship's engines made a *thrum-thrum* noise that made Tolver's ears ache and his eyes hurt.

"Don't worry," said the first mate beside him at the ship's stern. "You'll be able to earn time on shore in just a few months!"

Tolver tried not to cry as she sent him belowdecks to a small berth with a blanket and pillow.

The smell belowdecks was almost unbearable. This many goblins in a closed ship couldn't be otherwise. When Tolver found his berth, he saw that his mates there were young, just like him. Lucky. The smell was marginally better here, like spoiled milk.

His companions peered at him from the shadows. One resembled the kobold who had spoken to Tolver a few nights before, when he'd delivered the mail.

"I met your sister," Tolver whispered, "I think. On Brightside? They got your letter."

The boy sighed. "I miss my family."

"Me too," Tolver agreed.

"What do you owe?" the goblin asked.

The prospectors hadn't let Tolver keep the compass that had gotten him in trouble. He held out his hands. "I used one of their machines. They caught me at the Depository."

Another of the boglins in the berth's hammocks groaned. "They got me there too. I wasn't causing trouble, just went to get some words. They said I owed them for storage. And brought me here to pay it off."

"It's not fair! They can't patrol the Depository. The prospectors don't own that, we do." Tolver's chest swelled with righteous indignation.

"Now that the prospectors are supplying the city with fuel and upgrading the Depository, they're able to do anything they want."

Tolver deflated. He lay down on his bunk. "Then everything's lost." Not just Felicity and his dreams of adventure, but also Nana's island. "What do they make you do here?"

The Brightsider came to sit next to his berth. "We keep the word hogs polished and help cook. They've promised I'll get to go on a word hunt soon."

"Why would you want to go on a word hunt for the prospectors?" Tolver asked. "Don't they keep everything?"

"Sure," said the other boglin. "But we get credit for it, and eventually that adds up. That's how Captain Bellfont got his own ship! He found a whole gas bag full of hot air words once. Lucky goblin."

Tolver closed his eyes. That was a hopeful story. But he still turned his head to the wall of the berth to hide his sadness. There was nothing and no one who could get him out of this mess. Not even Nana.

His breath hitched. But Tolver promised himself that if he was stuck aboard *The Declension*, he'd find a way to earn a ship too. Just see if he didn't.

Chapter Ten

Sam

"I'm calling your parents," Mrs. Lockheart shouted. "I'm calling *everyone's* parents."

Ms. Malloy came out on her porch. "What happened?" But all Mrs. Lockheart could do was gesture to the wrecked Little Free Library.

"Maybe it wasn't them? I thought I heard a terrible wind earlier," Ms. Malloy said, not looking at Sam.

Mrs. Lockheart quieted slightly. "True, I heard that too." She put the phone down, but she didn't look like she wanted to.

Sam exhaled an anxious breath, and he and Bella hurried toward the baseball field. *That was close!* The warm summer breeze rattled the leaves of the oak tree as they sped away from it. Finally, they reached the big road. Bella held his hand and skipped beside him, her pigtails bouncing, as they crossed the street. "How did you get my word back?" she asked, Mrs. Lockheart already forgotten. "And why didn't you get yours?"

Sam realized as they reached the other side of the street that Bella could help him after all. "I have to get mine back by doing a treasure hunt. When I find the right things and bring them back to the library, the goblins will give my words back. Just like they gave me yours."

Sam told Bella about Tolver's list.

"Goblin word hunt!" She started skipping again, and Sam had to chase her down the hill to the fields.

"Bella, you can help, but you have to do what I tell you, okay?"

Bella agreed. But the two fields, separated by a long stretch of newly mown grass and a brown utility shed, took a while to trek through with a distractible five-year-old. "Helping" included butter-cups to pick and a monarch butterfly to chase. Sam tugged at her arm. "Come on, Bella!" Players were already gathering by the baseball diamond.

By the time they reached the chain-link fence that separated the team benches from the batter's box, Sam's sneakers were wet and green with grass clippings, and the team was already warming up. Mason waited in the batter's box, tense, bat at her shoulder. Dr. McGargee pitched a slow curve that broke right over home plate.

When the metal bat struck the leather baseball, the two made a distinctive *TINK*. Mason took off running. The five fifth and sixth graders on the bench cheered. Sam joined in too.

His parents hadn't said Sam couldn't cheer. He just wasn't allowed to play. Yet.

A row of aluminum bats leaned against the fence, next to the empty canvas bag that Coach Lockheart and Dr. McGargee had been carrying. Sam thought about the wooden bat that Nana had stolen from his house. His dad's bat. He was going to get *that* back too. But first, he had a bigger problem. Dr. Vane sat on the bench, watching the practice.

"Sam, I'm surprised to see you here," he said.

You and me both, Principal Vane. "We brought water bottles," Sam said, lifting the tote bag.

"Good job, you two." Coach Lockhart said, before Dr. Vane could ask Sam any more questions. "I was about to send someone up to the school to fill ours again. It's hot today. Going to get hotter still." He turned to Dr. Vane. "We decided that helping out on the weekend, while he's not playing, could be part of Sam's rehabilitation."

Dr. Vane smiled. "That sounds fine." But it didn't look fine.

"We can fill the other bottles," Bella said. "But first Tham has to find a—"

"Bellaaaaa." Sam elbowed her gently to stop her from saying too much.

"I'm tho—"

"Bella!"

Instead of finishing the sentence, Bella closed her mouth around the word, protecting it.

Good job, Bell.

TINK. A bat connected with another ball. Sam's teammates cheered, until it was caught and Gina got sent back to the bench.

Dr. Vane sat and watched, taking notes. "The scoreboard's definitely hard to see, and the seating could be improved," he murmured.

"Hey, Sam!" Suyi smiled at Sam, preparing to take the box and unconcerned by Gina's out. "You practicing?"

"Not today." Sam grinned back. He liked Suyi. "But my parents let me come and help." There was a soft tug at his sleeve, and Bella peered around him at the tall sixth grader. "Me and Bella."

Suyi grinned. "Hi, Bella!" Then he adjusted the batter's helmet and his gloves—pale white leather against his dark brown skin—and put the bat to his shoulder, ready for the pitcher.

Dr. McGargee threw a pitch straight down home plate, and Suyi swung and missed. Then he hit a curveball hard enough to send it into the outfield. "Great hit!" Coach Lockheart cheered as Suyi rounded the plates. Mason jumped on home plate as the outfielders scrambled to lob the ball in.

Sam's heart lifted like the ball, then sank again. He wanted to be out there on the field so much. But even if the coaches had let him try, just a little, Dr. Vane was sitting right there. Taking notes.

Sam had better things to do besides let the principal's raised eyebrow and loud, scratchy pen remind him that he was due at school on Monday. A list of things to find. Boglins and pookahs to send back where they belonged. Before Mrs. Lockheart could get mad or call his parents again.

How was he going to get into the classroom if Dr. Vane was watching? He couldn't wait until Monday. He needed Bella's help.

"Listen, Bell. Can I tell you more about the deal I made?"

She nodded, her eyes wide.

"I'm trading all those things for my words. We don't have much time to do it, because someone's going to meet me at the Little Free Library soon. Once I meet them, everything will be fixed."

"The fairies with the white pig are meeting you?" She *had* seen them. Not only the pig. Sam knew it.

"They're not fairies, they're goblins. And they *had* a white pig, but it's called something else."

Bella tugged on Sam's sleeve again. Then she pointed to the shed between the fields. "The goblin over *there* has a white pig. Look."

From the noon-thin shadows beside the shed, Nana waved at them. Tucked under one arm, a piglet wriggled. Beside her sat a white pig. *The* white pig, in fact: Starflake, the pookah that, only very recently, had been closed up in Sam's room.

"Don't move," Sam told Bella. Careful not to attract Dr. Vane's attention, Sam hurried over to the shed, trying to look like he was doing something important for the team.

As he approached, Nana looked up, her face creased and worn.

"I promised Tolver I'd bring Starflake and all the rest of the things he wanted to the library tonight—and then you two would give me my words and leave me alone! Why did you just go into my room and steal things?" Sam whispered furiously.

"Sam, it's terrible news, I'm afraid." Nana's voice was low and urgent. So much for Sam's hope.

Sam's anger dimmed as he remembered that the Little Free Library had looked like someone had crashed through it going really fast. "What happened? Are you okay?"

Nana nodded. "I didn't go in your room, Sam. Starflake came to me just now. She must have gotten loose. It's important you know that, because what I'm going to tell you next—" She hugged the piglet tight, and it nuzzled its snout in her hair. *Was Nana crying?*

"What happened?" Sam shut his eyes, trying not to imagine a goblin pig running through his parent's lunch date.

Bella ran across the field and breathlessly tugged on Sam's sleeve.

"Not right now, Bella, okay?"

She kept tugging, then pointed to the hilltop. "Mom and Dad are coming." Their parents held hands, walking the same way Bella and Sam had arrived, but faster. With Mrs. Lockheart.

Sam looked at Nana. "You have to get out of here or disappear."

Nana took the wooden bat out of her bag and waved it at Sam's parents. "Lente!" And pointed it at the Culvers. Sam pushed it away. "No, YOU disappear. Don't magic them."

But it was too late. Sam's parents had slowed considerably. So had the rest of that part of the field.

"It's only a temporary temporalism. They'll speed back up in a moment," Nana said. "Dear, would you take care of this pookah?" She handed Bella the piglet. Bella squeaked with delight and took the pig for a walk around the shed.

With Bella distracted, Sam braced for the terrible news. *Were the boglins going back on Tolver's deal? Why had he thought he could trust goblins?*

But what Nana said was worse. "Sam, we were at the Depository, trying to keep our words safe, and the prospectors took Tolver instead. They conscripted him! How will I ever get him back? They also put a hold on our safe deposit box." Her wrinkled cheeks were damp. "I couldn't get anything out."

She *was* crying. Sam didn't know quite what to do, so he patted her arm. "What can I do to help?"

Nana wiped her eyes on her sleeve. Her voice steadied into a firm resolve. "If you can get me the things Tolver asked for, I'll find a way to keep his bargain."

Did he believe the goblin? Sam wasn't sure. But Tolver had given Bella's word back. And Nana was here, letting Sam know what happened. "I will try, but—"

Suddenly, Nana and Starflake vanished, just as the Culvers finally made it to the shed and Mrs. Lockheart had turned to speak to the principal.

"Sam! Who told you that you could keep a grown pig in your room?" Mr. Culver asked, sounding more than a little frustrated. "And if what Mrs. Lockheart says is true, the Little Free Library's been vandalized again. Do you have any idea—wait." His dad stopped when he saw Bella with the piglet in her arms. "What is with the pigs?"

Sam sighed. *Couldn't Nana and the white pig have stuck around just once so someone would believe me?*

But Bella jumped in. "It's Tham's service project, for thchool."

Sam's dad tilted his head. Sam spoke fast, not wanting Bella to fib. "It's just for a couple of days? Ms. Malloy can explain." As long as Dr. Vane didn't hear about it, this should be all right. The principal was still watching the practice, jotting notes.

"Please, Dad. Just for a little while?" Bella said.

Sam's dad's eyes softened, even as his stepmom caught up to them, frowning. "I do have a few things I want to ask Ms. Malloy. Come on, you two. You have some cleaning up to do at the house, Sam. You can help out here later."

Sam had never felt so frustrated. His dad had no idea what type of pressure Sam was under. And things were only getting more muddled.

As they crossed the field, Mrs. Lockheart talked to Dr. Vane, then stormed away across the field, shaking her head. The principal waved them over, smiling at Sam's father.

"I'm making some notes for the community meeting on Monday!" Sam realized that he'd never heard Dr. Vane be excited, only strict.

"Wouldn't miss it," Sam's dad said.

"Is the scoreboard on the agenda for the meeting?" his stepmom asked.

"Yes!" The corners of Sam's dad's eyes crinkled as he turned on the charm for Dr. Vane. "Dr. Vane invited us to propose ways to improve the baseball fields and the community, and the scoreboard's part of that."

"Neighborhood improvement all around is much needed," the principal said, waving his clipboard. "Given what else has been going on. It sounds like the Little Free Library is a target for vandals."

Sam's heart sank. If everyone including Dr. Vane knew what was happening to the library, what would become of his and Mason's summer project? Ms. Malloy would be so upset. Worse, Mason would have another reason to be angry at Sam.

"Don't worry, Sam," Coach Lockheart said. "We have a plan to find out who's breaking the library. Ms. Malloy assures us it's not any of the students. So the Lockhearts are going to set up a camera."

Sam wanted to tell them all what was really happening to the library. But he couldn't. Not yet, not with Nana waiting. And now they were adding a camera? How was he going to get the pages and the pookah to Nana? He had to work faster.

Right then, a whistle blew, capturing Dr. Vane's and Coach Lockheart's attention. Dr. McGargee began to hand out blue-and-white jerseys to the players. They did that the day before the first game every year. Players pulled them over their regular shirts.

Sam wore his blue Ponyo shirt. No jersey, not yet.

"Let's go, Sam," his stepmom said. They walked back up the hill as a family, plus one piglet. Sam's dad kept looking at the piglet, then at him. He was still steamed.

The sun sank lower, and gnats hovered in a cloud near the crosswalk, blurring the air. The piglet squirmed in Bella's arms. Sam knew they'd been lucky his dad hadn't mentioned the "pig project" to Dr. Vane; still, he hoped Nana would take the little pookah back soon so he wouldn't be in trouble for that too.

But there was no sign of the older boglin anywhere.

At a loud *TINK* from the field, and the sound of cheering, Sam walked backward for a moment, watching the field grow smaller.

Chapter Eleven

Tolver

Tolver found the gentle rocking of the prospector's ship unsettling. He didn't like thinking about the long span of air between the ship's hull and the marshlands far below. But most of all, Tolver hated the food on *The Declension*. He missed his nana's cooking.

Many goblin kitchens were well-run affairs—Tolver's grandmother's being no exception. From them came fine breads, tea, and delicious cakes.

The mess on a prospector ship was a different story.

After following his kobold cabinmate down the length of the ship that first evening, Tolver knew before he stepped into the mess hall that he was in trouble. The place smelled like stewed socks. And the sounds of so many goblins slurping the green slop from metal cups and chewing what looked like beef jerky slathered with peanut butter was nauseating.

"I'm not hungry," Tolver whispered, his stomach churning. He was almost always hungry, but the ship seemed to have solved that problem.

"Come on, son!" A tall prospector missing several teeth and with breath that nearly knocked Tolver out clapped him hard on the shoulder. "Dig in!" He handed Tolver a bowl and spooned a gob of the gelatinous stew into it. Then he added a piece of jerky. "Everyone loves butter jerky!"

Tolver wobbled, and the bowl sloshed on his benefactor's arm and shoes. The prospector's cheerful face immediately transformed.

"You think that's funny?" the goblin growled. "We don't take kindly to waste around here."

Tolver reeled. "I'm sorry!"

"Sorry, *sir*!" the prospector snapped. "I'm your superior. Clean this up and then take yourself to the brig."

Oh no. Tolver hadn't thought things could possibly get worse. He'd been wrong.

"Wait! I know his grandmother," someone shouted in the crowded mess. "That boy does not need to be punished. He merely needs to gain his air legs. I'll look after him until he does!"

Tolver stood up from where he'd crouched to clean the floor. The voice sounded familiar.

Over the bent heads of eight hungry prospectors, he saw a lanky goblin wearing glasses and a big medallion around his neck. The goblin was obviously proud of it, given how he puffed his chest out to let it catch the last of the sunlight. The words "Ship's Inventor" gleamed.

It was Julius, Nana's friend. On *The Declension*. Tolver felt relief wash over him.

In sharp contrast to Tolver, whose skin was a miserable, mottled airsick green, Julius looked very well. His hair was slicked back. His brushed velvet jacket gleamed, just like the medallion, and Julius's skin shone with a confidence he'd never had on Brightside. There, the boglins had trod carefully around him, never sure if he was doing magic or science. And always whispering that he was a little strange.

Tolver wondered for a moment what Julius had done to earn a clean shirt and the decorations on his jacket.

But then Julius smiled at him. "There now, we can't have you telling Gwendoline that you've been treated poorly." He gave the boglin a chocolate bar. That, Tolver had to agree, looked more appetizing than butter jerky. "This will help your stomach settle."

The mess was silent, watching. When Tolver bit off the tiniest piece of chocolate, everyone began speaking again. The angry goblin shrugged and took a seat.

"That solves that," Julius said. "Prospector ships are rough on newcomers. I'm sure your bunkmates have told you?"

"How long have you been here?" Tolver asked. "We came to Brightside, looking for you. Nana needed help fixing a converter. Did you really send me that compass?"

"I've been helping with their machines on and off for a year or so. But only recently moved here. And soon your nana won't need my help—all of those problems will be quickly solved for everyone in the marshbogs!"

Tolver stared, another bite of chocolate halfway to his mouth. Julius continued brightly, although without really answering Tolver's question. "When you meet the captain, you'll understand—he's got a great mind. One of the greatest. We're going to make everything better. And yes, I did send you the compass, Tolver. You should be able to go out and have your own adventures. Gwendoline's been holding you back."

Julius's voice was kind, and he'd stretched out a welcoming arm to Tolver. But Tolver hesitated. "So much went wrong because of that compass."

The inventor caught his expression and grasped Tolver's elbow. Julius whispered sharply, his kind voice gone. "One can't blame a mere compass. Listen, you need to go along to get along here, got it? I'm just as much of a conscript as you are, Tolver. Smile, if your nana matters to you."

Tolver swallowed a half-chewed mouthful of chocolate and coughed until Julius clapped him hard on the back "Got it!" he said, choking. But he smiled.

Julius's voice smoothed. "Normally, you'd be assigned to a crew now, so you can start making a bit of your own back. But I'll tell the captain I'd like to have you as my apprentice. So you can tell your nana when you see her next that I took care of you. Would you like that?" Julius smiled, showing all his teeth at once. When a goblin does this, it is fairly spectacular and also a bit frightening, even to other goblins.

Tolver nodded miserably. Julius hadn't given him any choice in the matter.

As soon as Julius rose and walked from the mess, Tolver's tormenter from before turned to him. "Who else do you know on the ship, bright eyes?"

"I didn't know Julius would be here," Tolver protested.

"You think you're getting on a crew before I do?" The broad goblin bristled at him.

"No, I wouldn't want that." All Tolver wanted was to return to his berth and sleep. "I'm to be his assistant, anyway."

"Good. We'll get along fine, then. I've had my eye on a word-hog crew for weeks. I'm going to make enough to buy my own ship. Name's Broen." The goblin held out his hand and Tolver shook it. Everyone here seemed to want the same thing.

Tolver thought back to the dreams he'd been having. His own ship. Adventure.

Well, he'd gotten at least part of that: adventure.

Now he had to figure out how to get out of it in one piece.

The next day, the first mate called the entire crew of *The Declension* to attention.

Once they were assembled, the tallest goblin Tolver had ever seen paced the broad deck of the ship. All the prospectors aboard straightened when he passed, calling him captain. The goblin wore canvas pants and a vest over a white-and-blue striped shirt. His skin was the color of an unripe mango. His cheeks and hands were almost yellowish, and his silver hair curled down to his collar. He'd waxed his long mustache into silver commas that framed his mouth and cinched his belt so tight that everything looked squeezed.

The Declension too was bigger than any ship Tolver had seen. A giant gas bag held it aloft, while several big baffles at the back that opened and shut like accordions propelled it forward. On the sides, wide fins balanced the steering. *The Declension* moved through the air in sibilant curves. Its passage sounded like rippling water, as elegant as its well-heeled captain.

"You've all been called into service, in the interest of the marshbogs," Captain Bellfont said. "New recruits will help *The Declension* gather fuel for the city and for our ships. When you earn enough, you'll gain privileges and your right to disembark. Look around. Many onboard were once in your state and have risen through the ranks to great glory."

The captain sounded as if he gave this speech often.

"Do you have any questions? NO? GOOD." Captain Bellfont didn't give anyone time to ask anything. "We're approaching our next port of call, and you will pay attention and follow orders. Got it?"

Everyone on board replied yes, or aye, and Tolver rushed to do the same. The squeak of his voice hung in the air long after everyone else had stopped speaking.

As the giant ship turned in the air and began to chug its way toward a new floating city on the horizon, Tolver peeked over *The Declension*'s gunwales.

"The next port's Serendipity," said the goblin nearest him. The broad one from the night before, Tolver remembered: Broen. "Won't be here long. Captain Bellfont doesn't like to dawdle. Just don't cross him, stay out of the brig, and avoid angering the inventor! You might wind up stuffed *inside* his next invention if he gets mad at you!"

"Get to stations, swabs!" The first mate yelled. All the goblins on deck straightened up. The ones in the rigging began to sing as they approached Serendipity.

As the ship turned once more, Tolver saw the floating city was bigger than Felicity, and it was very close. Goblins working on the other side of the glass windows in the buildings stared back, and he could see the kinds of clothing they wore: suits and ties, nice patterns too. Very different from the canvas and cotton of the marshbogs.

A few moments later, the city extended a metal dock alongside the ship, and the goblin crew began carrying big sacks to the dock and baskets of word ribbons aboard.

"You! Julius's assistant! He's busy, so you'll help us for now." Broen prodded Tolver to grab a sack and follow them.

The sacks weren't heavy, but they were unwieldy. Tolver had to keep them from rising as much as falling as he walked down the gangway. *Hot air. They were delivering hot air!*

Even with all the excitement, Tolver worked very hard to keep his eyes off the big drop to the ground below the gangway. By the time he reached the deck of *The Declension* for the third time, carrying baskets, he was out of breath.

"You do this all the time?" he asked Broen.

The goblin nodded. "You get used to it. Not every city has their own prospectors. They're always glad to see us."

The Declension bustled as new items were stowed and as the goblins from the port—these wearing even nicer suits than the goblins Tolver had seen in the buildings—handed over sacks of tea and food in payment.

"Prices have gone up again," one goblin murmured to the captain. Her voice had an edge to it.

"Can't help it, so many need fuel," the captain said, shaking his head sympathetically. "Have we shown you our newest equipment? You might be interested, for your own needs. It converts any word."

She looked intrigued, so the captain beckoned Julius forward. The inventor winked at Tolver, and then he brought out a converter a bit more complicated than the one Nana had made for their island.

This machine was made of brass, with three cranks and a small trumpet for taking in word ribbons. The goblin touched it with a long fingernail. "I wouldn't have to trade for better words?"

"You'd still get the same fuel efficiency from your current

words, but you could use more kinds. Up to five different words per conversion." The captain patted the machine and beamed at Julius.

The goblin whistled. "Even goblin words?"

Captain Bellfont shook his head. "Those still don't convert."

"But our researchers hope to do that someday! Meantime, this is a very flexible tool." Julius patted the brass box.

The woman eyed Julius's medallion and seemed convinced. "How much?"

The captain whispered the price in the goblin's ear. She noted the long line of merchants behind her and sighed. "I'll take it. At least it keeps this lot from having it."

"Don't–" Tolver whispered.

Julius glared at him quickly, and the kobold grabbed his arm. "Do you want to be put in the brig?"

Tolver quieted. But then the merchant asked, "Do you have anything else?"

Julius clapped his hands together. "We do! We tested our latest invention last week. Highly successful!" He looked to the goblins on deck. "Bring me a piglet!"

A crewmember scrambled for the hatch and returned moments later carrying a brass animal about the same size as one of

Gilfillan's piglets. It had bulbs for eyes, and its joints were round like baseballs. Its round belly gleamed metallically in the setting sun. The woman squinted. "What does it do?"

When Julius said, "Put it down, show her, show her," Captain Bellfont sighed with delight, pulling on his long mustache with one hand and gesturing at the crew with the other. He was as proud of the inventions as Julius was.

The goblins put the piglet down and, with a tap from Julius, it walked forward, its head tilted. A corkscrew tail swayed in the wind.

"It's very cute," the woman said.

The pig sat by her feet and gave one loud, metallic oink.

Julius actually giggled. At this, the captain gave up on his mustache and strode over. "If you'd been human, that overused word of yours—cute—would have been mine."

The merchant blanched. "I'll take two. Do they also run on hot air?"

Captain Bellfont nodded. "Exclusively. No fuss. Generate it and capture it both."

"We can also show you . . ." Julius began excitedly, but the captain cut him off with two sharp words.

"Nothing else."

Tolver watched the exchange, wondering what else was in the hold. Had Julius made things that the captain didn't want anyone else to see? Nana had said Julius was powerful. Tolver watched the inventor closely for the rest of the day, but he saw only metal piglets. No new inventions emerged.

By the time they pulled away from the gangway, *The Declension* sat low in the air from the goods it had taken aboard, and the goblin crew had to add more fuel to the airbags. They did this with funnels, pushing some of the baskets of words through a large converter that was much more complex than the one the merchant had purchased.

"Why didn't the captain sell this machine in Serendipity?" Tolver asked aloud.

The captain twisted one half of his silver mustache with two fingers, pleased. "If we keep inventing new tools but only sell the small items, we gain power, my fellow prospectors. Progress!"

Tolver chewed on his lip, willing himself to stay quiet. "Permission to go below, sir?" he asked the inventor. *Progress!* didn't help him get home. Or help Nana buy her island.

"Granted. There's a lad," Julius said, then turned to the captain. "He'd be an asset to any ship."

Bellfont himself clapped Tolver on the shoulder so hard his teeth rattled. "Or perhaps someday he'll have his own ship!"

Tolver looked up at the captain and realized he could see right into the goblin's very hairy nose.

This was nothing like the adventures of his dreams.

Chapter Twelve

Sam

"Will you hold the piglet, Sam, while we cross the street?" Anita lifted the squirming pookah out of Bella's arms and handed it to Sam.

"MoooooOOoommm." Bella pouted all the way back to Mount Cloud village, until she could carry the piglet again. "What will we name it?"

"We are not naming it," Sam's dad said.

Of all Nana's half-baked ideas, leaving Bella with the pookah-piglet even for a moment might be the worst, Sam thought.

"We're going to have to give it back very soon," he said. "The project is almost over." At least, it was supposed to be. All he knew was that he had to get the dictionary pages, find Nana, and then fix the library so the Lockhearts wouldn't be upset. None of these plans included Bella continuing to own a pig.

Sam knew the only reason the pookah was here at all was because Nana needed one to get through the portal to find Starflake. Once she returned to the marshbogs, she'd take both pookahs with her. He hoped.

"I have to say, when it ran through the house, that piglet seemed much larger," his stepmom said. "I've had a lot on my mind lately, though. I could have imagined it." She looked at Sam as if he was part of what had been on her mind. Sam figured that was pretty likely. "I'll see you all back at the house!"

"Let's talk to Ms. Malloy about this." Mr. Culver turned off the sidewalk, and Bella, Sam, and the piglet followed. Ms. Malloy waved from her porch swing.

"Hello, James, Hi, Sam, Hi, Bella!"

She looked like she was feeling better. Sam was glad. He had so much to tell her. But Sam's dad barely said hello. "Why weren't parents given more notice about this pig project?"

"I'm so sorry about that." Ms. Malloy fanned herself and raised her eyebrows at Sam. "It was a last-minute opportunity, assigned to a few particular students. Animal care teaches the value of actions over words."

"Well. I guess that's a good lesson," Mr. Culver said. "How long will the, er, piglet be with us?"

Ms. Malloy's eyebrows couldn't get any higher.

"You said a day or two, for each of us," Sam interjected. "So we're almost finished."

She smiled, relieved. "Yes, exactly. James, do you mind if I speak with Sam about the project for a minute, since he's here? I'll send him right home. Bella, would you care for the piglet until then?"

Bella smiled in gap-toothed delight as she skipped back home. Mr. Culver followed, shaking his head at the sight.

"Whew, that was *close*," Sam said. Then he looked up, directly into his teacher's sternest expression.

"Sam, first. No more lying. Second…how did you come by a goblin pig?"

Sam owed her an answer, but he didn't have a great one. "Well, Nana—the older goblin…"

"You spoke to them?" The alarm in her voice carried out over her yard. Sam saw his dad pause near their door, but he and Ms. Malloy waved, and Mr. Culver went inside.

"I did—they're nice! Mostly. Just a little confused about ownership of things, I think." Sam really wanted his teacher to like the boglins, because he'd trusted them to return their words. "Did you know—"

"Sam! Wait. I don't think that hanging out with goblins is a good idea at all. We'll figure out another solution for Dr. Vane and Mason. Dr. Vane's a stickler for standards, and words mean a lot to him—as much as they do to me—but we'll sort it out. And as for Mrs. Lockheart—" She stared at Sam significantly.

Sam sighed. "I can't fix things with Mrs. Lockheart until I fix things in the marshbogs." Ms. Malloy wasn't going to like hearing about the marshbogs one bit.

That last thing was bad news, because Sam needed her help. More than that, he needed her dictionary. He took a deep breath and began telling Ms. Malloy about Bella's word and how he'd gotten it back. He told her a little about the prospectors. "And so the goblins need—" he began. But Ms. Malloy interrupted him.

"Goblins, still coming and going? Sam. I hate to think that we would ever have to get rid of a Little Free Library. But we must stop them from coming back. This is dangerous!"

How can I get you to understand? Sam crossed his fingers for luck and tried one more time. "I really want to get my words first, and they promised." The truth was, Sam kind of liked Tolver, and he wanted to help out Nana. Just like he wanted to help Ms. Malloy. "Getting Bella's words back proved I can do it. Plus, this is a good way to *really* fix things, right?"

"No, Sam. It's not. What if you get hurt? Or someone else does? I can't allow you to do any more." She wasn't buying it.

Sam's voice grew screechy as he panicked. "Do you think I'll be all right, then, not being able to say _____ or _____ or even _____ for the rest of my life?"

He couldn't keep still, thinking about it. The past couple of days had been really hard.

Ms. Malloy's expression changed. She shook her head side to side, slowly, her eyes soft. "How can I help?"

"If I can get the items on their list, they'll stop the prospectors, and then they can get our words to us. They promised."

"And you think a goblin's promise is worth trusting?" She frowned, doubtful.

Sam hadn't thought so a little while ago, no. But seeing Nana so upset had changed that. She needed help. She'd been as good as her word so far. Sam could be too. "I do."

Ms. Malloy looked away for a moment and dabbed at her nose with a tissue. *Was she crying?* But when she turned back and smiled at Sam, she looked just fine.

"Then we'll make sure they get what they need. And I'll try to help fix the library. So. What's on their list?"

"They want pages from a certain kind of dictionary—a big one. Like the one from the classroom."

Her face paled. "That's—Sam, you can't tear pages from the *Oxford English Dictionary*; it's very expensive. That's not even the school's. I bring it in especially for my classes."

Oh. "I understand." Sam's shoulders slumped. That was it then. Unless. "Does the school library have one? Can we ask Dr. Vane?"

"I'm afraid not." Her fingers wound and unwound the handkerchief she'd used on her nose a moment ago. The porch swing squeaked on its chains. "He wouldn't like that at all."

A shadow crossed the lawn between Ms. Malloy's house and the Lockhearts'. Overhead, clouds began to build again, and a few drops of rain hit the sidewalk.

Ms. Malloy sighed and brushed a drop off her skirt, thinking. Then she gave a big sigh. "All right. Okay." She rose from the porch swing. "A dictionary is replaceable, and people are not. I'll be right back."

Sam waited uncomfortably on the porch, thinking about the marshbogs and the prospectors who'd taken Tolver. People *were* more important than words. That was true for everyone.

The peak of the Little Free Library was visible over the hedge. More shadows crossed the lawn near Ms. Malloy's house, and Sam heard a soft *oink*. There, beneath the porch overhang, where he could barely see them unless he leaned out on the railing, were Nana and Starflake.

"There you are!" Nana said. "We had to dodge a lot of humans!" She held Mrs. Lockheart's plant sprayer in one hand—it looked a bit like a water pistol attached to a plastic bottle, and it had "Lockheart" written in black Sharpie down the side—and Sam's father's baseball bat in the other. A basket was slung over one shoulder, and Starflake's leash was around her wrist.

"You can't just take things…" Sam started, then looked closely at Nana's basket. A ribbon was coiled on the bottom. "What's that?"

She chuckled and stood in front of the basket. "A curse. Not a big one. Just for emergencies. The young lady playing catcher won't miss it, I'm fairly sure."

"You said those were really dangerous. Not for fuel." Sam leaned farther.

Nana nodded. "They can get away from you, for sure. Did you get what we need?"

He looked through the screen door at the house's inner hallway. Ms. Malloy hadn't reappeared. "She's worried. She doesn't want me to get hurt or in trouble. But she's helping."

Nana shook her head. "That's very sensible. Plus, I bet she's still mad at me, even though that was so long ago."

"Well, of course she is!" Sam whispered angrily. "You don't know how hard it is to be missing a word, Nana."

They hushed as Ms. Malloy came back out on the porch. She put the big navy book on the swing and sighed. "I love this dictionary." Then she opened it to the back and took a page in between her fingers. Paused. "Which words do you think they'd want, Sam?"

Nana had disappeared the moment Ms. Malloy had come back. Sam peered under the porch but couldn't see her or the pookah anywhere. So he guessed. "Something strong. For fighting with?"

"Fighting words. Okay. A lot of good fighting words start with un. Unravel, undo, unify . . ". Ms. Malloy turned to the *U* section and tore five pages in quick succession, as if she couldn't bear doing it slow. "Here, Sam. Take these."

"Thanks, Ms. Malloy."

"Keep me posted, all right? I don't want you or the library to experience any more damage, okay?" She rested her hand on the dictionary.

"Yes, Ms. Malloy." Sam leaned out over the porch and looked for Nana, but she and Starflake were gone. "That's great, just great."

"Oh, please be careful!" she reached out as if to pull Sam back.

He straightened up and brushed porch-railing dust off his shirt. Ms. Malloy looked so worried, he felt a pang.

Sam frowned as he folded the pages and put them in his bag. He wanted to convince the two boglins to stop stealing words, but if they couldn't, then he and Ms. Malloy would have to try something else. "We should block up the back of the library when this is all done."

Ms. Malloy frowned at Sam's tote bag. "Maybe so. I remember when my dad sealed the tree. It was just after." Then her face glowed. "Oh! He did that just after I lost my words. Maybe he *did* believe me. At least a little."

So that's how Nana had been stopped from coming over for so long. And if they couldn't come over, maybe that's why they didn't have a lot of fuel for the boat, Sam thought. *They couldn't come back until Mr. Lockheart put up the Little Free Library.*

As Sam considered this, Mason's friend Gina and her younger brother came by the Little Free Library. She picked the boy up. He pulled out a book with a bright yellow cover and chortled happily.

"What happened when your dad sealed the tree?" Sam asked Ms. Malloy. "Did your friends leave notes in other places?"

She shook her head. "We just stopped."

Sam didn't want to stop everyone—except the goblins—from using the Little Free Library. He bet Ms. Malloy didn't either. "Maybe we can talk them out of coming here," he finally said. "We only have these two goblins to deal with. And not for much longer, anyway."

Sam started down the steps, watching for Nana.

"I hope so, Sam," Ms. Malloy said. "But do me a favor? Try to stay out of Mrs. Lockheart's way until this is all over. She's very upset."

Despite the raindrops, which were coming a bit faster now, Mrs. Lockheart's gardening hat was visible over the hedge. It bobbed up and down as she packed dirt near the library's post.

Sam walked fast, hoping he could do as Ms. Malloy asked. He spotted the small black video camera she'd planted in the tulips, pointed up at the box, before he saw her waiting for him.

"I have no idea how this keeps getting smashed, *Sam*," she said. The emphasis she put on Sam's name seemed to say she had a whole bunch of ideas, all related to him. "Do you have any ideas? Because you've been nearby, 'taking care of the library' so frequently when it's been broken. You and your friend Mason too. If I have to keep planting new flowers here, I don't know what I'll do."

The last time Sam had trampled her flowers, she'd definitely gotten more and more angry when he'd apologized too fast. That wouldn't be a problem this time.

Maybe using that word all the time had weakened it.

He shook his head to clear it. He couldn't get stuck here,

talking to Mrs. Lockheart. He needed to find Nana and warn her about the camera.

"Maybe it's the weather, like Ms. Malloy said? Or an animal?" *Like a large white pig,* Sam thought, but didn't say.

"Whatever it was, they did quite a job this time. We'll catch them, though." She brushed a raindrop off her arm. "About time to go inside," she finally said. "I'll bring it up at the community meeting. We'll see if the camera records anything in the meantime." She waved her hand near the library and a red light turned on inside the lens. "See? Motion activated! Tell your parents I hope to see them Monday!"

"I will," Sam said. He understood Mrs. Lockhart's frustration, even if he couldn't tell her so. Having to keep fixing something that refused to be fixed was frustrating.

But that camera was going to be a problem.

As if in reply, the piglet squeaked from across the street.

Yup. A big problem.

Bella was waiting for Sam on the porch. "I talked to the fairi–... goblin, Tham," she whispered, big-eyed and serious.

The porch floor was spattered with dirt from a knocked-over plant. There were pig tracks everywhere. Anita laughed as she wiped one off the table while talking to someone on the phone. "And then the pig ran down the stairs and I didn't know what to make of it." She wiped tears from her eyes. "Hey, Sam, here's a broom."

Sam took the broom and turned back to Bella. "You did?" The broom handle got very slippery because Sam's hands started to sweat. "Bell, that's not funny."

"Nana's really nice. Thee thaid thorry about taking my word."

"She didn't take anything else, did she?"

Bella's pigtails swished as she shook her head no. "Thee promised not to anymore. As long as I promised not to try to follow her anywhere. And thee said you should meet her in the morning."

Not tonight? But what about the new camera? Sam groaned. The goblins could go invisible and not be caught on the video, but Sam couldn't.

"Thee thaw the camera and wants to put a thpell on the camera, But it only works at sunrise."

"Dinner!" Dad called up the stairs. "No pigs, please!"

Bella scampered to the kitchen, and Sam scanned the house for goblins. He didn't see any. Downstairs, cutlery jingled as Bella helped set the table.

"Interesting experiment, with the pig," their dad said. "Don't let your little sister do all the work for you, all right?"

"I promise, Dad. How was lunch?" he asked, trying to shift the conversation. "Aside from the interruption." Sam liked it when his dad talked to him like he was old enough to understand things. But over the past couple of days, they hadn't been doing much of that.

"Good. We needed to sit down and relax—it's been a long week. You know how it gets." Dad sighed. "Next week, with the community meeting, it's going to be even longer."

Anita brought out leftover sandwiches. The sauce for the meatball subs had soaked into the bread, and the cheese had melted when she reheated them. The meal warmed Sam's belly, and he relaxed as they ate. Together, they watched the fireflies come out in the yard.

Bella ran her tongue across the tooth just coming in. "How long until I can talk right again?"

"It takes the time it takes, Bell," their dad said. "You'll get used to it."

Sam wondered if Bella *would* get used to it. He hadn't gotten used to not being able to say the words the boglins stole. Bella's teeth would grow back. Sam's words wouldn't.

After dinner, Sam made a bed on the porch sofa—the porch being the only place the piglet was allowed.

When he woke up covered in dew, the pookah was nudging his fingers.

Oh no! Had he missed dawn? And Nana's spell?

The light was a soft pink. He hadn't missed it yet.

Sam grabbed the piglet and the tote bag, then scribbled his parents a quick note about working with friends on the library. He quietly closed the screen door as he left and ran down the street. When he reached the Little Free Library, the pale sun was rising. Sam eyed the camera, then waved his hand past its lens.

The camera lens had bubbles of dew on it, and the light didn't turn red. Nana's spell had worked. But there was another problem.

Mason leaned against the oak tree. Her hair was in a tight braid, her face was set in a glare, and her arms were crossed over her chest. "I knew it. You're the one messing up the library. You are in so much trouble, Sam."

On the other side of the library door, Nana and the pig crouched, panicked.

Mason paced, furious. "So you're trying to ruin our summer-project grade! Why?" Mason said. "Are you that mad at me?"

He shook his head, fast. "I'm not! I'm trying to make it better, Mason! Honest!"

"But Coach Lockheart told my dad that they're going to board up the library, and we're going to fail, because we can't take care of the library if it gets boarded up under our watch. Because *you* were sabotaging it."

"Mason, I am pretty sure Ms. Malloy will underst—"

"She might, but Mrs. Lockheart won't. She said she'd seen me and Gina *and* you out here messing with the library, but she didn't know who the main culprit was. So now WE'RE in trouble too, Sam!"

Behind Mason, Nana waved madly, trying to get Sam's attention. Her mouth was moving, but the closed door kept the sound in. Then she pointed at the camera. The spell. It was going to wear off.

"Sam!" Mason moved so she was between Sam and the door. "Do you hear what I'm saying? I don't want to be in trouble for something you did."

Sam understood. But he couldn't tell Mason, because he needed her to go away.

Nana started pulling the baseball bat out of her tote. Would she try to quiet Mason by taking her words? He couldn't let that happen, either.

The sun glittered through the tree, and the magic dew on the Lockhearts' security camera began to shrink. There wasn't any time to waste.

Could he say something so mean that it drove Mason away? Sam had done it before, but that had felt awful. But he didn't want Nana stealing Mason's words or Nana to use the curse on her. And he didn't want them to get caught on screen. And standing here not saying anything was making Mason just as mad.

She paced around the Little Free Library, looking at it. "If you're not trying to sabotage us, then something strange is going on."

Not too long ago, Sam would have told Mason exactly how strange.

Now, though? Now she'd tell Gina, and they'd whisper about Sam being a weirdo with dumb ideas and a worse imagination who wasn't good at math and made up stories about goblins. *No thank you.*

"I mean, you were in the box! How do you even fit in there anyway?" She looked like she was giving up on him.

And she might have, if Nana hadn't opened the Little Free Library's door. "Go away!" She waved the baseball bat—much smaller because of the Pookah—at Mason. In the shadows, with her arms waving, she looked like a large, talking bug.

Mason jumped, possibly at the thought of giant bugs in the library more than anything else. "What? WHO?"

For a moment, Mason, Sam, and Nana stared at each other.

Then Nana grabbed Sam's T-shirt and pulled, shouting, "I need your friend," by way of explanation, just before the last drop of dew dried on the camera.

Nana and Starflake pulled him back through the library before he could think to grab hold of anything. And he would have gone through straightaway too, except that Mason clutched Sam's T-shirt and the waistband of his shorts and tried to keep him on the sidewalk. "You're not taking him!"

And that's how Mason McGargee got pulled along with Sam into the Little Free Library by a goblin.

On the other side, tangled in a mud puddle with Starflake, on the boglin's small island, right next to the mail boat, Mason kicked Sam in the knee. "Get OFF!"

She pushed the large pig out of her way. Her hair was streaming, and splatters of mud dried pale on her face. She struggled to fight her way up and looked around, shocked. "Where are we?"

The wind blew across the marshes, rippling the water. The cottage door was broken, and household items were strewn everywhere. There was no sign of the prospectors, but the floating city could be seen above the islands farther south.

"This," Sam finally said, "is the marshbogs."

Mason dropped the book she'd been clutching under one arm. Her mouth hung open.

Marshbog breezes shifted reeds and moss hanging from the cottage into a soft rustle. In the distance, ships moved back and forth, shadows around the floating city. The piglet wriggled from Nana's arms and went to nudge Mason's ankle. Absently, she picked it up.

"Goblins," Mason said.

"Yep! Best of the lot—none of the mean ones, at least—live out here on the bog." Nana brushed herself off, looking proud.

"And steal children!" Mason's voice was a whisper.

"Given recent events, I can see how you might think so," Nana began. "But no, we gather words mostly, sometimes other items." Nana slipped the bat back in her satchel and put her basket down on the bench.

Sam handed her the tote bag with the dictionary pages in it. She looked through the contents, muttering. Sam bit his lip. *Would she keep Tolver's side of the deal? Especially now? Ms. Malloy will be so disappointed in me if she doesn't.* You can't trust them, Sam, *she'd said. Just yesterday.*

Nana squinted at the paper. "I guess these will have to do. Five pages—but, excellent words. Good enough for what we need. Good enough to earn back your words."

"What about the bat?" Sam asked. It was his dad's, after all.

Nana chuckled and patted the bat. "With the prospectors coming around, I wanted something a bit more substantial than my old willow switch." When she smiled at him, her eyes nearly disappeared in her wrinkles. "But I'll get it back to you, I promise."

Mason stared at her. "Bat? Prospectors? Sam, this is too weird. I want to go home now." Mason said. "We—I have a ball game today."

"We'll get you home as soon as we can, I promise," Nana said. "But Sam and I need to rescue my grandson, Tolver, first. You can help. If you don't want to do that, you can stay here on the island on your own until we get my grandson back. Those are your choices."

Mason's mouth opened and shut, like she wanted to ask for *more* choices but couldn't figure out how.

"The prospectors took Tolver," Sam said, hoping to convince her. "He's my goblin friend. They've got him on an airship and are making him mine hot air."

Goblin friend, Mason mouthed, her eyebrows raised. *Hot air.* He imagined Mason and Gina giggling in the future, behind his back, at school. He closed his eyes, waiting for the teasing to start.

"And once we have him, we can get Sam's words," Nana added.

"Sam's words?" Mason demanded. "What do you mean? That he really can't say sorry?"

Her eyes bored into Sam's, daring him to lie.

"It's real," Sam finally said. He didn't embellish.

"*This* is what was breaking the library to bits?" She gestured at Nana.

He nodded, speechless with surprise. She hadn't teased him.

"Boglins versus prospectors. Like a movie." Mason took one more long look around the island. "I guess we need to get your words back, Sam. And then we go *straight* home."

Nana clapped her hands. "Help me get the boat in the water, then." She was favoring her arm, so Mason and Sam both helped. She climbed in, then gestured for Sam and Mason to follow. But Mason still hesitated.

"What is the actual plan?" she asked.

Nana sighed. "Tolver is really the planner." Nana lifted the word she'd stolen from the baseball field from the basket. It glittered in the sun. "I was thinking I'd use this."

Sam remembered what Tolver had told him about the prospectors. "Can you bring down a ship with that?" He scanned the sky, wondering if she meant right then. But he didn't see any ships nearby.

"A ship?" Mason looked out over the bog.

"Ships fly here," Sam said. Mason didn't look half as surprised this time. Maybe she was getting used to things being weird.

"It's possible," Nana said. "But I don't want it to backfire, and curses often do."

"Then why don't we?" Sam said. "Once the ship is down, Tolver can escape. And we can go home." It was another kind of goblin trap—like he'd tried to make at home. Or at least, it was the start of one.

"That might attract *more* prospectors." Nana shook her head. "Though I hate it, I think we need to trade with them. A curse is valuable. The prospectors might give me Tolver for it. While we were at the Depository, I heard an old friend was on board *The Declension*, where Tolver is, so that may make bargaining go easier. But we have to find the ship first. We can't just sit here waiting." Nana looked toward the sky, then at the ripples in the water beside the mail boat.

"Okay." Without another word, Mason climbed in the boat and waited. "We can be heroes, like in a movie."

Once Sam was also settled aboard, they started to row. The boat wobbled—no one was very good at rowing. Nana pointed the direction they should go—right into the open water.

"My friend is an inventor. Someone who knows spell work and invents machines, like I did once," Nana said. "The prospectors seem to have conscripted him, and to hear people tell it, he was none too happy about it. So if we find the ship, and I can convince him to help us, perhaps we'll have an extra advantage when bargaining."

Mason's brow wrinkled. "And once we have Tolver?"

"We'll go straight to the Depository and get your words." Nana sounded so confident.

"But what if they don't want to bargain?"

"Then I'll use the words you brought, and the curse, and anything else I can think of," Nana said. "Words have a lot of power here. And while dictionary pages can't fuel a ship, they *can* do other magic. Most goblins don't remember how, but I do." She examined the pages again. "I think we have enough to make an undoing spray, because these are all un-words. That will come in handy if the prospectors don't want to bargain. I have a little bit of silverfish spell left as well. I'll get Tolver back, no matter what. Now please stop arguing and let's go!"

"We weren't arguing," Mason protested. "A good plan should stand up to some questions." But she bent into the rowing and the boat moved faster.

"True," Nana went to the bow of the boat and began tearing

one of Ms. Malloy's dictionary pages into tiny pieces. Sam winced, thinking what his teacher would say if she knew.

Mason struggled to row in time with Sam, and Sam tried to compensate, throwing them off rhythm even more. The boat veered across the marshes as Nana separated and murmured each word—*Unfurl, Unload, Unlock, Upend, Utilize*—while waving her bat over them. Then she put each into the plant-mister bottle. Once those words had dissolved, she tore the last pages to get more words. Finally, Nana scooped a bucketful of water from the marsh and poured it into the sprayer she'd taken from Mrs. Lockheart's gardening basket. As she worked, she murmured, "She's quite brilliant, your teacher."

Despite a crick in his neck from scanning the skies, an ache in his shoulders from rowing, and worry bubbling in his belly, Sam finally found a good rowing pace. He and Mason guided the boat past the islands as Nana finished the spell.

When the last page was gone, Nana added more saltwater and shook the bottle until the grayish water sparkled. Then she sprayed some on her bat. Sam held his breath, but the bat didn't break.

"It only works on objects with lots of parts," Nana said, winking at him. "Like a boat." She gestured with her chin. Far out on the horizon, where Nana pointed, Sam saw dark clouds that might be airships.

They kept rowing until Nana said, "Stop!" Sam's arms throbbed, and Mason was sweating so much her hair stuck to her cheeks. Both of them were plastered with salt spray. The boat spun in the current beneath a cloudy sky, and Mason trailed a finger in the water. Ripples spread across the reflected clouds.

"I promise," Sam said to her. "Once I get the words I need back, I'll fix everything. And maybe..."

"Maybe what." Mason looked doubtful again, as the reality of their adventure struck her fully.

"Maybe we can be friends again." He said it really fast, the way he'd pull off a Band-Aid.

Mason looked at Sam and then looked out at the marshbogs. And up at the clouds. Then at Sam again. "We'll see."

"Here they come," Nana whispered. She pointed at the large dark shape drifting closer to them like a cloud, blocking the sun.

"Put this in your bag," Nana said. She handed Sam the spray bottle. She leaned her bat on her shoulder. The closer the shape got, the less cloudlike it looked and the more it looked like a prospector's ship.

Only then did Sam worry that the mail boat held other things Nana might be willing to trade in order to get Tolver back. Like him and Mason.

Chapter Thirteen

Tolver

The prospector ship *Declension* caught up fast to the small mail boat. Its goblin crew peered over the gunwales.

Julius held his medallion to his chest as he leaned. Tolver looked too. His eyes widened as he spotted the occupants of the boat. Sam, a human girl, and Nana.

When the inventor spotted the dark-haired humans, he whispered to Tolver, "Those two down there aren't boglins, are they?"

Tolver shook his head, "But Nana's down there too. They must have—" he swallowed, thinking fast—"kidnapped her. They're probably dangerous. You should tell the crew to leave the boat alone."

Julius squinted and then held his hand out for Tolver's binoculars. When Tolver hesitated, Julius snapped his fingers. "Come on, be quick!"

Tolver unclipped the binoculars and held his breath as the inventor peered through them at the water below. "She doesn't seem to be kidnapped. She's even pointing her switch toward us."

"Perhaps she's coming to rescue us." Tolver hoped so.

"In that tiny boat?" Julius scoffed. "Even your grandmother couldn't take on a fully armed prospector ship under sail."

"Don't you want to be rescued?" Tolver had spent the entire day under the impression that Julius had been conscripted, just like him, because Julius had implied exactly that. "You're the most famous inventor in the marshbogs, even better than Nana."

"I'm getting along just fine here, actually," Julius said. "Being famous in the marshbogs isn't as exciting as being famous across the realms. You'll understand much better once you make your way on the ship like me." He absentmindedly brushed his hand over the fancy embroidery on his jacket.

"Plus," he added, "there's an unfortunate aspect to being the marshbogs' best inventor. You only get paid in eggs and mediocre words. Now?" He grinned. "I plan to be famous *and* rich."

Tolver's stomach dropped even farther. He watched with dread as his grandmother raised a small red flag on the mail boat's stern. It meant she had hot air she wanted to trade.

The setting sun cast a long shadow over the small boat as the prospector ship bore down fast on their position. "Get ready," Julius whispered, mostly to himself.

The prospector's vessel made loud clanging noises as its engines processed hot air and released it for propulsion. Tolver could feel the baffles stretching and compressing above as the breeze ruffled his hair.

The ship moved much faster than Nana could with the mail boat.

The young goblin felt ill. *Why hadn't he given Sam his words when he could have, back on the island? Why did he ever use the compass?* His eyes narrowed to slits and he blinked fast.

When the prospector ship caught up with its shadow, its crew dropped long boarding lines. The ropes slapped the water and splashed the little boat. A lime-skinned goblin wearing heavy canvas overalls and a striped shirt, his fists bound in brass knuckles, leaned over the bow. Near the bowsprit, a pair of silvered wings extended, slowing the ship. At its portholes, *The Declension* began to bristle with weapons.

Tolver whispered, "What are we doing? They're no danger to us! We're huge! They're tiny. They just want to trade!"

"We all heard what your nana did to *The Colophon*! Sent them all the way back to ground with her silverfish spell."

"But she used her words up! Tell the captain to leave her alone!" Tolver cried. He tried to reach for his binoculars, but Julius caught his wrist.

"You don't want to get sent to the brig before everything happens, do you?" the inventor whispered. "You're heading in that direction."

Tolver twisted, fighting down fear and anger. No, he didn't want to get sent to the brig, not if there was a chance he could help.

Below, Nana waited until the ship and the goblins hanging from its ropes were close enough. Then she waved a wooden base-ball bat. "If you come any closer, I'll be forced to use my words, not trade them."

Julius laughed, and the goblins kept coming.

"Fine then," Nana yelled. "You two, hold on to something," she told the children. "Tolver, we're coming!"

While Tolver could barely hear his grandmother, he did catch her meaning. The two humans grabbed each side of the small wooden hull. Nana slid to the middle of the little boat and raised her bat until it was pointed at the ship's airbag. "Undoooo!" she shouted. Tolver could barely hear her.

The mail boat rocked in the water, as if something powerful had pushed it. But only a clinking sound came from the bat.

Tolver looked more closely at *The Declension*'s hull. Instead of cannons, large wooden poles extended from the portals. Switches. Very big ones.

Words sounded from the two portals in the ship's sides. "Capture!"

"That's all she's got?" Julius clasped his hands. "Oh, Gwen-doline, how sad!"

The wind carried the ship's spells out across the water, where they splayed into translucent, glittering ropes. Soon, the little boat became entangled in sticky nets full of magic.

Sam, Nana, and the girl were trapped beneath the spells. They couldn't move.

Julius laughed and hopped from one foot to the other. "Perfect!"

Meantime, more nets wrapped around Nana's spell, still clattering through the air, and stopped it reaching *The Declension*. The entire spell dropped like a stone and hit the water with an enormous *GLUNK*. Copper-colored bubbles fizzed as it sank.

"Countermeasures. And ones I taught you!" Nana shook her fist from the boat. "Julius, how could you!"

Julius's silver hair blew every which way as he leaned over the gunwale. His brass medallion on its heavy chain thunked against the side of the boat. "It's all about progress, Gwendoline. I dare for progress! The prospectors are going to make me rich."

Nana struggled beneath the sticky net, trying to reach her bat. It had been knocked into the hull of the little boat. "Just as soon as I get up there, you're going to get a piece of progress so loud," Nana raged.

"Oh, I think not, dear." The first mate, her long silver braid tucked around her pointy ears, waved the idea away like a gnat. "You won't be coming with us."

Three goblins swung down from the ship on the sturdy ropes as Julius stepped away from the hull and clapped a hand firmly over Tolver's mouth as he struggled to keep an eye on his grandmother.

The descending goblins wore bandoliers with sticks tucked into them, goggles, and leather helmets. One was dressed in a dark cotton shirt and striped pants, another in overalls and a checked shirt. The third wore a long coat over skirts knotted to keep from tangling in the rigging. All of them had green skin of varying tones and bare feet thick with silver fuzz.

The two humans stared at the goblins, shocked. But as Tolver watched, the girl started shouting, then began to fend off the attackers with an oar. Her eyes were lit up, and she grimaced as the salt spray hit her face. She wasn't scared at all. She was furious. Sam began to do the same.

It didn't matter, though.

As Tolver struggled in Julius's grip, the first goblins boarded the mail boat and grabbed Nana's baseball bat. The broad goblin from the mess broke the bat in half, then half again, and passed the splinters to the first mate.

The first mate pointed the bat pieces at Nana and said, "Retrieve."

"Not my spells," Nana yelled.

"No!" Tolver said at the same time.

But it was too late. From Nana's lips spilled five word ribbons. More rose from her basket. They flew through the air and wrapped themselves around the pieces of Nana's broken bat.

Then the goblin prospector tucked the pieces into her top hat. "Thanks, ma'am," she drawled. "Julius and Captain Bellfont will appreciate these. That was for *The Colophon.*"

Nana glared at her. Up above, Tolver bit Julius's hand and struggled to free himself.

"You ingrate!" the inventor growled as he tucked Tolver tightly under his arm and shook his other hand in the air.

"Sam, jump!" Tolver yelled. "Swim away!"

But Sam didn't jump. "I'm not leaving the others!"

The second goblin, in overalls, pulled the girl from the nets and then out of the boat by the collar of her yellow T-shirt. "This one's fighty." The girl tried to jerk herself free, but the goblin was too strong.

With rough motions, the goblins bound the two humans and hauled them up toward *The Declension.*

"You can't do this!" The girl struggled against the rope and the air but then stopped once she got too high, afraid she might fall into the sea. Sam kicked at the goblins for as long as he could. Tolver worried they would get dropped. He didn't want to be responsible for any more harm that might come to the humans.

Below, Nana struggled and yelled beneath the enchanted nets.

"You can't just leave her there!" Tolver jerked against Julius's grip.

"Make nice, or we'll take *your* pretty words too," said the first mate as she brought Sam on board. The girl clamped her mouth shut and glared.

"You can't hold us," Sam said. But then he looked around the ship and saw Tolver and deflated.

"Prospectors decide what prospectors can do. You and your friend are hereby conscripted to help with the cause," the first mate said.

Julius finally let Tolver fall to the ground and strode toward the humans. "Well, what has Nana brought us," he murmured. Against Julius's now salt-stained sea coat, his medallion shone.

"You were her student!" Tolver cried. "You were her friend. How could you leave her lashed to the boat like that?"

"Nana? She'll get herself out of there at some point," Julius said. "She taught me so much over the years, from spells and making things to how to feel gratitude for all those eggs and fishes. I've exceeded her talents, obviously." His fingers tapped absently on his medallion. "But I won't show you any more of my ideas if you don't behave."

"No thank you," the girl said. She turned her face toward the sky.

Julius lifted the pieces of Nana's switch from his companion's hands. They glittered with spells. He raised an eyebrow at one of the words. "At least she can no longer curse our ship."

When a cabin door slammed open near the stern of the ship and Captain Bellfont emerged, Julius tucked the bat pieces into his coat pockets.

The prospectors who'd gathered Sam and his friend up from the boat below elbowed the humans into standing up straight. "Captain Bellfont, we found these two in the bog."

Julius added, "We left the older boglin floating."

Bellfont looked Sam and the girl up and down, squinting one dark eye at them and then the other. "You seem old enough to waste words." His voice was as bellowy as Nana's, but smoother. "How did you get to the marshbogs?"

"We have nothing to say to you." The girl pressed her lips together stubbornly. Tolver was impressed and frightened for her.

"On my ship, you'll answer when I ask," the captain growled. The girl frowned, furious, but didn't say anything more. "Take her to the brig." He looked at Sam. "She can rejoin you after our next word-gathering expedition, if the two of you behave."

"What? Wait!"

Broen restrained Sam and Tolver as Julius led Mason toward the bow of the ship. The first mate bent to unhook a well-oiled latch in the deck. When the hatch opened, a terrible stench wafted out. Julius dropped Mason inside and dusted off his hands, then kicked the hatch closed.

Sam turned green. Tolver turned even greener.

Far below, very tiny and getting smaller, Nana sat in the rowboat, furiously shaking her fist.

But she's sitting up, Tolver thought. *That was a start. I promise, Nana, we'll get your spells back.*

"Take your friend and get him something to eat," the first mate said to Tolver. "Now."

"Sorry about this," Tolver nudged the stunned boy ahead of him. They climbed down a rope ladder and into the dark mess. Belowdecks, *The Declension* smelled like a vegetable bin gone bad and old socks gone moldy. As Sam stumbled past the tables, grimacing at the odor, Tolver reached out and pulled at his sleeve.

"Sam! What happened? What was Nana thinking? It's going to take forever to earn her spells back. If they even let me try."

"We have to get them back, Tolver," Sam said. He stared at the plate before him. "And then my words too. I can't stay here forever! Mason and I have to go home!"

Tolver bit his lip and drummed his fingers on the table. "We have to work together. I haven't been exactly honest with you. I should have told you—"

"That you were going to take the words right off my cards? I'll say!" Sam growled. "You can't stop taking things, can you?"

On the contrary, Tolver thought. *Right now, after seeing Nana lose so much, I don't think I could stomach taking any more.* He spoke very quietly. "Sam, I promise, I won't take your words anymore. And I'll get yours back."

The mess was dim, especially with the portals blocked by

the weapons above. But Tolver watched Sam stare at table, holding his breath.

Finally, Sam said, "I don't know if I can believe you. You gave me your word last time."

"I am really sorry," Tolver said.

As he used the word, Sam sighed heavily. "At least you can say it."

"I'll work until I make everything better." Tolver knew that was the only way to really apologize. "Why were you on the mail boat?"

"We had a plan," Sam said. "We were going to trade some words for you, then go to the Depository. Obviously, we need a new plan now." Sam laid his head on the table with a thud.

Tolver groaned. "Nana's plans don't always go straight, but they're usually good. Tell me what else she said."

"Something about an undoing spray," Sam said. Sam tugged his bag open and very carefully showed Tolver what Nana had made. The bottle glittered with words. Sam lowered his voice. "Maybe we could take over the ship with it?"

Tolver laughed. "You can't commandeer a prospector ship,

Sam. You don't even know how to fly one. Besides, there are too many goblins."

"Do you know how to fly one?"

Tolver shook his head, then nodded, then shook it again. "Maybe a little? I've watched them enough. Look, what I'd do is go along with things for a little while. Eat the butter jerky." Tolver paused as Sam made a face. This, he understood. "But stay away from the stew. Do what you're told, then get off at the next port and find someone who will send you home. That's what I was planning on trying to do."

"But what about the Depository?" Sam whispered. "My words are there, you said."

They are now, Tolver thought regretfully. *They weren't when I told you that.* "They're lost, Sam. The prospectors are all over the Depository now. We have to work with what we've got." Tolver hated that he was starting to sound like Julius.

"But we've got to fight them! You need to go back to the island, Mason needs to go home, and I need to get my words back!" Sam said.

"Look at everyone down here," Tolver said. "They've all been trying to work their way home, some for years. Fighting gets you sent to the brig like your friend. And no one wants to be *there* long. So we buy our way out, word by word. I'm sorry, Sam. Normally I'm a hopeful boglin, but I'm flat broke. No words left."

Two goblins took seats next to them, setting down tin plates loaded with butter jerky. This time, Sam took a small piece. "Salty and takes a long time to chew," he finally said. "So. Let's solve this one thing at a time. How do we get Mason out of the brig?"

Tolver shook his head. "We could try to bribe the captain, if you have something he wants. Or you can wait until they let her out."

"I'll try anything." Sam raised his eyebrows and whispered, "Maybe we can visit Mason and use the undoing spray to free her?"

"You'd get caught. Too many people watching." But even as he said it, Tolver felt a small hope bloom in his chest. His nana had sent him a spell. Well, she'd given it to Sam, but that was almost the same. His despair vanished. Quickly, Tolver sprayed a corner of his sleeve with the glittering liquid. "Just in case."

When Sam tucked the spray bottle away, Tolver chewed more enthusiastically on his strip of butter jerky and scratched at his cheek. "Did you get Starflake back across?"

Sam nodded and sniffed at another piece of jerky before wrinkling his nose and putting it down.

"That's a relief. Listen, Sam, I know they're planning a raid. Julius can't stop talking about it. Once they've done it, they'll have to go to the Depository to weigh their words. It will be too much to process on the ship. Then we can–" Tolver stopped whispering right as the first mate appeared beside them.

"Do continue," the first mate said. "I am also very interested in hearing what you plan to do next. The captain will be too."

The Declension's first mate dragged Tolver and Sam to the captain's quarters and pushed them through the door without knocking. Unlike the rest of the ship, Captain Bellfont's berth was bright and fresh smelling. The wide glass windows behind his desk, where the captain sat glaring at Sam and Tolver, probably had something to do with the lack of stink.

But in her rush to present her prisoners, the first mate had burst through the door and caught the captain in the process of trying on business clothes that one of the merchants had traded him.

He'd taken off his sea jacket and replaced it with a leather prospector vest, but the tie—a bow decorated with stars—looked ridiculously out of place. A price tag for Macy's was still attached. Stolen.

The captain caught Tolver staring and pulled off the tie. "Watch it, kiddo. Or you'll be in the brig too."

Tolver's and Sam's seats, oak-barrel chairs old enough to have the names of another ship carved into their backs, creaked as *The Declension* wove its way through the sky. The captain's dark green leather vest made his skin look even more yellow. It was clean, though, and that was a big contrast to how dirty and wind-sprayed Tolver and Sam were. Sam was also mud-splashed, probably from his latest landing at the cottage. Tolver's clothes were creaky with salt. They both needed showers badly.

A swim in the water far below the ship was less than appealing, however, and that's what Tolver saw in their future, if they avoided the brig. *How much had the first mate heard?*

"These two were planning something," the first mate said. "Go ahead, tell them."

Think fast. What would Nana do? Tolver bet she'd just use the undoing spray, but Tolver knew the best way to get to the Depository was to try to make themselves useful to the prospectors. Julius had said that what the prospectors wanted most was more hot air. As much of it as possible. And Sam had said he'd do anything.

Tolver looked at Sam and then thought about his walks around Mount Cloud with Nana. There'd been a train station that went to the city, and they'd watched Sam's dad get on the train to go to work, carrying a tote bag. Sam was carrying that bag now. It said New City Design and Public Relations. The kind of business, Tolver thought, that probably used a lot of words.

"I've been thinking of ways to help the prospectors find more fuel, sir," Tolver began. "Better words. Lots of them. That's what we were talking about."

The first mate didn't disagree. Maybe she hadn't overheard much at all.

The captain smiled in a way that let Tolver and Sam see all his goblin teeth. It wasn't pretty. He pinched his mustache between his fingers. "Wonderful. But we already have Julius to create new inventions for getting words. We're establishing long-term supply lines. Why do we need a boglin word-gatherer and a young human?"

Tolver thought about all the bad things Nana had told him about the prospectors. "Don't you need new territories? What if we could help you find some?"

Sam looked confused.

Come on, Sam, work with me, Tolver thought. "Sam, you know places where people work with words all day, right?"

Sam frowned. "If I did, would you let us see Mason? And then take us to the Depository?"

The Declension began a slow turn in the air, and they heard the goblin crew calling out commands. Suddenly every sound the ship made, each clank and groan, seemed like a clock counting the captain's silence.

Finally, the captain sighed, frustrated. "We don't need territories. We need humans who waste words regularly, on a grand scale. *The Plumbline*—the ship I was on before I earned *The Declension*—mined several powerfully mis-used words from one of your weathermen last year. My cut was enough to buy this ship. What can you do for me that is as good?"

Tolver held his breath. *Would Sam help? Did he understand what the captain was asking?* Tolver stared hard at Sam's tote bag.

Sam's mouth made an O shape. "My dad's business works with a lot of words."

Tolver couldn't help smiling as Captain Bellfont leaned forward over the desk, his mustache dragging on its polished surface. "How wonderful. Does your father work with actors? Politicians?" The captain's teeth smelled bad, and his breath worse. Tolver held his breath.

Sam shook his head and spoke fast, like he was trying not to breathe either. "Nothing like that. He works in a PR and design firm."

The minute the words were out of Sam's mouth, the captain's eyes glowed. *Jackpot.*

Captain Bellfont jumped up from behind the desk. He came around to sit on the armrest of Sam's chair and patted Sam on the head. "Sam, you are a treasure."

Sam took a shallow breath. "But I won't tell you any more until you let Mason out of the brig."

The captain smiled even more. "Fair enough." He gestured to his first mate, who opened a side door and led Mason into the room. She smelled worse than belowdecks and looked madder than anything Tolver had ever seen—goblin or human. "But she goes right back unless you give us more. We will trade your friend's freedom for access to this resource."

"Wait a minute." Mason glared at the captain. He stared back, shocked. "You don't get to trade my freedom. I refuse to give it to you."

The goblins laughed. Tolver shivered right down to his toes, and Sam winced. Goblin laughter was unpleasant. "We're businessgoblins, young lady," the captain said. "The profitable kind. We don't negotiate. Sam, are you ready to tell us your plan and save your friend?"

"He's not my friend, he's—" The first mate shook Mason until she was quiet.

The captain stood. "That's not the matter at hand!"

But Sam turned to Mason. "I *am* your friend. But I was teasing too much. And I was mean. I won't do it again."

She nodded but still looked mad. "It wasn't *just* teasing, Sam. But…maybe I was mean too." Then she turned to Tolver. "And if you're the one who stole Sam's words, we are NOT friends."

Tolver hung his head.

Captain Bellfont smacked his hand on the desk again. "Enough. We need words we can *use*. Young man, you made a deal.

You tell us where your source is, and we'll keep your *friend* Mason safe, plus take you to the Depository." He rose and headed for the door and waved for his first mate.

Tolver shifted uncomfortably, growing increasingly worried. The captain was speaking only to Sam, not him. Tolver leaned close to the humans and whispered, "Don't say anything more, Sam! I don't trust him."

"But I promised Mason my help, and Tolver, you need it too," Sam whispered back.

"But, Sam!" Mason protested.

"I don't want you to go back to the brig," Sam told her.

"I don't want to go back either. They tried to feed me beef jerky with peanut butter!" she said, her eyebrows rising. "But still, Sam!"

"It's okay," Sam whispered. "I'm pretty sure even goblins could never get past my dad's secretary. I'll tell them where the agency is, and then we'll go to the Depository and get my words back, okay?"

Julius and the first mate entered and the captain returned to his desk, glowering. "This had better be a really good resource," he finally said. "Or else you'll be working off all of my wasted time."

Tolver watched as Sam tried not to squirm under the captain's gaze. "I'll show you where to go, you let us off at the Depository, and we'll go our separate ways. The three of us."

The three of them. Sam was bargaining for Tolver too. A human bargaining for a boglin. Nana, Tolver was sure, would be pleased. Meantime, the captain extended his hand, and Sam shook it.

"Deal," the captain said, smiling in a not-so-nice way, his eyes glittering. "Although you may yet come around to our ways. Julius here certainly has. All right, Sam, Tolver. Get ready to go on a raid."

"What? No! I'm just going to tell you where to go. That was the deal," Sam protested.

The captain grinned. "Not at all. You said *show*. Words matter. You'll stay with us until we're sure we've got the resource."

Sam sat down in the chair, hard. Beside him, Mason and Tolver slumped. A prospector raid. *This was terrible.* But then Tolver remembered that Nana had sometimes talked about how humans mis-used words so much as they got older that they threw piles of word-filled paper away. *Maybe,* Tolver thought, *he and Sam could lead the crew of* The Declension *to the trash no one wanted anyway, and Tolver wouldn't have broken the promise he'd just made to Sam.* Tolver hoped so. "We'll do it," he said.

"We will?" Sam said.

"Trust me," Tolver replied, hoping he was right.

And with that, the deal was struck. The first mate led them out on deck, where the captain placed a canvas map against the ship's big wooden wheel.

The map showed the boundaries of the marshbogs. Swirls in the water marked four big portals—one at each compass point: north, south, east, and west. Tolver had seen maps like this before, but Nana never used any of the big portals.

Between the portals, four floating cities were marked on the map and the marshbog archipelago spread below them. It was beautiful. Tolver spotted Felicity and Serendipity, the city *The Declension* had called at before it overtook the mail boat.

"Our ship has use of this portal," the captain pointed at the eastern swirl. "It reaches large mail rooms in many of your cities. We can generate our own portal if we're willing to burn enough words and go through smaller boxes, but I'd rather not. We're making so much progress—floating cities, ships, our inventions—that I need to optimize fuel as much as possible."

The captain tapped the portal, then flipped the canvas over. On the back, inverted, Tolver saw the human city Midtown, and Sam pointed a shaking finger at the street where his father's agency was.

"Well done, Sam," the captain said. "You're being very helpful. It's a good start. Inventor!" The captain roared so loud, Tolver jumped.

"Sir!" Julius sprang to the captain's side.

"Get the word hogs ready! The expedition will start immediately."

"An expedition," Tolver whispered. He did kind of want to see that. But he couldn't imagine an entire ship fitting through a mailbox, no matter how much magic the prospectors had.

The whole ship reverberated with loud metallic noises. The word hogs were coming. Tolver really wanted to see those too.

"Hop to it, Sam," the captain said. When Sam seemed confused, the captain pointed again, toward a large brass object being lifted from the hold. Julius hovered around the hatch protectively.

Mason grabbed Sam's sleeve. "You don't have to do this, Sam. Let *Tolver* do it."

"Sam doesn't have a choice in the matter," Captain Bellfont said. "If he helps willingly, I suspect we'll make less of a mess at his dad's office. Don't you think so, Julius? There's a chance no one will know we've been there at all."

Julius nodded. "We would try to be very careful."

Somehow, Tolver doubted that. The word hogs were enormous.

"You'll never be able to get in the building, though," Sam said triumphantly. "Your ship is too big."

"Oh, no. Ships rarely go over; they run out of fuel too fast, and it's impossible to make more fuel in the old world. We have alternatives." Julius rubbed his hands together. "To the hogs, please. Both of you."

The first of the word hogs came fully up on deck as he said it. It was raised by a hoist, six goblins working the ropes, backs tensing with each pull.

When the first hog rested on deck, Mason and Tolver went with Sam to look closer. Their faces were reflected in the polished surface. The word hog looked like a giant version of the piglet the captain had sold at the last port of call.

Except this one had gates in both sides that lowered and turned into ramps. And on the inside, there were wooden seats, lots of blinking lights, and control nobs and switches. The word hog's eyes were headlights. Its snout was a round grate. And it gleamed like Julius's brass medallion in the setting sun.

Chapter Fourteen

Sam

Sam didn't *want* to get in a word hog.

He was relieved they weren't taking *The Declension*. But even a few goblins appearing at his dad's office? That was going to be horrible. And one look at the word hogs made Sam realize there were going to be more than a few goblins.

By the time the second hog was on deck, prospectors had filled the seats in the first hog's belly and were starting to take their places in the other. A broad-shouldered goblin happily claimed a seat in the second ship and grinned at Tolver.

Three goblins, including the first mate, carried an ornately decorated crate with leather straps and brass corners to the captain.

They lifted the top off and took out a large spherical compass and leather-bound book.

With one hand on the map, the captain held the compass up to the sun. His assistants raised the book, which looked heavy, and all three said a word at the same time, and when they finished, it had burned clear off the page.

The compass lens was the kind that turned everything upside down, so Sam saw the goblin ship caught in it and the sun below that. Then he saw the big eastern portal open beside the ship's hull.

Sam held his breath. The portal was the size of the word hogs if they all traveled in a line. The pilot fed a paper strip through a slot on the word hog's dashboard. The machine's hatch slammed shut.

Brass propellers rose from the word hog's back. Wings extended from its sides. The creature lifted from the ship's deck and glided the distance from *The Declension* to the portal. Then it disappeared.

"Get in, Sam, Tolver." Julius gestured to two empty seats beside him. "I'm looking forward to this."

"Now?" Sam *really* didn't want to.

"NOW," Captain Bellfont roared. Goblin hands grabbed Sam's shoulders and pushed at Tolver's, and they found themselves stuffed into a word hog, buckled in next to Julius.

Then, with a lot of clatter, the word hog lifted and bounced through the sky. Mason watched from the ship's deck. Her face was one of the last things Sam saw out the slits in the machine's side as they flew off.

When that stretching feeling happened again, Sam knew he was heading home, but in completely the wrong way.

"There aren't real pookahs in here, right?" Tolver asked Julius as they traveled through the portal.

The first mate, who was sitting across from Tolver in order to keep an eye on Sam, laughed. "No. Pookahs don't like metal all that much. I hope we don't run out of fuel, though."

Julius dismissed her. "We won't." Then he preened. "I discovered, with the help of a few other boglins, that most mis-used words have a particular scent—like old roses mixed with orange juice and paint—and I was able to build very delicate detectors into the noses of the word hogs. Plus, with a particular magic spell of my own design, we were able to mimic the pookahs' shape-shifting powers. They're very efficient. That's the modern way to do it. Besides, pookahs make a mess on ships."

Tolver grumbled. "A few other boglins...like my nana—"

Julius shushed him. And then he hushed Sam for good measure.

With a pop, the word hog they rode in emerged inside a post office sorting room.

Sam could see people walking down the sidewalk, beyond the post office's glass doors. People. Not goblins. They wore summer clothes, not winter airship jackets.

He was home. Sort of.

When the post office door opened, summer heat blasted through the slats in the pig's side. The sun glared off the glass wall of his dad's building across the street.

"What floor is your dad's office?" The first mate poked Sam's ribs with a sharp finger.

Julius nudged his other side with a sharp elbow. "Tell her everything. Don't make her ask again."

"Twelfth floor."

There was a groan. "That's a long elevator ride. This had better be worth it."

"If my experiment works," Julius said with a tremor in his voice, "it will most certainly be worth it."

The goblins hung on Julius's pronouncements, but Tolver rolled his eyes. "Tolver," Julius announced, "I cannot trust you with important duties yet; that much is obvious. You will stay and watch the pigs."

Tolver fumed. "But…"

"No buts! Do as you're told." Julius's eyes flashed, and the first mate glared at Tolver until he bowed his head in agreement. Sam groaned. He was going to be alone up there.

Julius nearly sang with excitement. "I'm the first goblin who's thought of trying this. But that's why you all have me here. We're going to set up a few experimental tap lines. They're made of a special material that will let us siphon words from specific moments and projects, instead of removing them entirely. With a few adjustments and these new lines, we can create a constant drip of spoken, misused words, with infinite possibilities. You'll see." He absently rubbed his medallion, leaving streaky prints. Sam realized the inventor was nervous too.

Sam felt hope tickle the back of his brain. If the raid was too difficult, maybe they'd call it off.

The goblins pulled on heavy canvas coats, goggles, and packs carrying various tools. They pulled scarves up over their faces too, and practiced going invisible all together.

"One, two, three, think of the most embarrassing thing you've ever done," said the first mate. Every goblin disappeared.

Tolver did as well, then reappeared, scratching his scalp. "Why does that always itch?"

Sam tried to do it too, thinking of what he'd said to Mason on the last day of school, but he blushed bright red instead.

Maybe the office would be locked up. It was Sunday, after all. Maybe the goblin captain would let him and Mason go to the Depository, just for trying.

Somehow, Sam didn't think that was going to happen.

The other hogs arrived, and the mail bin they'd been balanced on tipped over, sending loose mail across the mailroom floor. Goblins spilled out of the hogs and scattered, while Tolver was stuck gathering up the letters and putting them back in the crate.

"This is prime ground for wasted words. Get them for the

captain!" The first mate pointed at the bank of lights on the word hog's inner wall. "The hog's reading very high for mis-used words across the street. The boy will show us where."

"Leave no trace when possible," Julius whispered. "Especially if we want to return. If they thought the mail was broken, they'd fix it."

They would, just like the tree had gotten fixed, and how Sam wanted to fix the Little Free Library. But given how technological the prospectors had gotten with Julius's help, Sam wasn't sure a quick fix would work anymore.

He helped Tolver pick up the scattered letters, and, after each of the goblins and their word hog disappeared, he opened the door to the post office. Tolver stopped him. "Just be careful, okay? Don't trust them."

Sam smiled grimly. "Got it!" Then he crossed the street with the goblins following and waited for the elevator in the lobby of his dad's building. To the entrance guard, he looked like one boy heading up to meet his parent. Not a goblin raiding party. The guard even recognized Sam and waved.

They all got in the elevator, which was a tight squeeze. The mirrored walls reflected only Sam, looking like he was holding his breath and trying to take up as little room as possible. Then the doors opened on the twelfth floor and everyone spilled out and Sam could breathe again.

Standing in the white-and-tan hallway of his dad's agency, Sam hoped to find the doors locked and everyone gone home. But the lights were on, the doors open. An intern—not the stern secretary—sat at the reception desk. "Hey, Sam!" She buzzed him in with a friendly wave.

"Hi!" Sam smiled weakly. "I forgot something in my dad's office the last time I was here. Need it for . . . homework," he said.

"Homework in summer! That's hard! Good luck finding it!" The intern logged him in as a visitor. "I'll print you out a badge. Just a minute. We're putting the finishing touches on your neighborhood's presentation—that's why it's so busy here. Your dad's so proud of this one."

She handed him a flyer that said, "Meet Mount Cloud's New Look! Field and Neighborhood Improvement Proposal Discussion with James Culver," with a photo of his dad, then went to find him a badge.

Sam heard the invisible goblins rustling and shushing each other right behind him.

Invisibility was a neat trick. One Sam wished very much that he had right then.

The gleaming metal reception desk showed Sam that he was turning a sickly green and shifting from foot to foot like he had to use the bathroom. Actually, he did have to use the bathroom. He put the flyer back on the desk.

By the time the intern returned, it was really urgent. But Sam wasn't going to the bathroom with a whole goblin raiding party tagging along.

Where could he send them while he went to the bathroom?

Down the hall, he heard loud voices. Behind the glass panels of a meeting room, two young writers worked, tablets out, paper and pencils strewn across the table. Sam put his ear to the door, which was unlocked and slightly ajar.

"We can use the word URGENT! People pay attention to that word."

"Or we could use EMERGENCY! People will click on that."

There was a snort and a snuffle. A prospector appeared enough for Sam to see the mechanical piglet he carried. Its eyes were glowing in definite interest. Then the prospector pushed the door open, and he could feel the draft as the goblins entered the meeting room. The writers didn't notice a thing.

Anita didn't like when businesses overused words like *urgent* and *emergency*. Maybe if that's all the goblins took, and it stopped there, everything would be all right.

And Sam really had to go.

"Don't break anything," he whispered. Then he ran to the bathroom.

When he got back, the meeting room was empty, and the raiding party either was being incredibly quiet—which was nearly impossible for goblins—or had moved on.

Oh no. Sam searched the entire hallway and every garbage can. The cans were very, very empty—suspiciously so. Most of the doors were locked, the lights off.

But then a door opened and—*nothing* spilled out, whispering loudly.

"Sam!" Julius appeared, waving his hands. "Come on! We've set tap lines—I sent the output ends back to the other side through the mail room! This place is great! The captain will be so pleased. The humans will barely notice because the lines look like spiderwebs—and we'll get years of words instead of having to store one entire utterance in the Depository. At least, that's the theory! So far, so good!" Julius gave Sam a big green thumbs-up.

Sam wilted with guilt as the goblins pulled him back into the elevator. He pushed the button to go back down. After the doors closed, several of the goblins reappeared, including the first mate. They carried satchels filled to bursting over their shoulders. Ribbons of glittering words spilled out. Paper ones too.

They'd done more than just set up tap lines and take a few words from the trash. "What did you take?"

"What *didn't* we take!" A big goblin laughed. Then they all disappeared again.

Sam winced. He led the now-invisible prospectors back outside and across the street to the post office. Then he opened the door and waited until everyone sounded like they were inside. When they were, Sam took a last look out at the city sidewalk and at the metro stop not that far down the street.

He could run down those stairs and go home. To his parents and sister. He could drink lemonade and catch fireflies with Bella instead of going back to *The Declension*.

In the pale reflection of the post office door, he stared himself down. Mason and Tolver were still in trouble on *The Declension* and in the post office. His words were still in the Depository.

He had to go back.

Sam squeezed into the mail crate with the rest of the raiding party, and, with Tolver, climbed into the word hog. "Thanks for coming back," Tolver whispered.

"Quiet!" The first mate pushed several buttons in the word hog's interior and recited the words of the spell again, feeding the paper into the hog's dashboard. The world stretched and skewed, and then there was a pop, and they were gliding through the sky, over the marshbog, and back to *The Declension*.

Sam put his head on his knees, queasy.

"It's a bit of a bumpy ride." The first mate patted him on his back after they climbed from the word hog back onto the deck of *The Declension*. "But you did very well."

I did not, Sam thought.

"Here's to you, Sam!" Julius added.

Sam sat on the ship's deck, head in his hands. He'd just helped prospectors do a terrible thing. "Bumpy ride" didn't contain nearly enough words to describe how he felt.

All around him, goblins high-fived and hip-bumped each other. The captain placed another brass medallion around Julius's neck. Tolver slipped away as the captain hung a medallion around Sam's neck too. The metal disk was so heavy.

When Sam finally caught up with Tolver, a broad goblin grabbed them both and pointed to a meter on the bag he carried. "Full to capacity in a single run! You're a genius, especially about the trash! I'm going to earn my way out of conscription with this." The joy on his face was immeasurable. "I'm going back home."

Beside Sam, Tolver watched the meter hungrily. But then he looked at Sam and blushed chartreuse. "I'm sorry."

But the prospector laughed as if Sam was their newfound piggy bank.

Sam was pretty sure he wasn't headed back home now. He swallowed hard. *What would happen to the agency? To his dad's presentation?* He needed to warn his dad, somehow. "What exactly did you take? I thought you were only doing an experiment."

"Isn't it wonderful? There were so many wasted words—in the trash, the email, a fancy presentation they were preparing. Thanks for getting us in there!" Julius couldn't stop pounding Sam on the back.

Sam narrowed his eyes, even as the first mate brought Mason up on deck. "Then you don't need the tap lines?"

"On the contrary, the tap lines are even more valuable now!"

Julius said. He waved his arms at the hogs and at Sam. "Don't worry, we'll be careful. We won't ruin a good source."

As the prospectors celebrated, Sam took off the brass medallion and tossed it over the side of the ship. But it didn't help. Every goblin who passed them and thanked Sam profusely made him feel more terrible.

There was a sudden stir as the captain brought Mason, Tolver, and Sam a platter of butter jerky. The big goblin smiled and said, "Anything you want, Sam. Anything at all."

"What have you done, Sam?" Mason said.

Sam didn't want to find out.

As the big airship circled over the archipelago, Mason, Tolver, and Sam walked the deck past gleaming word-hog hulls. They'd been back on the ship for a whole afternoon and they still hadn't turned toward Felicity. The floating city hovered out of reach on the horizon.

"You made a deal," Sam told the captain. "It's time to go to the Depository."

The big goblin chuckled. "We're headed there now, son. Didn't want anyone there to think this raid was easy." He hefted one of the bags of words as he said it.

Sam could see the first mate tallying more numbers from the meters and murmuring to herself. Captain Bellfont put on magnifying glasses to look more closely at the readouts the first mate carried over. His silver mustaches were starting to droop; he'd been focusing so hard. "So many different words. Such a joy. Some words are better for balloons and airships, you know. Other kinds work for pumps and pneumatics because they're already loud. Some are a bit odiferous, if I'm honest about it, but the ones from this territory? They are the best kind—universal-donor hot air, inoffensive to the nose or the ear."

"This is stealing!" Mason protested.

The captain of *The Declension* removed his glasses and grinned at Mason. It turned out, when they wanted to, goblins really could get quite big and scary. "This is business."

Mason said nothing. Her eyes spoke for her. Sam could see that she didn't like the prospectors at all.

Soon, the first mate shouted for everyone to go to their stations. Captain Bellfont summoned Sam to his quarters to watch the docking. Sam grabbed Mason and pulled her silently along. They had their first look at the Depository through the captain's windows as *The Declension* neared the port on the edge of the floating city. Two prospector ships were tied up to gangways. "That's my previous ship," Captain Bellfont said. "*The Plumbline*. Captain Geary's vessel."

On the city's far side, several more gangways extended. One was theirs, the captain explained.

"Closest dock to the Depository. In honor of our profitable raid."

Even in full sun, Felicity glowed softly. But to Sam, the city looked crowded up close.

"Do they ever go down into the islands?" Mason asked. "The marshbogs are so pretty."

"Rarely. We've grown beyond boglin cottages." The captain said, proudly. "Here, we·have everything we need airship-delivered: fish from the marsh, vegetables. We trade for fuel. Goblins who live in the cities know things are easier here and certainly drier. Away from the water, equipment doesn't rust or spoil. And that's important for progress."

Mason found a piece of paper in her pocket and drew

equations on it for a moment. She narrowed her eyes at the numbers, then at Captain Bellfont. "But you have a problem, don't you? The more fuel you use to stay up here, the more you need," she finally said. "So you need bigger ships and more storage."

The captain frowned. "Do you always ask so many questions?"

Sam hid a smile. She did. And it was wonderful.

Bellfont rose. "I'll show you what we're doing about that. The Depository is how goblins have always saved for lean times, when finding words is hard. And we are renovating it to keep the value of the words we mine at a strong, consistent peak. So we all benefit."

The Declension shuddered as it moored. Prospectors shouted to one another as those goblins who had earned leave pounded down the gangway. The rest of the crew carried Julius's spiderweb tap lines over their shoulders.

"What are they doing with those?" Mason asked.

"Not sure I want to know," Sam said.

But the captain chuckled. "We connect them in the Depository and run the dripped words through a converter. They're not nearly as powerful as truly mis-used words, but they don't run out, not for a long time."

But Mason glared from behind Sam's back. "If the prospectors start to hook up tap lines, will you need ships and crews then? Or pigs or word hogs?"

"Oh! We'll always need new crews. New lines to set, old ones to untangle. And when a supply point is running low, we'll need to be sure we take that last word, Mason. Never fear. This is the way of progress. The marshbogs will be converted to help outfit more prospector ships! It's all going to be very efficient." The captain ushered them out to *The Declension*'s gangplank. He pointed at the arc of the Depository in the distance. "There, my promise to you, about to be fulfilled."

"Where's Tolver?" Sam asked.

"In the brig, so that the rest of my goblins don't have to keep an eye on him."

Sam tried to argue, but the captain swept from the room, dragging him and Mason along.

When they disembarked and the Depository came fully into view, even Mason was stunned. It was Sam who spotted the construction equipment, including a few word hogs pulling heavy materials, all around the base of the structure. "Your modernizations?" He pointed.

"Yes! For those who can afford to pay," the captain said. The glee in his voice made Sam's skin crawl. The prospectors were terrible for the marshbogs, and for his world too.

He and Mason had to try to slow them down somehow.

Wait a minute. Nana's undoing spray was still in his bag. *It only works on objects with lots of parts,* she'd said. Would it work in the Depository? Sam's fingers twitched, waiting for the right moment. Nana had hated the prospectors' hold on the Depository. Sam owed it to her, and to both worlds, to try.

One of the Depository's glass doors slid open, and the goblins entered at a high-numbered level. "Now that the prospectors are reworking the Depository," Captain Bellfont continued, "we have progress! We're cataloging all of the boxes and assigning each a number as we modernize." The captain spoke about improvements as they ascended a network of stairs and ladders that seemed to go up and through and across the whole structure.

"Mmmm. Section 100, box 17A. Boglins, Nana and Tolver," the captain finally murmured. He showed Mason and Sam a stack of post office boxes surrounded by a wide balcony. "Just there, to the middle." He looked over the railing of the staircase and waved at the first mate, walking above. "I'll leave you here while I attend to ship business. You won't cause trouble. Not with your friend Tolver still on the ship. And there's only one way out."

Sam and Mason nodded that they understood. They were trapped here too. But when the captain had climbed the stairs several levels, Mason grinned and winked at Sam. He could tell she was still mad, but the plan was finally working. At least a little bit. They'd successfully infiltrated the Depository.

Except that Tolver was onboard *The Declension*, not here. That part was a problem.

But maybe, Sam thought, *Mason's my friend again.*

17A, Boglins, was an old-looking box, tiny in comparison to others. It had an antique-looking lock on it, stamped with USPS, 1901. Sam sprayed the Boglins' lock with the undoing spray. And waited.

Nothing happened.

So he sprayed a few more boxes too. A lot more.

On a staircase several levels above them, he and Mason could see the captain talking with his first mate. Then they disappeared into one of the larger glass rooms, with Julius following behind them carrying the tap lines.

Just then, and with a loud clanking noise, Tolver and Nana's depository box unlocked and swung open. A tangle of word ribbons nestled inside. Some whispered faintly. Others had fallen silent. Not knowing which was his, Sam grabbed them all and stuffed them in his bag. They made quiet rustling sounds, and the bag felt heavier.

The captain had been right. And Nana had kept her word.

Now Sam was going to keep his. He checked the box to make sure it was empty and shut the door. But the Boglins' box wouldn't stay shut. He tried to lock it, but it wouldn't lock, either.

Sam's thoughts were interrupted by more creaking and clanging from Section 100. At first just a few doors nearby rattled against their locks, but soon the noise spread, echoing metallically, until the Depository shuddered with the sound of a herd of squeaky doors, all opening.

"Sam, what did you DO!" Mason said. She didn't say *we*, but that was okay.

"It's not me! It's the undoing spray!" Sam said. Nana's spell was so powerful, it was spreading.

Chapter Fifteen

Sam

While Sam and Mason ran from Depository Section 100, the undo-ing spray spread, unlocking doors above and below them. Glittering word ribbons spilled everywhere.

Mason began gathering up as many words as she could, stuffing them into her pockets. "Maybe we can find who lost these and give them back."

Goblins began to shout, above and below. Some howled with glee as they scooped up words. Others, including the prospectors who were working on the new boxes, growled, outraged. A group of goblins led by a thin figure in a captain's coat began to descend the stairs toward Section 100.

"Mason, we have to go!" Sam tugged at her sleeve.

They scrambled up a ladder to Section 225, where the storage boxes looked like bamboo-and-willow containers, then through Section 314, which was filled with school lockers.

Finally they reached Section 500, part of the newly refurbished glass boxes. Inside, Captain Bellfont sat in front of a series of old computer towers, carefully inserting tap lines into a slot. Beside him sat the inventor and the first mate.

Each time the end of a tap line disappeared inside the slot, the computer tower glowed, and a number would appear on the glass. The captain chuckled as that number grew bigger and brighter. Beside him, Julius had attached tap lines to another hard-drive pile. The display above that group of storage boxes was spinning wildly. "It's working, it's working," Julius cackled.

The goblins were so caught up in the lights and numbers, they'd missed the tumult occurring below them.

Sam still gripped the bottle of undoing spray. *Only a little bit left.* He lifted the sprayer and took aim.

"No you don't!" The first mate stood. She grabbed a piece of Nana's spellbound bat from the inventor's coat pocket. Then she pointed it right at Sam and Mason.

As Julius reached out and said, "Wait!" the first mate spoke the curse that Nana had gathered on the baseball field.

Mason and Sam were blown back out of Section 500 by the force of the word. The bat splinter shot from the goblin's hand and smashed into one of the computer towers, which began to smoke. Words from Sam's father's office poured from the box, a river of them, running all the way to the ground, near the exit of the building.

"What have you done!" The captain shouted. They could hear him a long way down, which is where they'd landed, mostly unhurt, on top of a pile of word ribbons in many different languages.

"We have to get out of here," Mason said. She and Sam began climbing back up the staircases, and as they ran, they grabbed more words, especially from the growing pile near the door. Sam heard several from his father's office whispering "URGENT," and stuffed those in his bag and pockets too.

All the doors of the Depository were unlocking from the spread of the spray. The seams and hinges of some of the older boxes began to collapse.

"Nana made the spray really strong," Sam shouted. The noise of the falling words was loud enough to make his ears ring. He scrambled to his feet and pulled Mason up with him. Then they sprinted out of the Depository.

The thin captain that they'd seen earlier shouted from a balcony far below, "Bellfont, I see your humans!" Her voice rang clearly over the fading noise of opening doors and collapsing metal. All around, the Depository's spilled words whispered, feet clattered on stairs, and Sam's heart pounded in his ears.

As they ran from the Depository, Sam sprayed the rest of the undoing spell on the doors until they collapsed in a heap behind him and Mason. It wasn't much, but it would delay the pursuing goblins. Maybe long enough for them to figure out how to get away.

They ran out into the floating city of Felicity as the sun was rising.

"There!" Mason pointed at *The Declension*. The ship had cast off most of its lines, though Sam couldn't see the crew onboard.

He looked back and realized why. More than a dozen goblins were trying to clear the collapsed doorway all at once. "Mason, run faster! They're right behind us!"

When the goblins finally broke through, spilling onto the street, the two crews chased Sam and Mason all the way from the Depository to the gangway where *The Declension* had been docked.

Mason and Sam ran until their chests were on fire. "Who untied the ship?" Mason asked.

The Declension listed a little as its hull banged against the dock. It looked to Sam like no one was steering it.

But they could hear Captain Bellfont bellowing their names from down at the docks, so they couldn't stop. Soon, Bellfont began shouting at his crew too, because *The Declension* had clearly cast off and was pulling away. Mason ran up the gangway first, and then took a great leap. She yelled as she jumped, landing on the middle deck with an *oof*.

Tolver's spiky hair appeared, just barely above the helm of *The Declension*. "Get on!" he yelled. "Sam, hurry!" He gripped the wheel of *The Declension*, knuckles pale green, as the ship slowly turned, its stern just passing the gangway. A piece of his sleeve had been torn away.

The undoing spray—Tolver had used the tiny bit from his sleeve to unlock the brig. Sam laughed, even as he pushed himself to run faster. His feet pounded hard on the gangway, and as *The Declension* pulled away, he prepared to jump.

Five knobby, green goblin fingers grabbed his left arm and jerked him backward, so that he fell hard on the ramp. Words he'd gathered spilled from his pockets. Some ribbons glittered as they slipped through the dock and twisted in the air, headed straight for the water.

"Ungrateful goblin thief!" Captain Bellfont shouted at Tolver. The prospector captain lifted Sam high in the air.

"The best kind," Tolver yelled back. "We'll come back around for you, Sam!"

But the wind caught *The Declension*'s airbag and pushed the ship away from the city. Tolver's grin changed to alarm as he realized he couldn't turn fast enough. Sam was stranded with Captain Bellfont and his crew.

"NO!" Mason shouted. She leaned over the side of the ship, hands out, reaching for Sam. "Hurry! Do something!" Then she shouted at Tolver, "Go back!"

"I can't! I don't know how! I'm sorry!" Tolver sounded panicked. He tried to turn the wheel, but it was too big for him.

The Declension pulled away from the floating city's edge and headed out toward the archipelago.

As Sam watched the ship disappear, Captain Bellfont sat him up roughly on the gangway but didn't loosen his grip. "You lost me my words, my ship! You terrible human!"

He stood over Sam, blocking out the sun. His silver mustache was speckled with spit. "You'll spend the rest of your years earning back every bit of fuel and the cost of my ship."

"You were never going to let me go home," Sam said quietly.

"Well, I'm certainly not now!" The captain watched his ship grow smaller as it sailed away. "You're worth more to me here. Who knows where else you can help us get in." His eyes glowed red. An angry goblin was never pretty, Sam realized, and this one was furious. His eyebrows soared to his hairline, and he showed his pointed teeth. "We'll be enjoying your company for a long time, Sam."

Behind him, the other captain Sam had spotted in the Depository called out, "We'll chase them with my ship, Bellfont!"

Without letting Sam go, Captain Bellfont turned to her. "Perfect." Then he lifted Sam in the air and threw him over one shoulder. Sam stuffed his hands in his pockets to keep the words from falling out.

Meantime, both crews began to move very fast toward the other ship in port. The captain spoke as he ran, jostling Sam hard. "I used to serve on *The Plumbline*. You won't enjoy Captain Geary's brig, though that's where you're going." Sam gulped, but he couldn't get free of Bellfont's grip.

The goblin hauled Sam aboard as Captain Geary bellowed orders. Then the ship cast off its lines and turned to pursue *The Declension*, which was already far from the city.

"Use all the resources you need," she told her crew. "Just catch that ship."

Sam watched from Bellfont's shoulder as both crews filled the baffles with hot air. The ship's first mate began to chant speed words, and the boat roared through the sky.

The Declension wobbled in its route. They were slowly closing on Tolver and Mason.

"Ready the weapons!" Captain Geary shouted. "Bring the

hogs on deck!" Her goblin crew scrambled to obey, and Bellfont's crew tried to help. As *The Plumbline* hurtled toward the horizon, *The Declension* slowed once again. Tolver's lack of experience piloting a ship was showing.

But then Tolver carefully lowered a thick line toward the marshbogs. Far below, the commander of a small boat rowed closer and seized it. *Nana.*

. *The Plumbline* tacked and picked up speed, bearing down on the other vessel. Julius yelled, "Capture," and a net flew.

Ahead, *The Declension* hauled Nana—with a small pookah under one arm—up the rope, and the ship's motor thrummed. *The Declension* zoomed forward again, and the magical net from *The Plumbline* fell, empty, to the water.

"They can't get very far," Captain Geary said. "Your airbags weren't but three-quarters filled, and they've been burning fuel like mad."

Sam struggled against Captain Bellfont's grip. "I hope you never catch them," he said.

"Your words are not *currently* needed, child." Bellfont turned to his host. "May I use your brig?"

The *Plumbline*'s captain shook her head. "Sadly, our brig is full, but I have another option." She opened the hatch of one of her word hogs, which Julius was inspecting for scratches.

"Put him in here, out of the way. I need all hands, including yours, Bellfont."

Captain Geary stuffed Sam inside the brass pig while Bellfont grumbled and glared at him. Despite his delight at seeing the captain upset at being demoted to Geary's second in command, Sam still banged on the insides of the machine until his hands went numb.

The pig swayed as they left the city behind and pursued *The Declension* in the open air.

Inside the word hog, *The Plumbline*'s rocking motion was sickening. The smell of hard use by goblins was even worse.

Sam pressed himself close to the slats of the nearest air vent, hoping for fresh air.

From his vantage point, the horizon lurched and rolled, and the crew ran past on the deck.

As he peered through the side of the brass word hog, *The*

Declension passed beyond the farthest island, and a bright spark gleamed for a moment before a large portal opened.

"That's a rogue portal!" Captain Geary said. "They're going through!"

"They have help!" Captain Bellfont said angrily. He stood so close to the word hog, Sam could smell his breath.

Then he tapped the metal side of the pig with a long fingernail. "Your friends have made a terrible mistake, Sam. They're running, in the ship, straight through to the old world. And we're going to catch them. You'll be reunited with them soon, never fear."

"Make sure that portal stays open," Captain Geary instructed her spellcaster. "We're going in after them."

"The whole ship?" Julius said. "Both crews? Think about the cost in fuel—"

Sam heard the swish of the long skirts Captain Geary wore beneath her canvas jacket. Through the side of his prison, he caught a glimpse of her silver hair tangled around green-and-silver goggles. She reached out and patted Julius's cheek. "We are taking the whole ship."

Her crew fired up the baffles, and the ship leapt forward, even as the portal began closing behind *The Declension*.

Beyond the portal, Sam glimpsed the roof of Ursula K. Le Guin Elementary and the trees surrounding Mount Cloud's park. He heard cheering from a ball game. Smoke rose from a barbecue grill. Then *The Plumbline* entered the portal.

~⌐

Sam would never get used to passing through a goblin portal. But the feeling of going through one onboard a ship, in the belly of a brass word hog, was even worse.

The Plumbline creaked and shook all around him. The word hog shrieked metallically and tried to lift from the deck. He clapped his hands over his ears. And then the terrible stretching and compressing feeling began.

The dizziness hit him first, and his stomach flipped over. This kind of portal crossing wasn't meant to happen. Looking out the air vent, Sam saw the goblins were similarly affected and turning the color of paste that's been left sitting out with the lid off.

"Stop slacking, prospectors! This is for progress!" The captain of *The Plumbline* urged them on. "We'll capture those two mutineers and show them what happens to goblins who run off with ships."

The doubled goblin crew rallied and shouted agreement.

"And while we're there, we'll take all the mis-used words we want!" the captain added. "Plenty for everyone!"

Through the cheers, Sam saw one particularly thrilled face: Julius's. The inventor began to unroll a spool of tap lines.

No. They couldn't. Not in Mount Cloud. My sister's only just gotten her word back. And Ms. Malloy... Sam banged on the hatch of the pig again. He had to stop them.

When the ship emerged on the other side of the portal, *The Declension* was nowhere to be seen. Meantime, *The Plumbline*'s air pumps faltered and weakened. The gas bag slumped over the ship. They'd used up most of their fuel in the pursuit.

The vessel wobbled in the air until the captain ordered the first mate to render it invisible, and all the goblins quickly disappeared. Everything around Sam went transparent too, although he was still stuck inside the pig. He could see quite clearly now.

The ship teetered in the air, sinking rapidly toward the park.

Tree branches brushed the hull and then cracked and bent as *The Plumbline* came to rest atop a big tree. From here, Sam could see all over Mount Cloud, at least until the airbag, low on fuel, collapsed over the deck. Even then, he could make out blurry forms through the layers of transparent brass and canvas. The airbag sank onto a thick bough of leaves, and a nesting sparrow erupted in anger.

The bird screeched at the invisible ship as the branches bent in new ways, making the deck creak ominously.

"Bring the rest of the word hogs on deck. Julius, bring your tap lines," the captain addressed the assembled goblins. Through the slats in the pig's sides, Sam could hear the crew's canvas overalls rasping and their boots squeaking and clomping. Then the captain cleared her throat so that everyone could hear her. "Below is an entire neighborhood of word wasters, plus two escaped goblins and a stolen ship. The goblins must be captured and brought back home to face consequences. The ship will be rescued. The humans? You keep what you steal once we have enough fuel to get home again. Stay out of sight and report back by nightfall."

The Plumbline and *Declension* crews cheered once more. They made ready to scour Mount Cloud on their captain's orders.

Sam knew he had to get out of there and warn Bella and Ms. Malloy.

The crew lifted the canvas gas bag from the deck carefully. Then they fired up four of the hogs and took off in them. Sam heard the propellers spinning fainter and fainter. Before long, there would be goblins all over Mount Cloud.

Sam ran to what he thought was the front of the word hog. When he crashed into the controls, he started pushing buttons. "Come on, work." Eventually, he remembered what the first mate had done the last time they'd flown. He took a slip of paper from his pocket and wrote "Little Free Library."

When he fed that through the dashboard, the pig's propellers clattered into motion, and the brass word hog lifted from *The Plumbline*'s deck. Then it wobbled precariously in the air.

I'm flying it! Sam could hear the captain yelling as he carefully steered away, until he could see the crosswalk and then his street. But then there was a clank and a bang. The pig began spinning out of control, and no matter what Sam pushed, he couldn't get it back on track.

Dizzyingly, he pitched toward the street and landed with a crash in Mrs. Lockheart's hedge. The hatch of the word hog popped open, and Sam climbed out.

Behind him, what was left of the Little Free Library, the hedge, and Mrs. Lockheart's tulips were all crushed beneath a massive, invisible pig. Everything was flattened, but what was doing the flattening couldn't be seen.

Before Mrs. Lockheart could come outside to yell at him, Sam ran across the street and right up to his front door as if goblins were still chasing him. The door was locked. He sped around the side of the house and squeezed through the dog door. And he was home.

Relief gave way quickly when he realized how empty the house sounded.

"Dad? Bella?"

Silence. On the fridge, where his stepmom always left information and instructions, there was Sam's note from earlier that morning. Just below it, under a strawberry magnet sticker, his stepmom's handwriting: *Gone to the Blue Lake/Mount Cloud baseball game and then the community picnic! See you there!*

Oh no. That's why the street was empty. Everyone was at the game. Sam felt like it had been forever since he'd seen his family. He ran upstairs to his room. Starflake's pig tracks still marked the carpet.

After trying to scrub the mud off his face in the bathroom, he grabbed a clean T-shirt and shorts and a new pair of shoes. At least these didn't smell like goblins and saltwater.

Sam reached inside his pockets and searched his bag. He still had handfuls of words, including two whispering, familiar-sounding things: "regret" and "sorry." His words. Sam put the one that said "regret" in his mouth and chewed fast. It tasted like damp chewing gum. Not sweet at all.

He tied the other word around his wrist. Tolver had said words could be taken more than once. He was going to be careful. But he had to move fast. Sam took off running for the baseball field.

He didn't know how he'd find *The Declension* or his friends. He didn't know how he'd locate the rest of the prospectors. But he did know one awful thing: his second and third plans had back-fired terribly.

Instead of defeating the prospectors, he'd accidentally set them loose in Mount Cloud. And he had to warn Bella.

Part Three

Chapter Sixteen

Tolver

Tolver woke, groggy, still holding on to the wheel of *The Declension*. The ship wasn't moving. Everything looked so green. What had happened?

He shook himself and his eyes cleared. But everything still looked green.

He remembered now. They'd fled Felicity, and at first, he hadn't been sure if he was steering *The Declension* or if the ship was steering him.

The ship had rolled in the air, and each new gust of wind pushed it farther from where Tolver wanted to go, which was back to Felicity to get Sam.

He'd heard Captain Bellfont shouting at the boy, but Tolver

could barely steer, much less manage all the air funnels and gadgets. Ropes swung loose from the bow of the boat and trailed in the ship's wake.

And Mason, who'd leapt aboard at the last minute, had pulled herself upright. "You have to go back! They grabbed Sam!"

"I'm trying!" Tolver shouted. "This is too much for one goblin!" He pointed Mason to where the ship's wings were tightly tucked against the bow. "Try to unfurl those. We'll have more control and can come about!"

Mason tugged against the pulleys, but they wouldn't budge. Then she looked back over Tolver's shoulder. "They're coming!"

Tolver checked. *The Plumbline* had also cast off from the city. Its baffles pumped and the ship wove across the sky, coming for *The Declension. What could he do?* Tolver had watched ships sail the clouds so often, he felt like he should know. But with the wheel in his hands, he knew watching was different than doing. He still had to try.

"Open that, fast!" Tolver pointed at the ship's fuel dispenser. Mason scrambled for it, and she yanked on its catches. The baffles and fans began to groan loudly.

As the boat picked up speed, Tolver found it grew easier to

steer. He loosened his grip on the wheel, just enough to shake some feeling back into his fingers.

"Look! Down on the marsh!" Mason leaned out over the bow and pointed at the water. She came astern to hold the wheel while Tolver looked.

Among the small islands of the marshbogs, a mail boat headed their way. "Nana!" he said. "Turn the ship! Turn the wheel!"

Mason did as he asked, and Tolver lowered a basket to Nana, who caught it. Then Tolver hauled on the rope until he got Nana and a smallish black pookah to the side of the ship and then aboard.

He was drenched from the effort, but when he saw Nana's face, he yelled with relief. She dropped the pookah on deck and wrapped her arms around him. "Oh, I'm so glad to see you again!"

But the relief was short-lived.

"Tolver!" Mason shouted and pointed astern. Tolver could see the bowsprit of *The Plumbline* aimed at them like a wasp's stinger. "They're still chasing us!"

Nana took charge of the bow wings and the baffles. "I remember a thing or two about sailing." She grinned. "And I'm not about to let the prospectors get the best of us."

With three sets of hands onboard, the ship steadied. They carried less weight than the other ship, and as they crossed the marshbogs, *The Declension* slowly expanded its lead.

The black pookah slowly grew until a full-size Gilfillan roamed the deck of the ship. "We need to get you home," Nana said to Mason. "The closest portal is just a few leagues away. We'll get close and send you through with Gilfillan. We don't want to take a whole ship through. That would cause too much disruption."

Mason bit her lip. Then she shook her head. "I don't want to go without Sam."

Tolver checked the wind and looked back at the other ship. "They're getting their word hogs ready to launch—we won't be able to get close enough to rescue him. We have to send you home first."

Nana put her arm around Mason's shoulders. "It's the wisest course," she said. "We'll help get Sam back too. I promise."

As they approached the whirling sea below the portal, Nana began to ready Gilfillan, and Tolver tried to tell Mason what to expect. "It's going to feel pretty weird," he started to explain, before he heard *The Plumbline*'s cannons.

A net of spells sailed toward them and fell just short of the boat. *The Plumbline* had put on a sudden burst of speed. In moments, it was close enough to fire more spells.

Nana turned the ship's fuel lines all the way up.

"We all have to go," Tolver said. "We have to take *The Declension* through the portal or they'll catch us all."

"Tolver, taking a ship like this through is dangerous," Nana cautioned.

"But those prospectors are more dangerous!" He pointed back at *The Plumbline*. He wrapped his fingers around the wheel and began to turn the ship toward the portal. "I choose the lesser danger."

The wheel and then the ship groaned.

Mason ran to Tolver's side and helped the boglin steer. *The Declension* shuddered loudly as it closed in on the portal. Amid the whirl of wind and sea, Tolver listened as Nana pulled a word from her bag and held it, along with the magnifying lens, up to the sun. "Revolve!" she shouted.

The portal opened, and Tolver saw the rooftops of Mount Cloud on the other side of the turbulent vortex. The ship shook, and Gilfillan grunted. Then everything began to shrink and shiver. Tolver watched as Mason turned as green as the rest of them.

As they began to pass through, *The Plumbline* drew close astern again. The two goblin captains shouted furiously at their crews. They fired another spell but missed. Then the portal took hold of *The Declension*, just as Nana turned them all invisible.

Tolver felt the ship all around them, but he couldn't see anything. With the turbulence in the portal, he felt dizzier than he ever had. His skin itched. Beside him, he heard Mason groan. "This is awful."

"We're going to make it, though," Nana shouted as the ship shot out the other side of the portal and right into Mount Cloud on a bright, green day.

And then *The Declension* came to a sudden, lurching, crunching stop. The last thing Tolver heard was a bird screeching, outraged.

Now he realized that the day was green because they were completely surrounded by leaves. The ship's airbag was tangled high above them, slowly and loudly leaking hot air.

They'd landed in a tree. A big one.

Nana picked twigs out of her hair. Mason pulled a glowing machine from her pocket. All around them, the light was growing dimmer. As Tolver watched, worried, the airbag deflated and draped itself over the ship, trapping everyone inside.

⟿

"I'm glad to be home, but can't be stuck here—" Mason pulled herself upright and pressed blearily on the airbag. "We're so close to the field. I'm going to miss the first game!" The girl shook her head, then turned to the boglins. "But... We made it though! Thank you for that!" The green-shrouded deck of the boat glowed as Mason began pushing buttons on her machine. "Only a little battery left. Enough to text my parents. I can let them know I'm okay."

Tolver winced at Mason's idea of "okay." "We can't be trapped here. Didn't you see? *The Plumbline* came through just after we did—its hull went right over the tree line. Wherever they land is going to be filled with prospectors. We have to get out of here and send those prospectors back where they came from."

Together, the three of them pulled and pushed at the hissing airbag.

Gilfillan even tried to chew at the fabric, but the canvas envelope held fast.

"You don't happen to have any more silverfish, do you, Nan?" Tolver said.

"Not that we can use without also setting them lose on ourselves! We're stuck here." She looked at her grandson sternly. "Magic doesn't solve every problem, you know. Sometimes it even makes things worse."

Tolver looked at his bare feet, then up into the leaves of the tree that held them fast. "I know. I'm sorry, Nan."

"And with us stuck here, this is as good a time as any to give you a piece of my mind. Accepting prospector technology. What were you thinking?"

Tolver ducked his head. "I wanted to give you your island. To do it fast enough that I'd have time to have adventures too."

"And to go against everything I've taught you?" Nana chewed her lip, visibly upset. Mason looked away from them, focusing intently on her phone. The device went dark, out of charge. She shook it once, then put it away.

"I'm so sorry, Nana," Tolver said. "I thought I could handle it."

"And I thought I was doing the right thing by protecting you," Nana finally said. Her eyes softened, and her wrinkles seemed more pronounced. "I was wrong about so much. Julius, for one." She put her arm around Tolver. "We'll find our way out of here. Hopefully. Together."

There was a loud sniffle from Mason at that. "Goblin thieves. Being nice to each other." She wiped her eyes.

Nana laughed. "We're always nice!" But then her smile dimmed. "When it was just gathering a word here and there, I didn't realize the damage it caused. But stealing everyone's words? We have to stop the prospectors and send them home."

But then how will we save our island? Tolver thought. "Sending them all home through the library will take a lot of pookahs," he finally said, looking doubtfully at Gilfillan.

The black pig snorted at him, as if to say, "Totally doable."

Nana coughed. "We have to find them first. Then catch them. Once we find a way to do that, since we've got several pookahs on this side already, we can shuttle them back, I think. But first, we have to get out of here."

"Maybe we can loosen a line and sneak out. Or maybe …" Tolver tried prying at ropes again. But none of it worked.

As the morning grew a little warmer, the shrink-wrapped goblin prospector ship began to heat up. Tolver paced to keep awake.

"What are we going to do?" Mason said. "We have to get out of here."

A branch cracked below them. "We might be getting out—and by that, I mean down the hard way—sooner than we think," Tolver whimpered.

Chapter Seventeen

Sam

Sam caught the light at the crosswalk and ran as fast as he could past the school to the baseball field.

Away from the shaded sidewalks, the muggy summer air soaked his T-shirt. He didn't slow down, even though moving fast felt like struggling through wet laundry. Overhead, clouds swelled in a sky currently free of goblin ships.

Before he made it to the top of the hill, the rise and fall of cheers reached him in waves. The noise sounded joyfully familiar: families rooting for their kids, having fun, and not being attacked by goblins. Still, he pushed himself to go faster, until he could see the baseball diamond and the field.

A small bounce house distracted players' siblings in the grassy stretch beside the supply shed. A face painter had set up her table close to where families sat and clapped for both teams. The cotton candy machine leaned against the shed, awaiting the picnic. The benches were filled with blue-and-white uniforms: Mount Cloud's team wore white jerseys with navy lettering. Blue Lake's shirts were turquoise with white lettering.

Everything looked completely normal.

Suyi pitched a slow-breaking curveball as Sam approached. A Blue Lake player swung wildly, then dropped their bat on home plate and walked back to the bench as the umpire called, "Strike three!"

The Mount Cloud team cheered and high-fived as they ran in from the field.

Once Sam got close enough, he could read the portable scorecards on the chain-link fence: eighth inning and the teams were tied. He didn't see a single goblin.

This was not reassuring.

"Tham!"

Bella waved at him from the bounce-house line. She had a cloud painted on her left cheek. "You almost mithed it! We're winning!"

No, we're not, Sam thought.

She spun, and Sam saw the right side of her face had a gray-and-white mountain, even though the closest thing Mount Cloud had to anything like a mountain was the small hill where people sat now.

"I came as fast as I could!" he said, his chest heaving. "Bella, you've got to—" He reached for her as the line moved, and Bella dove into the bounce house with Mason's sister.

Too tired to chase her, Sam scanned the crowd for goblins, trying to think where they might have gone first. How far did they land from the fields? When *The Plumbline* had crashed in the park, he'd been too busy trying to escape a word hog to see where they landed in the trees.

The trees. That was the answer. He ran up the hill.

From his viewpoint, Sam could see treetops of the neighborhood park. Branches and leaves rose behind the rooftop of the elementary school, a mottled wall of dark and light green. Among the trees, although a little hard to spot, the crown of the big tulip poplar bent sideways much like a storm had broken its branches. The poplar's big green leaves were mashed together as if something heavy still rested on them.

That had to be *The Plumbline*. And if that ship had come to rest there, maybe *The Declension* was nearby.

But none of the other trees looked similarly bent.

Where had Mason and Tolver landed? Were they okay? Sam's stomach churned on pure worry. *Worse, where had the rest of the goblins gone?* He half expected to see prospectors lurking near the game and to hear the metallic sounds of word hogs running across the baseball fields. Instead, the Mount Cloud team cheered from its bench, joking and yelling. Parents clapped and called out encouragement. And the birds that usually swooped around the fields looking for spilled snacks still swooped. Nothing had spooked them.

Where had the prospectors gone?

The next Mount Cloud player—a sixth grader named Ben—struck out, and the Blue Lake players ran off the field. Everyone clapped and cheered some more.

"Tham, are Nana and Tolver okay?" Bella found him again. "And the pigs?"

Sam bit his lip, unable to give her a good answer. "Bella, I need you to keep an eye out for anything strange. Don't DO anything. Just watch, okay? And if I'm not around and you need to tell someone, find Ms. Malloy. And DON'T say any important words. Promise me? Stay close."

She hugged him. "I promise."

Blue Lake's coach asked for a time out, and as she knelt by the team's bench, giving a pep talk, Coach McGargee spotted Sam on the hill. "Hey Sam! You seen Mason? She texted to say she had to run an errand and might be late, but this game is almost over."

Sam shook his head. He saw Dr. Vane and his father approaching. "Not yet!"

"Having both of you miss the game is really hurting our team! Better not miss the picnic too." Dr. McGargee went back to psyching up the team for the last half of the inning.

Sam winced. Coach Lockheart wasn't going to be happy when he saw what had happened in front of his house. And the McGargees weren't going to be happy about Mason taking off and not telling them where she was going. And Dr. Vane definitely didn't look happy about seeing Sam at the game. At all. His eyebrows had nearly met his hairline, he'd raised them so high. And Sam's dad was right behind him.

Sam tried to smile, but it only made Dr. Vane walk faster.

"Sam! If you want back on the team so badly, there's just one thing you have to do. Are you ready to say you're sorry?"

Sam's father nodded encouragingly at him. Bella clutched his hand.

Despite everything, Sam *was* ready. He'd have said the word a million times to get back on the field. "Yes sir. I regret–" But he'd barely spoken the word when he felt the familiarly awful sensation of a tooth being pulled from his mouth again. A smaller ribbon than before drifted on the air and disappeared. He heard the clanking sound of a word hog.

No. The goblins *were* here. Sam began coughing to cover the noise and his own alarm.

"What did you say, Sam? Out with it." Dr. Vane looked mad.

Sam shook his head. "I said I _____, Dr. Vane." Tears pricked at his eyes.

"Not again, Sam?" His dad spoke as if a lot was riding on Sam saying one word. Bella stared up at him.

Sam wanted to make his dad happy and to set a good example for his sister. But the prospector goblins had made that so difficult.

He had no idea how to tell his dad that. "I'm working on it. I promise, Dad." He considered the one more ribbon still tied to his wrist.

"Ahhhh, not 'can't,' Mr. Culver. A *can't* is just a *won't* all tangled up." Dr. Vane wagged his finger and smiled at Sam's father, but that expression fell away when he looked at Sam. "Can you imagine," the principal said, "what would happen if everyone had to be more careful the first time or faced the proper consequences when they spoke rashly? Just think of how much more pleasant things would be."

Sam's throat felt dry. There was no way to be certain, but Dr. Vane sounded a lot like the goblin captains Bellfont and Geary. No. Sam *wouldn't* say the word the principal wanted now. He couldn't chew the last ribbon. That way, he wouldn't lose another word to roaming prospectors, even if Dr. Vane turned up the pressure or his dad did.

Mr. Culver frowned for just a second. Then he turned to Dr. Vane. "Isn't that a little harsh? A lot of people learn how to use language correctly by misusing it first." Mr. Culver folded his arms across his chest, and then, with a sigh, unfolded them again. "It's all part of growing up."

"True, true," Dr. Vane said. He raised both hands like he held great, disappointing weights and frowned. "Enjoy your picnic, Sam. I'll expect you tomorrow. And I'll see you in the afternoon, James." He shook the Sam's father's hand.

"You're not coming to the picnic?" Sam tried to keep the relief out of his voice.

"I have to meet with some important businesspeople about another project."

The gleam in the principal's eyes made Sam worry even more.

"Come on, Tham," Bella pulled at Sam's shirt. "Mom made so much food for the picnic."

"One's your favorite," their dad said. "Barbecue chicken salad!" He still looked disappointed.

Sam smiled sadly. *Chicken salad should sound delicious, but my stomach isn't interested.* And the park was the last place he wanted anyone to go.

His dad clapped him on the shoulder. "Sam." He wore a Mets T-shirt and a blue Mount Cloud baseball hat. Beneath the hat's brim, his eyes were deep with concern. "I don't mean to press you, but with the school hosting the community meeting, I'd like to stay on

Dr. Vane's good side. He seems very strict, and I'll continue to support you. But if it's the matter of a simple word, perhaps you could help me out?"

A simple word. Sam plucked at his sweat-drenched T-shirt, wishing anything was simple. Mason's mom joined them, to retrieve Mason's sister from the bounce house. "James. I'm sure Sam will sort it out. And Mason too."

"I saw her earlier. I'll go find her now," Sam said, eager to escape. "Bella, remember what I said."

Bella nodded solemnly, and Mrs. McGargee smiled. "Thanks, Sam."

Mr. Culver grinned and rubbed his belly, making Bella laugh. "Let's grab some food!"

Both teams and their parents crossed the road back to the village together: a large blue-and-white cloud. Sam trudged behind, listening for word hogs and prospectors.

The park occupied the center of the village, about a block from Sam's house. A covered gazebo sheltered two big silver grills, and several picnic tables sat in the shadow of the big trees—Anita said they were tulip poplars and oaks, mostly. The picnic tables were weatherworn and splintered, but parents spread cloths over the wooden slats. Blue and white balloons bobbed cheerfully by the tables and the gazebo.

Bowls of coleslaw, macaroni salad, and hot dog and hamburger buns sat on a long table. A few flies buzzed the slices of thick farm tomatoes and cheddar cheese. Sweating plastic jugs of lemonade sat on each table beside stacks of blue cups.

The whole park smelled like summer. It sounded like summer too, as the baseball team players lined up first for burgers, giggling and teasing each other. Coach Lockheart took his usual place at the grill, setting a row of patties over the flame. He congratulated each player on their runs and catches as they came through the line.

Anita grabbed Sam a plate. "You look like you haven't eaten for days."

Sam's stomach growled, but not in a good way. To humor his stepmother, he took the plate. He was just about to reach for a burger when he spotted the nearly invisible prospector tap line glittering in the shadows behind the second grill like a spiderweb.

Sam dropped his plate. It landed unbroken in the dirt, but

Sam didn't stop to pick it up. He ran to the tap line and stomped on it. Hard.

"Sam! What in the world?" Coach Lockheart paused, his spatula raised.

"A spider—a big one." Sam made a face and Bella and Mason's sister, Spot, screeched.

Mrs. McGargee shuddered. "Oh! Thank you!"

Sam tracked the broken tap line toward the trees. Where there was a tap line, goblins couldn't be far away.

Beneath the trees, the light grew speckled, then shadowed. When he tilted his head, Sam could see the shadow of *The Plumbline*, pressing on the leaves and blocking out the sun, right above him. He'd been right.

"Sam!" Ms. Malloy caught up with him. "Are you all right?" She held a plate of brownies, but she nearly dropped it when she looked up. "What's up there?"

Ms. Malloy has believed me so far, Sam thought. *But she also told me to stay away from the goblins, because she thought they were dangerous. And I haven't . . . stayed anywhere.*

He couldn't meet her eyes.

"Sam?"

He took a deep breath, his throat suddenly really dry. "Goblins," Sam said. "Bad ones and good ones, loose in Mount Cloud. And I need to find the good goblins, Ms. Malloy."

"*Good* goblins?" She sounded doubtful, until she saw Sam's expression.

"Mason is with the good goblins, in a stolen prospector airship."

She sighed. "You went after them."

Sam nodded. His frustration came out in one big whoosh of breath. "I keep trying to fix things, Ms. Malloy, but first, the pig got loose in my room, then I led a whole mess of goblin prospectors to Mount Cloud, and now they're trying to steal enough fuel for their ship—and I crashed a goblin machine into the library."

"Not the library again." She looked very worried now. "How big is their ship?"

Sam pointed up and Ms. Malloy squinted. "Are you sure?"

He nodded. "I'm pretty sure."

She gasped and pointed down at a shadow below the trees. "It's enormous. And how many goblins, do you think?"

The two crews and their captains. "Fifteen, maybe, plus their scientist—a weird goblin with crazy silver hair."

She squinted at Sam, tapping her finger to her lips. "Hmmmm. And they're roaming all over? We'll need to trap them. In a very big trap. I've done some research, but I bet you and Mason know more about catching monsters or goblins than I do. Think about all the movies you watch."

The thing Sam liked best about Ms. Malloy, it turned out, was that she was really practical in an emergency. He and Mason *had* watched a lot of monster movies, some of which had traps. They might be able to figure something out. But he had to find Mason before he could ask her for help.

The clank of a word hog just behind him made him jump. "Don't say anything, Ms. Malloy. The prospectors are hiding in the park, stealing people's words." Sam couldn't bear to tell her he'd already lost one of his. Again.

Ms. Malloy looked around. "I don't see anything."

Sam didn't need to see them. He could *smell* them just fine. No one's words were safe here until the prospectors left.

If they ever left.

Above, the clouds were piling thicker in the sky and beginning to turn gray. Sam wished they'd hurry up about raining before something else went really wrong.

Ms. Malloy noticed. "Go, Sam. I'll come by your house later and we'll make a plan. Meantime, I'll get some supplies to fix the library." She hurried away as Sam turned back to the picnic tables, where Bella was still toying with the remains of her cheeseburger. Sam's stomach turned over. "You're not hungry either?"

She shook her head, glum.

"What's wrong?"

"Dad and Mr. Lockheart are angry," she whispered. "They've been over by the grill arguing for a while. About beautify-something. What's that?"

Uh oh. Sam's dad had relieved Mrs. McGargee at the second grill. And as he turned hot dogs, he and Coach Lockheart were having a heated conversation. The burgers and hot dogs were getting really smoky.

Members of both baseball teams quieted as Mr. Culver said, "There must be some kind of mistake. We wouldn't have sent anything of the sort out. Especially not today."

"The flyer implied you're going to be doing more than a scoreboard. Beautification, in fact. Without discussion! That sounds an awful lot like you want to get rid of things that make Mount Cloud unique. I like how quirky we are. Especially things like our library. I thought you did too." So this was about the presentation. Sam edged closer.

"That's not what the flyer was supposed to say—I'm sorry. I do very much like the library. The presentation and discussion are merely—"

Sam couldn't hear anything but the clanking of a passing word hog. The ground rumbled. His dad scooped the last of the hot dogs off his grill and dumped them into the trash can, too burned to eat. Sam saw a word ribbon drift, glittering, to the ground, then disappear.

Although he couldn't see them, he could hear the goblin prospectors working the park, stealing words. He imagined their sacks beginning to fill.

Anita looked up from where she was serving seconds on salads—the barbecue chicken, plus a three bean, to the baseball teams. Mrs. Lockheart brushed past her as something jostled them into each other. The bowl tipped, and Sam caught it before it could spill too badly. "Thank you, Sam," his stepmom said. But Mrs. Lockheart had walked away without saying anything to either of them. Like she'd done it on purpose. Anita blushed bright red.

The friendly summer picnic noise grew charged, like the

air before a storm. Sam's dad came over. "Come on," he said. "Let's go home."

Sam couldn't agree more. He helped Anita pack up the food, and when Bella and his parents were safely away from the park, he called, "I'll be right there." Then he turned toward the Little Free Library.

Sam knew he needed more help. Now that Bella was safe, he had look for Mason, Nana, and Tolver. When you were looking for someone, you went back to the last place you'd seen them. That was—at least on this side of the portal—the Little Free Library. Or where the library had been.

When he got close to the Lockhearts' yard, Sam couldn't see anyone. But the oak tree's upper limbs were bent in a very particular way.

He'd been right underneath that tree when he crashed, and he hadn't seen or heard anything. But he hadn't been looking up. That had to be *The Declension*.

Sam's heart was in his throat as he tried to figure out how to reach the lowest branch of the oak tree.

Chapter Eighteen

Sam

The oak tree was broad at the bottom but had few footholds for climbing. That was one reason Sam had never climbed it. The tree technically belonged to Mrs. Lockheart, and he'd been in enough trouble for trampling her plants. That was the other reason.

Now Sam stretched one foot up to the oak's cemented knot, grabbed a branch with his opposite hand, and pulled himself up the trunk. Then he grabbed a higher branch and kept going. Branches cracked on the way up. He thought he heard muffled voices.

He found the ship by knocking his head right into the hull.

"OW!" Sam could almost see it too, or at least the shape the ship pressed into the leaves. But *The Declension* had buried itself deep in the branches, pushing them into a thicket that made climbing any higher impossible.

"Mason? Tolver?" he whispered. Then louder. "Nana?" He hoped they could hear him. "Are you guys up there?"

"Sam?" Mason's voice came muffled, from inside. "Is that you? We can't get out!"

He tried to scramble higher. His fingers touched the canvas airbag. It had gotten tangled in the tree branches and wrapped tight over the hull too. His friends were trapped inside.

"I've been looking for you!" Sam had never felt so relieved. But the canvas was on so tight he couldn't pull it off without sliding down the tree. How was he going to help them?

Then he remembered the word hog hidden in the hedge.

"Hang on!" Sam scrambled back down the tree. On the ground, he kicked at the dirt and bushes until his foot struck something hard, with a clang. "Ow!" He put his hand out and felt the cold, smooth surface of goblin brass.

Once he found the hatch of the word hog, Sam let himself inside. Then he hesitated.

He still had no idea how to pilot the thing. None. *But all I have to do is go up, right?* He thought. *And avoid the tree.*

He wrote "up" on a piece of paper and fed it to the machine. The propellers began to spin, and the word hog rose in the air. When Sam was above the oak tree, he fed it "hover" until the hog hovered evenly. Then he lowered a rope with a hook on the bottom to as near the deflated canvas airbag as he could get it.

It took him a couple tries to find and grab the invisible airbag, but he finally managed to hook it.

He fed the word hog another "up" and it rose a few more feet, then lurched slightly as the airbag resisted. While he pulled at the canvas, his friends pushed from the ship's deck. Together they got it loose enough that they could squeeze out. Once they were on top of the hull, they climbed up the rope and into the word hog one by one. Tolver took over the controls.

A few minutes later, they were all safely on the ground. Nana and Tolver hugged Sam. Everyone looked relieved.

Everyone but Mason.

Mason stared at the Little Free Library.

"I know, it's trashed," Sam said. "I landed a word hog on it. Ms. Malloy is getting supplies to fix everything."

"No, Sam. That isn't what I'm looking at." Mason pointed at the camera, which was aimed at the two humans and two goblins, its red light still on.

How much had the Lockhearts' camera seen? Sam was willing to bet on *everything*. And there was nothing he could do to fix it.

"The prospectors are probably delighted by all of this," Nana said morosely. "This was our territory, Tolver. But now we can never come back." She lifted a broken oak branch the size of her arm from the ground.

"Hey!" Mason said. "This is our *home*. Not your territory."

Nana smiled sadly. "You're right."

Then Mason turned to Sam, shaking off her despair. "Took you long enough, Sam!"

"I'm _____." Sam fidgeted with the ribbon on his wrist. He wasn't going to risk using his last word yet. Not when he might get it wrong or lose it to the prospectors. Besides, she was teasing. He could see it in her eyes.

Still, he didn't have time to tease back. He was relieved at having found his friends, but now he needed their help. All of them. "I came as soon as I realized where you probably were. Can you come to our house tonight?"

Mason frowned. "Why me?"

"I need your math brain…and a lot of luck." Sam said.

Mason narrowed her eyes. "You're not going to try to 'fix' the library again, are you?"

Sam grinned. "No. We're gonna build the best goblin trap ever." As he said it, he hoped he looked more confident than he felt.

She brightened. "I am definitely up for that."

All four of them worked together to push the word hog back behind the oak tree. Nana looked up for a long moment at the branches and *The Declension* hidden there. "We were pretty well trapped. And that's what we'll do to the prospectors," she finally chuckled. "We need a lid on whatever it is we build, Sam."

"I'll add it to the brainstorming list." This was going to be a big list.

Right as they'd gotten the word hog well hidden, Ms. Malloy pulled up in a taxi. The driver brought out a bag that read MT. CLOUD HARDWARE. He pulled several pieces of wood and two buckets of paint from the trunk, then put those down next to the crushed library. "Kids should be more careful," he said, looking at the destruction. Then he got back in the cab and drove off.

Ms. Malloy stepped around the pile of supplies when she saw Mason, then hugged her fiercely. "No more pirate ships!"

"They aren't–" Mason began. But her teacher had turned to the rest of the group.

Tolver and Nana took one look at the expression on Ms. Malloy's face and went invisible. Sam could hear Gilfillan fleeing with them before she could scold them too.

"Ms. Malloy, if you give them a chance…" Mason said.

Ms. Malloy put both hands on her cane and leaned on it. "Mason, if they had stayed on *their* side and not stolen any words– Sam's or mine–do you think I would be here, repairing this Little Free Library right now?" She was fuming.

"No," both Mason and Sam said at the same time.

"And do you think that Sam and I would have to go back to school tomorrow to meet with Dr. Vane? And Sam's parents?"

"NO," Sam said.

"Probably not," said Mason.

Ms. Malloy rolled her eyes. "And do you think if they hadn't done what they'd done, that there would be *any* invisible giant brass mechanical pigs crushing Mrs. Lockheart's garden?"

"Well, actually, that was my fault, Ms.–" Sam stopped when she held up her hand. Her neatly pinned bun was coming undone, and wisps of brown hair stuck to her cheek in the pre-storm humidity.

"Enough. I'm going to work on this now. I'll try to get it fixed as best I can."

"I'll help, Ms. Malloy," Mason said. "I told my parents I was doing a Little Free Library errand anyway. I should get it done!"

"I need to get back to my family–" Sam wanted to make sure Bella hadn't lost any words.

"Go, Sam. We'll meet at your house," Mason said.

Sweating, Sam sped across the street and around to the back of his house. The sky was growing darker. Behind the bushes, Sam heard rustling, then a real pookah *oink*. Tolver, Nana, and Gilfillan were following him. He peered through the leaves. Nana was angrily stripping the oak branch into a switch as she walked.

"She'll understand you didn't mean it," Sam finally said. "Someday."

"Maybe," Nana answered. And Sam thought for a moment he heard real sorrow in her voice.

He went through the kitchen door and found his family sitting morosely at the table.

"Did you find Mason?" Anita asked.

"Yeah," he said and sat down, exhausted.

"Don't worry, Sam." His dad put a hand on Sam's shoulder. "You'll get that figured out, just like I'll work things out with Coach Lockheart."

"But... can Mason come over tonight?" Sam asked.

"It's probably not the best idea." His dad shook his head. "Today was a lot."

"But...!"

"What's up, Sam?" Anita asked.

"I just asked Mason to come over, and Ms. Malloy's coming too."

Suddenly beaming, his dad patted Sam on the shoulder. "I knew you could do it."

"Really proud of you, Sam." His stepmom kissed him on the forehead.

She wasn't always that affectionate. She liked to give him his space. So Sam was confused for a minute.

"Thanks," he said. He wanted to say _____–for lots of things, including keeping her at arm's length for a long time. When she and his dad had gotten married, Sam was happy, but he'd still felt like he was supposed to be missing his own mom. Even though the only thing he had to remember his own mom by was a postcard. But he couldn't make amends to his stepmom like he wanted to either, not with the prospectors everywhere.

And then he realized the reason they were so happy: they thought he'd finally said the word. He tugged at the ribbon on his wrist again.

They were going to be so mad when they found out he hadn't said anything yet.

Sam could chew the ribbon if he had to, but losing the other word that afternoon at the game made him extra cautious. Who knew where the prospectors had gotten to by now? If he had to risk losing the word again, it was going to be at the perfect moment. When he really meant to say it. He had to distract them.

"Dad? What did Coach Lockheart mean about the sidewalks and the Lockhearts' library? I thought you liked it?"

One of the flyers for the community meeting sat on the kitchen table. But the paper looked strange. There were words missing. Sam looked closer and saw the problem immediately.

Meet Mount Cloud's New Look! Field and Neighborhood with James Culver

The words *proposal* and *improvement* were gone.

"Dad, I think I know what Mr. Lockheart's upset about. The flyer is wrong—"

"Sam, my firm has worked on this flyer for a week. It's fine." His fingers tapped the paper, unseeing. His tone had shifted back to gruff, and Sam stopped talking.

But Anita looked at his dad. "Ouch. Sam was trying to tell you something important. He wanted you to listen."

"Oh, Anita, Sam, I'm so _____." His father tried to say the word, and his eyes grew big. "I'm so _____."

He gaped like a fish. Sam recalled the word ribbons flying at the park and totally understood. But his dad didn't. Not yet.

Mr. Culver sat down at the breakfast nook, his hand on his head.

"What is happening? The word—it's gone."

"I know how that feels, Dad," Sam finally said. It felt risky to even say that.

His dad blinked. "Sam. You and Bella really weren't kidding. The word is completely gone. What is happening?" His head sank. "How can I do my job if I can't find the words to help people find compromise?"

He tapped his fingers on the table, then lifted the flyer. Squinted at it. "You know what upset Lockheart? This flyer's missing enough words to make it sound like we're not willing to discuss anything. That's the problem. How did this happen?"

Bella slid in beside her dad at the table. Sam sat next to her. "It's boglinths, Dad."

Anita looked from the flyer to Sam, and back. "Goblins? Bella, honestly."

But she and Mr. Culver both yelled in surprise when Nana and Tolver appeared next to Sam. Very green, and very real.

"Dad," Sam said. "Part of what's happening is my fault. And I'm going to make it right. This is Nana, and this is Tolver." Below the table, Gilfillan grunted. "And that's Gilfillan."

"Another pig?" Anita stared at all of them. "This can't be happening."

"Dad, Mom, listen," Bella whispered. "It's important."

Anita shook her head slowly back and forth as Sam told his story. His parents occasionally stared at the goblins sitting at the table. But they listened. Sam's dad leaned forward as Sam finished with "and they said because I was careless with my words, it made really good hot air for their machines and... when you–"

"What do you mean, 'careless'? I'm a professional word arranger. I'm *never* careless." He was growing mad again. "Why did they take my words? And also the agency's words. How did that part happen exactly, Sam?" Mr. Culver squinted at the goblins suspiciously, still unsure they were real.

"Well..."

"SAM."

"Try not to get too mad?" Sam said, hopefully. "You know how the pig got loose in the house earlier?" Gilfillan grunted happily. "And how Mr. Lockheart's Little Free Library keeps getting broken?"

His parents nodded. Bella leaned against him, and he put his arm around her. It felt good to have someone on his side when he said the next part. "Goblins have been raiding the neighborhood, stealing words for a long time. Then they stole Bella's word and I went to get it back."

"Goblins"—his dad frowned at the two goblins sitting at the breakfast nook—"have been raiding...Mount Cloud?"

Nana and Tolver nodded emphatically, their silver heads bobbing up and down.

"Years," Tolver said.

"Decades, really." Nana smiled cheerfully.

Gilfillan squealed.

"Tell me the pig's not a goblin too?" Sam's dad had his head in his hands.

"It's a pookah, which is a sort of goblin," Nana said proudly. "But the mechanical hogs aren't—"

"Mechanical goblin pigs?" Sam's dad took off his glasses to rub his nose. "And that's why I can't say ___? Did they go near the proposal?"

Sam nodded. "That about sums it up."

"SAM. And you two." Sam's father glared at the goblins. Gilfil-lan squealed. "You THREE. If you are what you say you are—" He sounded so angry and confounded.

Sam's heart sank. He plucked at the word ribbon. Should he risk it now? He felt awful.

"It's really not his fault this time, Mr. Culver," Mason said from the other side of the porch screen. Ms. Malloy stood behind her. "It's the goblins' fault. For real."

Still shaking her head as if to clear it, Anita let them in, and everyone made room for them at the table.

"But it's fixable!" Bella sang. "That's the best news. Tham fixed my words. He chased the goblins down and grabbed my thorry back."

Sam's stepmom gathered his sister in her arms. Bella nod-ded very seriously. "Oh, my sweet girl. Sam, you are a really good big brother."

A week ago, Sam would have felt relieved. Now that wasn't good enough. "I think we managed to recover a lot of the agency's words this morning too, Dad."

Mason reached in her pockets, and Sam reached in his bag,

325

and they piled word ribbons on the table. "They're in there some-where."

Anita lifted a ribbon from the pile "So many. And what do they do?"

"You eat them!" Bella clapped her hands. "They're sweet!"

"Well, yours was, dear child," Nana said. "Not all careless words are."

Don't I know it, Sam thought.

His father stared at the pile of glittering words on his kitchen table. "They sound like they're whispering…"

"Well, yes," Nana said. "That's how you tell if they're still fresh. Words get stale, you know."

"They sound—like familiar voices. But I'll have to give these to the account reps to sort through tomorrow." Sam's dad gathered the ribbons into a bag. "What do we do about the rest? How do we stop the—what did you call them?"

"Prospectors," Nana, Tolver, and Sam said all at once.

"They sound like pirates," said his dad.

"They can't be pirates. They wear suits sometimes," Sam pointed out.

His stepmom guffawed, and Ms. Malloy started giggling.

"What's so funny?" Nana asked. She'd edged as far as she could away from Ms. Malloy, who'd been glaring at her earlier, and now started squeezing even more into the wall.

"Occasionally, pirates wear suits in our world too," Ms. Malloy said. "And occasionally, they steal words."

Tolver ducked his head.

"So how do we get our ___ –our words back too?" Sam's dad asked, as though he was really taking Sam seriously.

He is, actually. Because it's happening to him.

Sam wished he had a better answer for his dad. "I'm not sure we can get them all back," Sam said. "Especially if they've already been turned to hot air." He glanced at Ms. Malloy. She seemed worried about the same thing with her words.

Sam's dad groaned. Then he put his head in his hands. "We've got the community meeting coming up, not to mention the rest of our lives...What am I going to do?"

"I know exactly how you feel," Sam said. He patted his dad on the back.

"Oh Sam, I'm so _____," he said.

"I know, Dad." Sam smiled sadly. "And you know what? Our problems are nothing that a decent, well-thought-through goblin trap can't cure."

Even as he said this, Sam realized he couldn't do it on his own. "But we're going to need Anita's tools, your presentation, Nana's magic, Mason's questions, Tolver's planning, and Bella's imagination to make sure we build the trap right."

Chapter Nineteen

Tolver

"We need..." Tolver listened as Mason listed tools and Sam wrote them down using one of Bella's crayons. "A bunch of safety equipment—goggles and gloves, and one of those traps they put ghosts in..."

"Proton packs and ecto-containment boxes! Yes!" Sam cheered.

"No electricity." Anita shook her head. "It's too dangerous."

Mason groaned. "The Ghostbusters didn't think so, and they weren't even trying to catch goblins!"

"Only some goblins," Tolver whispered. He hoped the humans would only trap *some*, anyway.

"What do you need us to do?" Sam's dad said.

That was hopeful. "Give us your vacuum and your leaf blower?" Tolver asked.

"No," both Sam's parents said at the same time.

Adults were kind of no fun, Tolver thought.

"For the community meeting, are you going to be up on the stage at school? When?" Sam tried again.

"Yes. At four p.m. I thought we could show some posters up there, of the scoreboard and things like that," Mr. Culver said.

Tolver snapped his fingers. "Sam said Ms. Malloy had wondered if we could build a goblin trap at the school. Maybe the auditorium could even *be* the goblin trap!"

"That's a great idea," Sam said. "Dad, can we help you set up for the meeting? So we can build the trap there? And as a way to make up for all the trouble?" Sam looked apologetic.

His dad's forehead wrinkled, but when he saw Anita smiling, he sighed. "I expect you can, son."

Nana reached out for a crayon. Ms. Malloy looked at her and at the small oak tree branch the boglin had tucked into her bag.

"Are these two staying?" Ms. Malloy twisted a piece of paper between her fingers.

"They've helped us a lot, Ms. Malloy," Mason said.

She nodded sadly. "I'm going to go back and work on the library, then. It's hard for me to be here. I'm not sure I can explain." Her eyes were red.

Tolver realized they'd been red for some time.

"Are you sure?" Sam's dad asked.

"I think it would be best, yes." The teacher got up from the table and pushed the kitchen door open. "I'll see you tomorrow, Sam."

As Sam watched her go, his stepmom knelt down to eye level with him. Tolver knew this was serious. Adults-and-eye-level serious.

"Sam," she said. "Ms. Malloy's been your biggest advocate through this. I think she can help you now. But you've got to help her too."

Sam nodded. "There's definitely something Ms. Malloy needs to say."

He pushed back from the breakfast nook and caught her on the porch. "Ms. Malloy, wait! Please stay."

Tolver followed them, feeling worried. What if she yelled at

Nana or at him? He tried to stand in front of his grandmother, just in case.

But behind Tolver, Nana spoke. "Wait, please."

Ms. Malloy froze on the stairs, her cane clutched tight.

Nana stepped in front of Tolver. "Maybe I have some apologizing to do first, before anyone else." She held out a very old-looking ribbon. "This is yours. It was my first word. I didn't want to give it up. We told Sam I'd given it away, but it was something I was both proud of and very embarrassed by getting so wrong. So much so that I never used it."

Ms. Malloy's voice shook. "Do you know how hard it's been without this word?"

"We do, yes," Nana said. She glanced at Tolver, until he agreed with a nod. "We're going to try to figure out how we can avoid taking so many, or only when they're being really badly used. We'll work with the other boglins too. We don't want to hurt you."

Gilfillan made a loud snort of agreement.

"And the pookahs—we'll train them differently. Once we've stopped the prospectors." Nana held out the ribbon. Only Tolver could see her hand shake. The ribbon's edges were frayed, and it only sparkled a little, but he could hear it whispering. "Will you accept this? With my apologies for all the hurt I've caused?"

Ms. Malloy reached out a hand and touched the ribbon and lifted it from Nana's palms. She put it to her lips, then ate the whole thing in a few bites.

"What happens now?"

"You wait. Sometimes old words can take longer to come back," Nana said.

"Will you stay and help us, Ms. Malloy?" Sam asked.

Mason stood behind Sam, watching. "Please?" she said.

"Yes, thank you all. I think I will." Her eyes snapped wide open. "Thank you! Oh my goodness." She grabbed Nana and hugged her until the goblin grumbled in protest.

Tolver and Sam both blinked. So those were the words Nana had taken: *Thank you.*

Ms. Malloy came back inside. Mr. Culver made them fresh lemonade.

"What we need to do," Tolver said, "is make sure the goblins can't fuel up the ships by stealing more words."

"But to make a big enough trap, we're going to need a whole lot of math," Mason added.

Tolver's eyes grew wide when she pulled a protractor, two rulers, and a compass from her backpack. "What magic do those do?"

"Ships?" Sam's dad was still having trouble absorbing basic word-stealing goblin stuff.

Tolver sighed. *This was going to take a while.* "One's in the crepe myrtle tree in the park. The big one. And one's in the oak near the Lockhearts.' So is the—"

Mr. Culver got up and made himself another cup of coffee. "Ships in trees. Next you're going to tell me that pigs can fly."

Sam stepped on Tolver's foot to stop his glee. *Ouch!* "Well, actually..."

"The big pigs can. The metal ones!" Bella shrieked. "And Tham got to fly one!"

Now all the adults stared at the goblins again. Not in a nice way.

"It wasn't...that...dangerous...not all the goblins are dangerous!" Tolver smiled in what he hoped was a nonscary way.

Mason held up her drawings. "They won't be dangerous if we find them and trap them in the school."

"And put them in boxthes!" Bella said.

"Not all of them, right?" Tolver said, a little louder.

"Just the prospectors." Nana leaned in, eyes sparkling. "And then we take them back home."

Sam nodded at Nana and Tolver. "Mason, what do you think?"

"I have a few questions and ideas so far." Mason laid out her drawings. She'd sketched pictures of goblins in nets hanging above the stage and pictures of goblins below the stage.

"What about a catapult?" Tolver asked. He liked the idea of a catapult, as long as he wasn't in one.

"A catapult would just make a mess," Mason said. "What we need is a way for all the goblins to fall into something."

"We could shove them off the stage into a box?" Sam pushed his hair out of his eyes, trying to concentrate.

"They'd be really hard to shove," Tolver reminded them. "Some of them are pretty big. And there are a lot of them."

"What about the trapdoors on the stage?" Anita asked.

"There are trapdoors?" Mason yelled. "Why didn't anyone tell me!" She put a big red line through her sketches and began drawing again.

"The parents' committee had them installed so sets could be raised up from below the stage when you all do your big sixth-grade musical next year," said Sam's stepmom. She wiggled her eyebrows. "I helped make sure the stage was sturdy enough for students."

"But not for goblins!" Bella said.

"What if this goblin trap doesn't work? Every plan I've tried so far has made everything worse," Sam said.

"Sometimes things don't work when you're first learning," Anita said. She tilted her head and smiled. "We keep trying, right?"

Tolver looked at Nana, thinking about the mistakes he'd made with the compass. To his relief, she was smiling too. "We keep trying, and we keep learning."

Sam got his Lego set from the closet and put it on the table next to Mason. "Let's test some of your ideas."

"How big are the goblins?" Anita asked. "We can set the floor doors to open if all of them add up to a certain weight."

"They're not always very big, but there are a lot of them," Sam said. "Two whole ships, thanks to us." Tolver felt himself fading with embarrassment.

"And how many hypothetical goblins is that?" Sam's dad still had questions too.

"We should plan for eighteen?" Mason said, counting on her fingers. "I think we're going to need a really big box to hold them— more than a shoebox for sure." She was teasing Sam.

Tolver remembered the morning when he'd taken Sam's words and how much teasing had bothered the boy then. He fidgeted, nervous. But Sam wasn't upset. He was smiling.

Then Ms. Malloy said, "Mason's right. If we knew their average size and number, we could multiply the two and have a pretty good idea of how much space they'll take up."

"This is just like school," Sam laughed.

"Cool." Mason grinned. "Good thinking, Ms. Malloy." She began to build a Lego stage with a trapdoor. Tolver picked up a Lego, but then put it right back when Mason shook her head. "Sam's going to help me with this, okay?"

Tolver didn't mind one bit. He hadn't been interested in the Lego. His fingers had twitched at the way Mason had said "cool," like it almost didn't matter. But he looked up to find the teacher frowning at him as if she was very disappointed. He disappeared and then reappeared. "Sorry, Ms. Malloy. A habit I'm trying to break."

"Well." She smiled tightly. "At least you can say it."

"Tham can say thorry too." Bella said from the other side of the table. "He's just frightened."

"I am not!"

Everyone in the room stared at Sam.

"What do you mean? I thought you said you couldn't get the words back, Sam?" His dad said. "What was all that at the baseball game today?"

Sam drew slow circles on his paper. "I couldn't get all the words back. I got Bella's and mine. But I lost one again today, and I don't want to lose any more. Not with the prospectors loose. I'm not sure I can get my words back again. I couldn't even get your words back by myself, Ms. Malloy." He sounded ashamed.

Ms. Malloy's eyes softened. "First, Sam, Nana wouldn't have returned my words without you doing everything you did. So you *did* get my words back. Second, I'm not going to force you to say anything you're not ready to. But I hope you'll find a way soon."

She really understands him, Tolver thought.

But Mason stared at Sam, shaking her head. "Why are you like this?"

"Like what?"

"You're so stubborn. Just say it and get it over with. In front of Dr. Vane."

"I tried!" Sam crumpled a piece of paper in frustration. "Besides, what if that's the last time I can ever say it? I want it to count. And not because Dr. Vane is making me."

Mason stared hard at her drawings, blinking. Even Tolver understood she was wrestling with something. "You want me to tell him that you did apologize?"

Sam shook his head. "Mason—I don't want you to lie." Tolver noticed Sam had twisted the corner of his shirt into a ball. The boglin realized he'd done the same.

"I know, Sam. I don't want to lie, either. But you being in trouble is a huge pain. If you can't risk saying it, it's almost like not being able to say it."

Tolver took a deep breath so noisily that everyone stared at him. "Sam, I want to give you *my* apology—maybe that way you'll feel like you have two, kind of like a spare." He laughed uncomfortably. Nana frowned at him.

"What do you mean?" Sam looked confused.

"I didn't tell you the truth, back in the marshbogs. I had your words then, and I didn't give them to you because I was afraid I would need them more." The words came out in a rush and Tolver felt himself going invisible. "But what I needed was you guys," he whispered.

"Thanks, Tolver," Sam said. He elbowed his friend. "That really helps. I accept your ____. Once we trap some of the not-good goblins, I won't be so worried."

They borrowed Sam's parents' bathroom scale and figured out how much an average goblin weighed (forty-one pounds, give or take, without the pig).

"So," Mason did the math in her head, "Seven hundred thirty-eight pounds? How are we going to get them all in the same spot?"

Tolver snapped his fingers. "You need bait."

"The community meeting's going to be filled with people misusing words. That should tempt them," Anita said.

"Exactly, but I don't think random words are going to get them all the way into the trap onstage. We need to make sure we have their attention," Mason said.

"What would the best bait be?" Sam mused out loud. "Beef jerky and peanut butter? Old student notebooks? Maybe there are still paper copies somewhere?"

Ms. Malloy's face lit up. "I think I know where to find something good," she said. "But it has to wait for tomorrow at school."

"Ugh," Sam said. "I don't want to go see Dr. Vane."

"At least it gives us a good excuse to be at the school," Mason said.

"We?" Sam's face looked hopeful.

"Yup," Mason said, elbowing Tolver and winking at Nana. "Definitely. Those bad goblins aren't going to catch themselves."

Maybe Mason still isn't my friend, Tolver thought, *but this is pretty close. And she's definitely Sam's friend again.*

Chapter Twenty

Sam

The next day, the hottest day of the summer so far, Mason and Sam walked together to the elementary school without seeing a single pig.

Not Gilfillan, who'd been happily snoring in Bella's room, despite their parents' efforts to keep the pookah out on the porch. Not the big metal word hogs that Sam knew were roaming the neighborhood. He could hear them clanking. But they stayed out of sight.

They passed the oak tree and the rebuilt Little Free Library. The night before, all their parents, plus Nana, had come out to rebuild it while Sam and Mason refined their trap ideas. The library looked better, though there were cracks up the side, and the paint was a bit patchy where the caulk was still drying.

Mrs. Lockheart, in a big sun hat, stood next to it, holding the security camera. She watched Sam and Mason pass, her lips pursed like she wanted to say something but was not sure what.

They waved and walked as quickly as they could to the corner.

"What are you going to do about Dr. Vane, Sam?" Mason said.

Sam chewed his lip. "I wish I had the cards Bella made for me."

"Sorry about that," Tolver said. Sam couldn't see him at all, but it sounded like the goblin was walking right beside them. "But we're even now, right?"

"Not anywhere close to even," Mason laughed. The three of them crossed the street, and she pulled a list of supplies to get from Sam's bag. "Let me know if you think of more things you need. Your stepmom and I are going to go to the hardware store when it opens. Then if you want me to come talk to Dr. Vane with you, I will."

"You're not going to lie for me, Mason. I told you." Sam wouldn't let Mason get in trouble too.

"I know. But he's so focused on words, not actual apologies. I think it's ridiculous. There's a big difference." Mason's cheeks were rosy with outrage.

"Once we get rid of the prospectors, it will all be fine," Sam said. He faced where Tolver was probably standing. "Won't it?"

"Absolutely," Tolver said. "Let's go to school! There should be a lot of careless words in the garbage cans, at least."

Sam shook his head: *no*. Tolver chuckled. "Can't fault me for trying. We need hot air to get back home, just like the prospectors."

"Maybe you should wait outside," Mason suggested firmly. "Until Ms. Malloy says okay."

Sam stopped and waited until, with a rustle and a thump, Tolver sat down hard on the elementary school steps. "Fine. Fiiiine."

And with that, Sam trudged through the door alone and ran smack into Dr. Vane.

He wore a suit, even though it was already hot. And a bow tie, tied so tight the stars on it seemed to stretch. "Hello, Sam. Anything you want to say to me?"

Ms. Malloy came out of Dr. Vane's office, looking frustrated. "I tried to talk to him, Sam. But he insists on doing this by the book."

Which book was that, exactly? There were so many different ways to say I'm ___. "I'm working on it, Dr. Vane. I want you to know that I do feel badly about what happened." Sam had practiced that phrase with his dad at breakfast, before Mr. Culver went in to fix things at the office.

Dr. Vane shook his head slowly. "That's not 'sorry,' Sam. Or 'apologies.' I've given you plenty of options." He sighed. "The words, Sam. The words are important. You show others you mean to change with words *and* deeds."

"I think Sam is well on his way to the latter," Ms. Malloy protested. "He walked here with Mason today, and I—"

Dr. Vane held up a hand and Ms. Malloy's cheeks turned an angry red. Sam's hands curled tight around his backpack strap. *Why was Dr. Vane being so mean?*

The principal opened his office door. "I'll be right here, all day. You should know, Sam, that every minute you delay doesn't just reflect poorly on you. It impacts Ms. Malloy as well. I feel I'm doing your job for you, Ms. Malloy. You could say thank you."

Ms. Malloy pressed her lips tight in a frustrated line. She was also not saying what Dr. Vane was demanding. *Interesting*, Sam thought.

Once the principal closed his office door, Ms. Malloy took Sam's elbow and propelled him fast down the muggy school hallway to her classroom. "Is Tolver outside?"

Sam was pretty sure, despite Tolver's theatrics, that the boglin had snuck in right behind him. "Maybe?"

"I need his help. There was a device on Dr. Vane's desk today that wasn't there last week. It looked like something you'd described from the prospector's ship. All brass, with a trumpet and a bunch of clear cables running from it?"

Tolver appeared. "That sounds bad."

Sam lowered his voice to match Ms. Malloy's "Tolver, I saw your grandmother's friend Julius on board *The Plumbline*, working on something like that. If Dr. Vane's been tapped by the prospectors, the community meeting is going to be even more terrible."

But as Sam thought about it, he realized that he already knew Dr. Vane wasn't being mined for his words. The prospectors' machine was *sitting* on *his* desk. And the tie he'd been wearing that morning, a bow tie, with stars? Sam had seen that before too. On *The Declension*.

It was from the suit Captain Bellfont had been trying on. "What if Dr. Vane is working with the prospectors?"

"You don't think . . ." Ms. Malloy looked horrified. "I'm going to go back and speak to him right now."

Tolver put out a hand, blocking her. "You can't risk it. He could tell the prospectors everything and we'd lose our element of surprise."

"Then I need to tell the school board," she said.

With a buzz, Ms. Malloy's intercom clicked on. The red light had been on when they'd walked into the room, but now it was green.

"Ms. Malloy?" Dr. Vane said. His voice filled the room with static. "The school board will be at the meeting; can you be sure to make them welcome?"

Ms. Malloy's eyes went wide. She found a pencil and wrote: *I think he's listening to us*, on a blank piece of paper. Her hand shook while she did it. Sam put his finger to his lips to show her he understood. Tolver did the same.

"Come to think of it, Sam," Dr. Vane continued, the intercom whistling because the principal was too close to the microphone. "I do need your help this afternoon, and your friends too. The community meeting has been moved to two p.m. due to some rather large concerns by the neighbors. Your father suggested you could help set up the auditorium."

"Okay," Sam said.

"Thank you." Dr. Vane clicked the intercom off. Ms. Malloy, Sam, and Tolver sat together in the hot, silent classroom.

Oh no. Two p.m., not four.

Ms. Malloy looked heartbroken. "Sam, do you think it will be enough time?"

Sam played with the pencil stub he'd been writing with, thinking, *All of my plans so far had gone pretty terribly, and I want to make sure this one works.* "Tolver, find Mason and Anita. And get Bella and Nana too."

Tolver went invisible as he climbed out the classroom window. Sam could see his path through the unmowed grass, across the field, and to the hardware store near the Mount Cloud train station. He hoped the boglin found everyone in time.

They were going to need to all work together in order to pull this off.

Ms. Malloy smiled at Sam nervously. "I really liked this job," she said aloud.

Sam wished he could say something to make her feel better.

Instead, for the rest of the morning, the two of them strategized silently, testing and retesting the goblin trap plans Sam and Mason had refined the night before.

When Tolver returned with Mason, they snuck in through the window. Ms. Malloy pointed at the intercom and put her finger to her lips.

"Bella's with your stepmom," Tolver whispered. "They're down by the auditorium."

Have you seen any prospectors? Sam wrote on his scrap of paper. *Anywhere?*

The boglin nodded, his dark eyes wide. He borrowed the pencil and paper. *A word hog was hidden behind the dumpsters near the train station. Maybe they went downtown?*

Uh oh. Not back to Sam's dad's office. "We have to warn my dad," he said aloud.

Sam, Ms. Malloy wrote, *Mount Cloud can't be the only small neighborhood the goblins have been mining.* She looked over her glasses at Tolver.

Tolver looked sheepish. *I don't think they could have gotten far, to be honest. They used up most of their fuel chasing us here, didn't they? They're stuck too.* Tolver wrote quickly. *We don't often get stuck over here. Only lately.*

Before Sam could write back, Nana appeared and thwacked them both gently with the oak switch. She took the pencil and wrote, *Boys. This is a serious matter. We won't be going back home until we sort this all out.*

Tolver ducked his head. "Okay, Nan."

"Yes, Nana," Sam said, feeling guilty until he saw Ms. Malloy wink at Nana.

Let's go get them, Mason wrote.

Down the hall from Ms. Malloy's room, the doors to the school's auditorium were wide open. The room had been modernized the year before to add air conditioning in addition to the special stage with a trapdoor that let the chorus appear and disappear during plays.

Sam, Mason, Tolver, and Ms. Malloy slowly walked down the hall and into the auditorium. Inside, the air conditioning felt cool against Sam's skin. Mason shivered.

His stepmom and Bella stood on the stage, looking at the trapdoor.

Anita pulled a screwdriver from her tool belt. "I'm going to make some adjustments. Want to help?" she winked.

She showed Sam and Mason how to set the computerized scale on the floor so that it would sink when it hit a particular weight. Then she hesitated. "Did you calculate for the bait, or just the goblins?"

"We still have to get the bait," Ms. Malloy said. "Once we have it, we'll add that weight to the calculations from last night. It will be fine as long as there are exactly twenty goblins, and if they don't bring any word hogs."

That was a big if. Sam hoped they were right.

"But how are you going to get them on stage, Sam?" His stepmom stared out over the empty auditorium seating. Then she whispered, "Are any of them already here?"

Nana shook her head. "They're not. I've ... distracted them for a few hours."

"Good," Sam said.

"How?" Mason asked, her eyes narrowing.

Nana blushed. "I disabled their word hogs and had Gilfillan run through a bunch of tap lines we found. They're chasing the pig all around the neighborhood."

"I thaw it," Bella said. "It looked like a tornado blowing down the road. All the trash cans got knocked over."

Ms. Malloy covered her eyes. "I hope they stay well away from the Little Free Library. We just fixed that again."

Sam hoped so as well. Emphatically.

Once his stepmother had the trapdoor primed and the video monitor set up the way Dr. Vane had requested, they took a break to eat lunch. Anita had brought leftover chicken from the ruined picnic and a big thermos of cold lemonade.

"Now we just need to bait the trap," Mason said after she swallowed.

Tolver, digging in the auditorium's waste bins for words, said, "It had better be really good."

"It will be." Ms. Malloy smiled.

"Like what?" Mason asked. "One of us?"

"No. None of us," Ms. Malloy said. "I have something else in mind: Old essay papers. With circles drawn in red ink around careless words. I keep several years' worth in boxes in the base-ment archives."

A light dawned in Tolver's eyes. "Can I have them when we're done?"

Ms. Malloy rolled her eyes to the ceiling, pointedly ignoring Tolver's request. But then she frowned. "Oh. But the keys are in Dr. Vane's office."

"Sam and I can get them, Ms. Malloy!" Mason said. "I have the perfect idea."

⟝⟞

"You can't," Sam said. "I won't let you."

Mason walked ahead of him all the way to Dr. Vane's office, making Sam nearly run to keep up. "You can't exactly stop me, you know."

"But what if you lose your words? What if the prospectors' machine takes them?" Sam wasn't going to let that happen. Not to any of his friends.

"Sam, when the first mate took me out of the brig, she said something. I thought she was just celebrating your raid, but I don't think so now."

Sam frowned. "What did the first mate say, exactly?"

"She said there were a lot of potential resources that had gone untapped so far, but that Julius's new inventions would make every-one rich. She was hoping to get her own ship someday."

All the prospectors had the same dream, Sam realized. *And it's one that requires a lot of hot air.* The prospectors wouldn't stop at just a few baskets of words if they had the chance. They'd keep going. *And I'm not going to let that happen.* "I still don't want you to risk your words, Mason. I should be the one to do that. Slow down!"

"This isn't about a few words anymore, Sam. This is about saving Mount Cloud! And maybe other places. A few words are worth that." She grinned.

But Mason hadn't been missing several important words all weekend. She didn't know the trouble it caused. Not firsthand. Sam didn't want her to find out.

They were nearly at the office.

The door was open, and someone was talking loudly and a bit pompously to Dr. Vane.

"Imagine, Vane. If you could keep kids from trash-talking each other on the field. What an improvement that would be to the game! This machine," Sam and Mason heard a hand thump the machine, "is capable of that very thing!"

The voice was Captain Geary's.

"How can you prove it?" Dr. Vane said. "I've been playing with this thing all day and I can't get it to work."

Bellfont, who sat next to Captain Geary, flicked the machine on, then off again. Sam heard it *whirr* softly, then stop. There was feedback from the intercom every time he did it.

"We'll bring it to your community meeting this afternoon. You can watch us test it there and enjoy the results. Then we'll teach you. Anyone back talks or interrupts, you'll see the power of this technology immediately."

Mason stared at Sam, wide-eyed. "They can't do that."

"The meeting is about beautification and standards," the principal protested. "Not about restricting students' self-expression."

"Libraries and scoreboards, we know. We heard you all yesterday." Captain Geary said. "I know how business works, and you've said yourself that you need parents' buy-in. You can't have the kids interrupting you during your statement. That's all I'm saying. You bring us enough kids who mis-use words, and we'll prove its value to you."

"It may even," Bellfont chuckled, "take sincere words, if you target it right. Experimentally, of course. My scientists are very skilled."

Vane frowned. "I'm not convinced. But if you'll keep it to the kids who've been breaking the Lockhearts' library and getting in trouble, I won't fight it."

Sam and Mason hid behind the office secretary's desk as the two prospector captains emerged from his office. They both wore suits this time. And shoes. They didn't smell. It was hard to tell that they were goblins, if you didn't look too closely.

When they heard the double doors of the school swing shut, Mason stood up. Sam followed.

Dr. Vane sat staring into the mid-distance. The machine that had been on his desk was gone. "Would be nice," he murmured.

Then Mason knocked hard on the doorframe, and the principal jumped. "Just a moment!"

"Mason, NO!"

"Trust me, Sam." Mason punched his arm lightly. "Play along, okay?"

Sam realized he did trust her. "Okay," he whispered.

Dr. Vane came to the door. "I'm in a meeting, kids. If you need me, I can come in a few minutes."

They both knew he wasn't in a meeting. But he didn't know they knew. "We're sorry to interrupt you, sir," Mason said. "We need you to come now, Dr. Vane. Ms. Malloy's gone silent."

She nudged Sam and he added, "She keeps trying to say things, but nothing's coming out. It started this morning, when you were talking to us over the intercom, but now it's getting worse."

"We weren't sure if we should take her to the hospital?" Mason said.

Sam admired Mason even more. She was brilliant at thinking on her feet.

There was a rustle behind them. Tolver had heard the whole thing. Now the boglin went running to the auditorium to tell Ms. Malloy what she needed to do.

"No, no hospital." Dr. Vane frowned at the place where the machine had been on his desk. "That's not supposed to happen. Is it possible she's got laryngitis?"

Mason and Sam both shook their heads: *no*.

Dr. Vane had a hard time not running down the hall. They watched him speed up, straighten his tie or his hair, slow down, then speed up again. All the way to the auditorium.

Meantime, Mason went around to the other side of Dr. Vane's desk and found the keys to the basement in the top drawer. "Mission accomplished!"

"Mason," Sam said, "we have to find that machine too. Before the meeting."

"What do you mean?"

"Did you hear what they said? He thinks we're the kids who've been messing with the Lockhearts' library."

"We kind of are," she pointed out.

"Mason, Dr. Vane's fine with the goblins taking our words forever. Starting at the meeting. We have to warn everyone." Sam looked up at the wall clock. They were running out of time.

Chapter Twenty-One

Tolver

Tolver sped back to the auditorium and found Sam's stepmom and Bella working on the stage, with Nana helping, while Ms. Malloy guarded the door.

"What's taking Mason and Sam so long?" she asked as Tolver tugged invisibly on her sleeve.

"Principal Vane is coming," the boglin said. "You have to pretend you've lost all your words. Mason said you'd understand."

Ms. Malloy nodded slowly, trying to comprehend. "All of them? Not just one or two, like before?"

"The prospectors have a new tool and are hoping to steal a bunch of hot air fast. So they're teaming up with the principal. He was testing the machine earlier, and Mason and Sam need him to think he accidentally took all of your words."

"What new tool?" Nana asked.

"Something of Julius's—it takes all the words, not just the overused ones," Tolver said, getting so upset he reappeared. He was scratching his ear when he popped into view.

"I regret the day I ever taught him anything," Nana seethed. "We'll fix him when we get home. The whole city needs to understand the risks here."

"Soon, Nana," Tolver said. "But first we have to stop the principal and the captains. Right, Ms. Malloy?"

To Tolver's astonishment, Ms. Malloy opened her mouth to say something and then looked frustrated when nothing came out. She tried harder.

"Did it really work?" Tolver whispered.

Ms. Malloy laughed quietly. "No, Tolver," she whispered back. "But we can pretend it did."

Tolver's cheeks glowed nearly purple. "You're really good at that," he said. "Nana, she's marvelous—"

"Yes, she is," Nana agreed.

They heard footsteps approaching rapidly down the hall. "Hurry, everyone."

Tolver and Nana hid at the back of the stage near the basement stairs to wait for Mason and Sam. "I hope they hurry."

"Ms. Malloy!" Principal Vane burst through the auditorium doors. "May I speak with you? Oh, hello Mrs. Culver-Vasquez." He rolled his "r" dramatically and completely unnecessarily.

"Hello, Principal Vane." Sam's stepmother waved cheerfully. "Almost done here!"

"Good, good." He turned to Ms. Malloy. "How about you?"

Ms. Malloy smiled and opened her mouth, but no sound emerged. Vane turned even paler than he already was. The teacher put her hand to her throat and looked slightly panicked.

"Now, Ms. Malloy, please do sit down. This is likely temporary—perhaps some tea?" He looked like he wanted to run back and hide in his office.

Tolver had to squelch a giggle as Ms. Malloy waved off the offer of tea and reached for a notepad. On it she wrote, *It's been like this since I left your office, sir.*

"Do you think you're ill?" Vane asked hopefully.

Not at all—fit as a fiddle, Ms. Malloy wrote. *Only my voice—well, not exactly. My throat feels fine; it feels more like my words are gone than my voice.*

"That's impossible." Vane said, taking a seat very quickly in the first row of auditorium seats. "Come now, you must please try again, Ms. Malloy."

Ms. Malloy gamely opened her mouth and formed a word with her lips, but no sound came out. Tolver almost laughed, but Nana invisibly stepped on his foot. "Hush, you," she whispered. "Try to hold your tongue before I have to hold it for you."

Tolver squirmed. That sounded like an uncomfortable spell.

Moments later, he was saved when Sam and Mason burst into the auditorium and ran down the aisle, skidding to a stop in front of their teacher and principal. "Oh good, you found her," Mason said. Her eyes widened with concern. "Could you help her?"

"Not yet, I'm afraid," Dr. Vane said. "But we're working on it. Why don't you kids move along." The principal was so distracted, he waved Sam and Mason in the direction of the stage.

They were happy to oblige.

Tolver and Nana followed them to the basement door,

hidden behind a stage curtain. Mason unlocked the door and quietly slid it open, and then all four of them descended the stairs. The boglins reappeared midway down, just as Mason opened the door to the storage room and turned on the lights.

Tolver scratched his elbow as they moved among the crates and containers, past shelves of old computer drives and screens. Sam came to a stop when he found Ms. Malloy's neat handwriting on the fronts of six boxes of term papers.

Tolver's green fingertips brushed the boxes. "Lots of good words in there. Even I can smell them."

Mason smacked his hand lightly. "Those are for the trap, Tolver."

Chastened, the boglin dragged his foot across the dust on the storage room floor. "None of this would have happened if you hadn't trapped Starflake ... or hadn't chased us through the Little Free Library, or ... or if I had magic." Tolver's expression filled with yearning.

Mason overheard him and glared. "Or if you didn't steal words?"

"Or that." Tolver had to agree. "But maybe ... just maybe there's a way to use heaps of mis-used words—like these—instead of just one at a time. If there is, we won't have to steal any others." He looked toward Nana to see what she thought.

"We've always worked by not taking enough to be noticed," Nana protested. "But, especially if the words were really, really wrong, we might be able to use written ones. We'll fix the converter and give it a try once we trap the prospectors, all right?"

The four of them examined the boxes on the shelves. There were decades' worth of old essays, dating back to when Ms. Malloy was a new teacher.

They each lifted a box from the shelf and carried them out to the space below the stage. Mason sneezed from the dust. Sam's arms were streaked with sweat and dirt.

Tolver couldn't stop sniffing the boxes. "There are so many words in here no one will ever miss!"

"Focus, Tolver," Nana said.

Sam's stepmother waited for them below the stage with a scale. Together with Bella, Nana and Tolver helped set aside the best papers, their fingers twitching over red pen marks and highlighted paragraphs. Meantime, Sam and Mason began to slowly build the goblin trap, placing the essays on top of the piles of boxes. Soon they had nearly fifty pounds of bait.

"That will have to do," Anita said.

Ms. Malloy whispered down the stairs that Principal Vane had gone back to his office. They raised the boxes to the stage, and Anita made some final adjustments to the trapdoor equipment.

It was nearly time for the meeting. Tolver hid in the wings, stage left. Nana and Anita stayed below the stage. Sam and Bella went back to find their dad.

Tolver paced nervously as he waited. He really wanted this to work, more than he'd wanted anything in a long time.

Human parents began to find seats in the auditorium. As Tolver peered out, he saw adults in suits sitting in the front row. Mr. Culver, sitting next to Sam and Bella, kept adjusting his tie nervously.

Behind them, Dr. Vane sat next to Ms. Malloy, talking. Except Ms. Malloy wasn't responding. She gestured silently when Dr. Vane spoke. Occasionally she would try to say something, only to have no sound come out. The more she did that, the guiltier Dr. Vane looked, and the faster he talked.

Then Sam's dad stood up. Tolver wiped his sweating palms on his canvas vest.

With a word from Nana, Tolver went invisible and sat near the boxes, in case the doors didn't open at the right time. Or the prospectors tried to steal them. *But hopefully they wouldn't be able to do that,* he thought. *The papers in the boxes were heavy. It would take all of the prospectors to carry them away. Which they would be unable to resist trying.*

Tolver heard the clanking sound of a word hog approaching soon after the air conditioning kicked on high. He looked out into the darkened auditorium, but with the stage lights on he couldn't see anything. The prospectors were trying to sneak invisibly into the auditorium, but the sound of hatches opening and shutting gave them away.

From the sound (and, unfortunately, the smell), Tolver could tell that a lot of prospectors had come to the meeting. He was pretty sure he heard the two captains whispering nearby too, ready to steal words away with their new machine.

Below Tolver, Anita and Nana moved, almost visible, through the crack in the trapdoor.

The auditorium seats filled with the parents of every student Tolver had seen at the Mount Cloud school the day he'd stolen his first word. Suyi, Mason's friend Gina. Their families. Mrs. Lockheart, with a small video camera.

Word had spread that something big was going to happen at the meeting, and everyone wanted to be in the air-conditioned auditorium when it did.

"Your words aren't going to get stolen today," Tolver whispered. "I promise."

And then Sam's father took the stage. Standing near the crates of papers, he pointed at the posters of new scoreboards as people began to murmur.

They didn't sound happy at all.

Chapter Twenty-Two

Sam

"What we wanted to do with the scoreboards was give people a way to see the Mount Cloud teamwork on display. I'm happy to announce that, instead of the parents' association or the school board paying for it, my agency will be picking up the tab."

Sam sat up. He didn't know that was the plan. It sounded like a good idea.

About half the room clapped when Mr. Culver finished. Then he cleared his throat and said, "I had intended to speak about neighborhood beautification, but my partners and I feel it best to wait. Suffice it to say that a bit of confusion here is my own fault, and we would appreciate time to make it right."

The other half of the adults in the room grumbled. Coach Lockheart stood. "I'd like a chance to speak."

"This doesn't sound good," Mason whispered from behind Sam.

Sam thought of the cookout and the arguments.

"Maybe," Sam whispered back. "Give my dad a chance. He's really good with words."

But Mr. Lockheart got up on stage, staring straight at Sam's dad. "And, I'd like an apology from you, on behalf of your firm."

Sam leaned forward as his dad turned pale.

In the wings, the prospectors' machine powered up with a sound like a leaf blower. The static from it raised the hair on Sam's arms. He got up from his seat and climbed to the stage too, coming to stop near the boxes of papers.

"It's okay, Dad," he said. "I can help too."

"Sam," Coach Lockheart said. "You can't be up here. We have video of you on my security camera. You and your friends destroyed my library. You are a danger to Mount Cloud."

Sam stared at his shoes. Coach wasn't wrong—he just didn't know what kind of danger.

Then Sam raised his chin. The whole neighborhood watched him from the auditorium seats. There was Mrs. Lockheart looking like she'd just sucked on a lemon. There was Gina, rolling her eyes at Sam and trying to whisper to Mason.

But then there was Mason shushing Gina. She gave Sam a giant thumbs-up.

Deep breath, Sam. You can do this.

"Coach, my dad was just trying to help. He's not to blame for the misprinted flyers or what happened to your library." Sam untied the word ribbon from around his wrist and held it tight.

"You shouldn't feel pushed to replace your library with something more standard," Sam's dad said. "It's an asset to the town."

Coach Lockheart nodded. "I still want an apology. From both of you."

The hum from the prospectors' machine grew even louder. Sam could hear Julius whispering near the stage and the captains hushing him. It dawned on Sam that it wasn't entirely the pull of old essays attracting the goblins. It was that they hoped Sam and his dad would waste more words to escape the neighborhood's anger, but without being sincere.

Well, if that's what they want, Sam thought, *I'll give it to them.* The word ribbon whispered as he put it in his mouth and chewed once. It tasted sawdusty.

Then he stepped forward. "It's important for me to say right now how much I'm..." and he dropped his voice to a whisper. The goblin smell became overwhelming as prospectors drew closer. They were almost standing on the trapdoor.

"What did you say, Sam? Speak up!" Dr. Vane said.

Sam thought of baseball players striking out, of puppies and chocolate. His eyes actually got teary; he was trying so hard to be insincere. And that was the hardest part, because Sam really did feel bad. But feeling bad would destroy the trap. He had to fake this better than he'd ever done before.

The sound of the machine grew louder. Sam felt a gust of foul-smelling air on his cheek, like one of the goblin captains was breathing down his neck.

"With all my heart—" Sam said, ending in a whisper again. The prospectors' machine was right by his ear now, and he felt the trap under the stage creak. He stepped away from the platform. Tolver gave him a thumbs-up from just offstage. They were all there, even the captains. "I apologi—"

With the feeling of a tooth coming loose, Sam could see the word begin to slip from between his lips: a faded, glittering ribbon. And then he bit down.

The machine hummed louder, working hard to pull the word from between Sam's teeth. The goblins crowded closer, all clustered on the trapdoor. Tolver disappeared below.

And Sam took two steps forward.

Suddenly, with a huge *thunk*, the trapdoor dropped. Sam hadn't moved far enough away, and he fought to keep his balance at the trap's edge.

His dad grasped his arm and held on as the papers and the goblins all tumbled into the basement. Julius screeched, "Not my machine!" Then came a sound like a broken piano. Sam heard more scuffling, and then a lid slammed.

"Got them!" Mason yelled.

Sam slurped his word back quickly. Bella was right, it did taste sweet.

Nana climbed on top of the crate and poked a hand from the orchestra pit. She passed a glittering ribbon to Sam's dad. Mr. Culver took it and chewed it.

"What's going on?" Coach Lockheart called when the dust cleared. "Is everyone all right?"

"We are," Sam's dad said. "And I am sorry for the confusion. We'll work hard to communicate with you and won't make any plans without consulting with the community beforehand."

Coach Lockheart smiled, his shoulders relaxed. "Thank you. That's all I wanted to hear."

They shook hands, and the meeting concluded without a hitch.

No one noticed when Dr. Vane slipped from the auditorium, except for the boglins and Sam.

Compared to the crowded air-conditioned auditorium and the dusty stage, the hallway outside was steamy and hot.

Dr. Vane strode the corridor, phone in hand, muttering, "I don't even know how to contact you."

"I'll take care of this one, Sam," Nana said. But when Tolver and Gilfillan emerged from the side door, Nana held up her hand. "Wait just a moment."

She turned to Tolver and passed him the oak branch. Then she whispered in his ear and gave him a slip of paper. The younger boglin's eyes widened.

Nana took Gilfillan's leash, and they pulled the crate filled with prospectors out the side door. The box rocked on the cart they'd stolen from backstage.

Tolver raised the oak switch and pointed it at Principal Vane.

"Wait!" Sam held out his hand. "You can't take his words."

"Even though he was going to take yours?" Tolver looked outraged.

Sam knew that it might have felt fair to get even, just like with teasing. But this wasn't about getting even. "He's not a very good principal, but no one should have their words stolen."

"But he was working with the prospectors, who are headed back to the marsh to work off some debts." Tolver whistled. "Oh, I know! Do you think we should take your principal back to the marsh too?"

"No, I don't think that's any better," Sam said.

While Tolver narrowed his eyes, thinking, Dr. Vane, in his perfect suit, spotted Sam. "Oh hello, Sam! I was just…gathering my thoughts." He looked so uncomfortable.

Sam stayed silent.

Dr. Vane shifted from one foot to the other. "You, ahhh, heard about the machine?"

Sam nodded and crossed his arms over his chest. He raised an eyebrow.

"I just want people to use words properly," the principal said. "Like you—if you would only—" He raised his hands. "Well, the truth is, wasted words are valuable! Businessmen wanted all the hot air generated in this school. And they promised to help me make this school a model of propriety."

"Why would you do that?" Ms. Malloy came up behind Sam and Tolver. "Students need to be able to experiment. They learn that words have value over time. You can't force it."

"She really is the best teacher," Tolver whispered. Sam nodded enthusiastic agreement.

"Because, dear Ms. Malloy," Dr. Vane said. "It's too slow a process. Why wait, when we can streamline? It's called progress."

The auditorium doors opened, and neighbors began to emerge. The meeting was finished.

"I've heard enough," Tolver said. He cleared his throat and waved the oak switch. Then he said, loudly, "Begone!"

Instead of stealing Dr. Vane's words, the switch sent puffs of tiny silver wings toward the principal.

The fancy suit and the star bow tie began to unravel. The principal squeaked and tried to slap the wings away, but they followed him.

Sam looked on, amazed. "Tolver, you did it! You did magic!"

Tolver had disappeared before the adults could notice him. "I did," he whispered.

By the time the last board member had emerged from the cool auditorium and into the heat of the hallway, Dr. Vane had run down the hall and out the double doors of the school. He made it to the parking lot, clutching the remains of his coat and trying to cover the holes in his pants, where his striped underwear showed.

"What in the world," said a school board member, looking at the retreating principal, not at Sam.

"Sam!" Bella burst through the auditorium door as they walked back down the hall. "You did it! You said it!" She ran up to hug her brother. "And the goblins didn't steal the word!"

Looking down at his little sister, Sam swallowed. The taste of the apology leaving his mouth was still there on his lips. He'd almost lost the words he'd fought so hard for. It would have been worth it, but it was scary—even though he hadn't actually risked the word.

"I didn't really say it," Sam admitted.

Bella looked confused.

"It was kind of a trick," Mason said. "Sam almost said it, but he bit down on the last syllable. So the goblins technically couldn't take it." She half smiled at Sam. "Pretty smart."

Sam grinned. "Thanks."

His sister scuffed her shoe on the linoleum. "Oh, okay. But when do you think it will be safe to say the whole thing?"

Sam scuffed the floor with a sneaker. "I'm working on it." Bella squeezed his hand.

"Bella!" Mason picked her up and swung her around. "You said 's'!"

She looked delighted. "I did!"

After the community meeting let out, neighbors left the building, still talking, as Sam and Bella walked back down the aisle into the auditorium.

Mrs. Lockheart had found Anita. She was smiling. "Can we try another potluck tonight at the park? The last one didn't end so well. And we have a lot to celebrate. I'll bring brownies." Anita smiled and agreed.

Sam's dad came out of the auditorium and patted Sam on the shoulder. "The city—our client—has agreed to work with neighborhoods to teach people how to establish their own beautification standards creatively. And they've asked the Lockhearts to help!"

That sounded fantastic.

"Plus, the community unanimously approved the scoreboard! And," Coach Lockheart said, with Ms. Malloy standing next to him, "Ms. Malloy explained what's been happening, or tried to. In any case, she advocated strongly for you to return to the team. Would you be willing to stay in the outfield another year and help me keep fixing the library for as long as it needs it?"

Sam smiled. "Okay, coach!" He hoped the library wouldn't need much fixing.

As his parents headed home to get ice cream for the dessert potluck and the Lockhearts strolled toward the park with Ms. Malloy to set up the tables, Mason and Bella and Sam walked together down the sidewalk.

When they got close enough, they noticed the flowers

around the Little Free Library, which their parents had replanted the night before, were already trampled.

"Oh, great," Sam said. "So much for Mrs. Lockheart not being angry with me."

"Nope, this time it was my fault, Sam." Tolver appeared, grinning. He picked the yellow petal of a tulip off his heel. "I'll help you fix it. We're just sending the last of them over now."

Beside him, Gilfillan and Starflake pulled sleds made from pieces of *The Declension*. Crates on each sled contained many prospectors each, from the sound inside. When Tolver gave the signal, each pig leapt into the Little Free Library and, with a pop, disappeared.

"What will happen to them?" Mason asked.

"They'll have to repay their transport home, to start with. Gilfillan and Starflake are very expensive. No more fancy prospector ships for a long time." Tolver chuckled. "Meantime, Nana and I will try to teach everyone in Felicity and the marshbogs how to use printed words—which don't permanently leave those who write them. Ms. Malloy was right. There were a lot of careless words in the basement! We can compress them so they'll last us for a while."

Mason crossed her arms and smiled at the green boy with the silver hair as he climbed into the Little Free Library behind the pigs. "So no more stealing?"

Tolver gave Sam and Mason a mostly convincing thumbs-up. "You know it! We don't steal from our friends!" Then he disappeared.

In the shade of the big tulip poplar tree at the park, as neighbors began to arrive with plates of dessert, Sam gathered his thoughts.

There might still be goblins in the trees. He might have mis-counted the number of crates Tolver and Nana and the pookahs had taken back over.

And others might return sometime for the word hogs. Sam couldn't seal up all the Little Free Libraries and post office boxes to keep word-stealing goblins out.

But Nana had said words were magic. That they were some of the last magic left in the world. Sam believed her. And Bella was right to be disappointed that he hadn't actually apologized at the meeting. It had been a good trick, but he hadn't finished what he'd promised to do yet. Not the way he wanted to. He kicked at the dirt.

Glanced up at the branches of the tree still bent funny from the crash of *The Plumbline*.

"What are you waiting for, Sam?" Mason called from a picnic bench. "Get some ice cream!"

Words had mattered to Coach Lockheart. When Sam's dad apologized, the meeting went better. And even if she hadn't said so, Sam knew they mattered to Mason too.

"We'll see," she'd said when he'd asked her to be friends again. And then "definitely" when he'd asked her about working together. Could he risk being honest now? His hands stuck in his pockets, Sam walked over to the picnic table where Mason sat.

"What?" she raised her eyebrows.

"So, it doesn't matter anymore if a goblin steals my words," Sam finally said. "And I'm not doing this to get out of trouble. I just want you to know."

"Know what," Mason said. She put down her spoon.

"I'm truly sorry," Sam said quietly. His cheeks went red again, but he decided he didn't care. He didn't want to be invisible. Not while he was saying important things. "I didn't mean to hurt your feelings. I got too caught up in the teasing, and I won't do it again. I know how important your grandmother was to you."

Mason's face lit up, and her eyes got sad all at the same time. "Thank you, Sam. She was really wonderful." She slid over on the bench to make room for him. "Do you think we'll see them again? The goblins, I mean?"

"Maybe. Maybe we should go into goblin-removal services as a summer job."

"Maybe we should." She elbowed him. "I'll consider it if you'll teach me how to fly one of those word hogs."

That night, Sam ate two brownies topped with ice cream. He, Mason, Bella, and Mason's sister, Spot, caught fireflies in the park. Ms. Malloy told his parents that Principal Vane had left the district and that Sam was no longer in trouble at school. To celebrate, they all sat in Sam's backyard and watched *Ghostbusters IV,* singing along with the music until Mrs. Lockheart yelled at them to be quiet.

And the next morning, Sam put on his navy-and-white Mount Cloud jersey and went to play baseball.

Chapter Twenty-Three

Sam

A few days later, the Mets played the Phillies on the Mets' home turf.

Sam's dad's company got box seats for all of them. Sam, Bella, Mason and the rest of the McGargees, and Coach and Mrs. Lockheart. The box had a fancy shelf where they could get candy and popcorn. Mason and Sam filled up on junk food and lemonade. The lemonade wasn't anywhere near as good as Anita's, though.

It was cool in the stadium box. Cold, actually, Sam decided. The air conditioning was cranked high. At first he thought he was going to have to sit behind glass the whole time, like at school.

But then Mr. Culver pointed to the door and to the seats

outside. Sam opened it and summer heat blasted through. It was wonderful.

"Close the door, Sam! Sheesh." Anita went to sit with Mrs. Lockheart.

Sam couldn't take his eyes off the heat shimmering on the baseball mound, or the players in their red-and-white and blue-and-white uniforms. And the teams' mascots started leaping around, fuzzy green fur, big eyebrows, and jiggly eyeballs and bellies.

They looked a little like giant monsters in person. Seeing them on television always seemed a little weird, but here it made Sam laugh hard.

Mason was laughing too and not teasing him at all. Then she spotted someone familiar in the crowd. "Ms. Malloy!"

"That's Acting Principal Malloy now!" Sam's dad waved her over. "Congratulations!"

Ms. Malloy waved back and pointed to two seats, one that looked empty, next to hers. She put a box of popcorn on the seat and, as they watched, the popcorn disappeared rapidly. Bella giggled until Anita swooped in to smear them with sunscreen.

"Mom, quit it," Sam finally said. Her hands hovered over his face and she blinked a couple times. Then she hugged Sam and left him with the bottle of sunscreen, a huge smile on her face.

"I've never heard you call her that before," Mason said. "And I've known you practically the whole time you've known her."

"I guess you're right?" Sam stuffed a handful of popcorn in his mouth so he could chew while he considered it. "Maybe."

He hadn't thought of saying it before, but the word had just sounded right that time. Like he really meant it. "I won't be careless with it," he whispered.

"Aw," whispered Tolver, snacking on popcorn on the back of his seat. His feet were invisible, but Sam could hear them swish. "That's all right, though. I'd never steal a word like that." Then the boglin nudged Sam with a sharp elbow and jumped off his seat, whispering "Oh, would you look at that."

Before Sam could ask what he'd seen, Tolver climbed over the edge of the box. Sam could just barely see the ripple of his silver hair. The adults couldn't see him at all. And then Tolver whistled. "Do you see that ad! They don't mean *any* of those words!" Then he jumped over the rail, headed for the outfield.

"Let's play ball!" The announcer roared, and the fans cheered.

As the teams ran out onto the field, Mason, Bella, and Sam cheered too while sitting in the warm sun under a perfect blue sky. It was really—finally—summer.

Acknowledgments

"Word-stealing goblins…" I said. Then I waited a moment, breath held. Would my editor like the idea? It was so different from my first middle-grade book, *Riverland*.

"Oh! YES! With truffle-pigs?" she replied.

Reader, I love working with editor Maggie Lehrman. Gilfillan and Starflake are, in my mind, her talented pets that I've just borrowed, brought into being through that first conversation about *The Ship of Stolen Words*. To her credit, Maggie barely batted an eyelash when she discovered that I'd built mechanical flying word hogs into the story too.

These and a thousand other thank-yous go to Maggie, Emily Daluga, Brooke Shearhouse, Jenny Choy, and the entire team at Abrams for supporting my portal-hopping books. To cover artist Shan Jiang and designer Marcie Lawrence, I love how you've captured Tolver and Sam's story—thank you so much for your beauti-ful work.

In portal narratives, characters go from one world to another in order to work through big issues. In the case of *The Ship of Stolen Words*, what began as my own problem (I have on occasion apolo-gized way too much for things that aren't my doing, like the weather!) became a discussion about what language means, the importance of practicing different approaches, and even getting things wrong, and the magic that words (and dictionaries, and mail) have when they're meaningful. It doesn't go without saying that a book is its own kind of portal. I love the adventure of passing through a story, and the surprises I find (even as—especially as) an author.

To those who've accompanied me on this adventure—especially Tom, Iris, Susan & Chris, Beth, Jeff & Kalliope; my early readers Carlos Hernandez, Aliette de Bodard, Kenna Blaylock, Ellen Klages, Rachel Hartman, Kelly Lagor, Marissa Lingen, A.C. Wise, and Rachel Winchester; and the community of librarians, booksellers, authors, and educators that brings so much joy to my world—from the Philadelphia kidlit community to MG BookVillage, MG LitChat, and my Patreons, to those who have written, emailed, and posted amazing things online. To my professional communities, and the teachers within all of them, from Bruisers, Sparklepony, and b.org, to all the discussions on the Internet. To Elizabeth Bear, who once took my sorries away so I could practice other words. And to my colleagues at Western Colorado University MFA, SFWA's YA and Middle Grade group, and especially my fantastic agent, Andrea Somberg, who also doesn't blink (much) when I come to her with the next wild idea. A heartfelt thank you. I couldn't do this without you.

To the summer camp by the Chesapeake Bay in Worton, Maryland, where I first found my voice, thank you always. And to you, reading this book, I wish you many adventures and wonderful words.